A MATTER OF MOTIVE

A MATTER OF MOTIVE

•

Michael Hachey

AVALON BOOKS
NEW YORK

Hac

Library of Congress Catalog Card Number: 2004093954
ISBN 0-8034-9688-5

Published by Thomas Bouregy & Co., Inc.
160 Madison Avenue, New York, NY 10016

PRINTED IN THE UNITED STATES OF AMERICA
ON ACID-FREE PAPER
BY HADDON CRAFTSMEN, BLOOMSBURG, PENNSYLVANIA

For Kathie

Special thanks to: Liz Feagles, James Dorsey, Richard Trende, Joe Pelton, Jeffrey Henn, Bruce Peterson, Susan Peck, Mary Cunningham, Peter Jackson, Tony & Sally Manzara, Clark Leeson, Erin Cartwright, and Kathie.

Chapter One

The deputy was on a 'welfare check'—police jargon for requesting an officer to check on the well-being of an individual; in this case, Paul Summer, an investigator with the Curran County Sheriff's Department. His daughter, Ann, had called from Madison and asked if someone could drive out to his cabin to see if he was there. Paul's cabin was half-an-hour north of Higgins Point, near the northern border of Curran County in west central Wisconsin and had no phone service. The deputy, who knew Paul's daughter did something with the DCI, had no idea why she was looking for him, but he was more than happy to take a drive in the country. It was 6:30 AM when he pulled into Paul's driveway. He hung his arm out the window and drove slowly up the quarter-mile dirt road that wound through a stand of evergreens and led to the cabin. Above him, the canopy of branches thrashed in the high, early morning wind.

The deputy knew Paul Summer, but not well. He'd heard talk about the poker games that Paul hosted from time to time at his cabin, but he'd never been out here before, the invite list was short, only a few of the department's old-timers. He rounded the last curve, and the driveway fanned out into a clearing. The small, one-story, wood-framed house, what they called a 'cabin' in Wisconsin, was settled in among close pines at the far end. Summer's dark blue Dodge Intrepid, the car the deputy had been told to look for, sat in the small parking area in front. He verified the plate number and then grabbed his radio handset.

"Eighty-eight eleven to dispatch."

"Go ahead, eighty-eight eleven."

"I'm at Paul Summer's premises. His car's parked in front; I'm going in."

The cabin was closed up and absolutely still as the deputy approached the front door. There was no response to his knock, so he walked around the house checking for other possible points of entry or windows that would let him see inside. The window curtains were all drawn shut. He made plenty of noise rapping on the back door, but there was still no reply. Arriving back at the front door, he was faced with a decision: have the office try to reach the daughter in Madison and request permission to enter or kick the door in. If this had involved someone he didn't know he might have waited, but Paul Summer was a fellow officer, so he didn't hesitate. He took a stance and kicked the door sharply next to the lock. It flew open with no trouble.

The interior of the cabin was dark; the only light coming in was through the open front door. He reached over and flipped the light switch and an old wagon wheel chandelier hanging in the center of the main room came to life. He couldn't see anything unusual from where he stood, so he walked across the room toward the back of the cabin, where the kitchen was separated by a waist-high counter. A quick glance told him there was nothing there. He turned left and pushed open one of the two remaining doors. It was a small, dark bedroom—empty. When he pushed open the last door, he froze.

The room was set up as an office with a desk and a filing cabinet. Paul Summer lay on the floor behind his desk next to his overturned chair. The deputy moved quickly across the small room, taking care not to step in the pool of blood. When he bent over and reached behind the desk to check Paul's neck for a pulse, he saw the chest wound and knew he was dead. He backed out of the room as carefully as possible, trying not to disturb anything. He returned to his car and grabbed the radio handset, taking a deep breath to steady his voice.

"Eighty-eight eleven to dispatch."

"Go ahead eighty-eight eleven."

"I'm at Paul Summer's cabin. I have a ten ninety-nine. I need investigators and supervisors."

"Do you need medical assistance?"

"I need a medical examiner."

At 7:30 AM, Officer Dexter Loomis sat at his gray metal desk in the Village Government Center on Cherry Street, his fingers immobile on his computer keyboard. Currently Higgins Point's only cop, he was trying to fill out a stolen property report for Mrs. Daniels, who had called in to report that someone had stolen her underwear off the clothesline in her backyard. She was demanding that something be done about the sex pervert who was roaming unchecked through Higgins Point. But Dexter was familiar with the woman and her planetsized proportions and was of the opinion that the motive for the theft probably had more to do with humor than perversion. Of course, he couldn't tell Mrs. Daniels that; he had to keep her mollified and, at the same time, prevent a prank from escalating into community panic. Phyllis, the town clerk, who also provided secretarial assistance to both Dexter and the mayor, was gone for the day on a canoe outing with her self-discovery group from Roberts, leaving Dexter alone in the office. The only sounds came from the clock ticking on the wall, accompanied by the constantly whistling wind trying to get in through the windows.

While he sat there, Dexter gradually became aware of a third sound, a rhythmic, metallic clanging. Welcoming any excuse for a break, he rose from his desk, went to the front door, and opened it. The metal chain on the aluminum flagpole on the front lawn had worked its way loose and was flapping back and forth in the stiff wind. Dexter walked out to reattach the chain and turned around just in time to see a gust blow the front door of his office closed.

He stood next to the flagpole staring at the building, and the clumsy yellow brick and white plywood façade stared back. Intended to mimic a colonial style of architecture, the Government Center featured square white posts supporting a second story overhang. Brass lamps attached to the brick face hung on either side of the front door, and a brass plaque informed all who approached that this was the office of the 'HIGGINS POINT POLICE DEPARTMENT'. Dexter walked back to the door and jiggled the knob to confirm his suspicion that he had locked himself out of his office. The wind whipped his pants legs, while he stood there considering his options. The Government Center consisted of a one-room police station on the first floor, the mayor's office on the second floor, and the city maintenance garage in back. The windows and doors were all locked, and there was no one in the mayor's office or the maintenance garage at this hour of the morning.

He was still standing there five minutes later wondering how much more foolish a forty-year-old man could feel, when Mayor Dick Evenson came walking up the sidewalk. Evenson, looking tan and healthy, if just a bit stout, was fond of telling everyone that he was waiting for his age to catch up with his weight. Dexter was a little surprised to see the mayor, who usually spent mornings at his hardware store, preferring to leave town matters for the afternoon. When Evenson stepped up onto the porch, he was displaying one of his campaign smiles, which immediately put Dexter on guard. He was at least half a foot shy of Dexter's six-foot-three-inch height, and when he spoke, he cocked his head up like a baby robin waiting for a worm, raising his voice in the wind.

"Morning, Dex, got some good news for you."

"Hey, Dick." Dexter wondered what additional duties this 'good news' was going to entail.

"I'm promoting you to Chief."

Old newsreel footage of Chief Sitting Bull in a full, ceremonial headdress flashed through Dexter's mind.

Evenson looked around. "What're you doing out here?" He tried the door, unsuccessfully. "What'd you do, lock yourself out?"

"Dick, what are you talking about?"

"I'm talking about why the door's locked."

"I mean the *Chief* business."

"Lewis Coffers has been gone for almost two weeks. You're the only cop we have now." Evenson fished his keys out of his pocket and unlocked the door. "The town needs a police chief, and since I'm the mayor, you're it—congratulations."

They both entered the office and Dexter closed the door, cutting the sound of wind.

"Just like that? Dick, isn't the city council supposed to have something to say about this?"

"Aw, Dex, you don't want to go and wake them up. They're old, leave em alone."

"You sure you've thought this one through? You said yourself, I'm the only cop in town."

"Which makes you numero uno in the seniority department."

"So who am I supposed to be the chief of?"

"Hasn't been the boss for thirty seconds, and already he's lobbying for more staff. You're a natural, Dex."

"What about the issue of credentials; namely, my lack of any?"

"You've got a lot of natural ability." Evenson reached

up and patted Dexter's shoulder. "Don't sell yourself short."

"I don't think you appreciate how spectacularly unqualified I am to be a cop, even in a town as small as Higgins Point."

"Relax, it's only temporary, until we can get an experienced cop from the cities to help us out part-time."

Suddenly, the volume of the wind spiked when Grady Penz opened the door and walked in. Partially bald with a salt and pepper beard, he wore the gray uniform of the New Richmond EMS. His skin was somewhere between milk chocolate and dark chocolate, and he was tall enough so he almost had to duck when he came through the door. He had moved to Higgins Point from Chicago four years earlier, looking for what he referred to as a 'higher intensity of serenity.' Grady knew both Dexter and the mayor well and skipped the preliminaries.

"You guys know an investigator with the county named Summer?"

"You mean Paul Summer?" Dexter said. "I used to."

"A real old-timer," Evenson added.

"Well, he's dead. They found his body about an hour ago."

They both stared at Grady, and finally Dexter asked, "How?"

"Gunshot. I don't know the details, but I heard it was suicide."

Dexter recalled Paul Summer's quiet smile, never given too freely, and his hard-nosed reputation. Last fall, when Dexter was still an engineer for the county, he'd run into Paul when they were repairing a storm sewer on Hoage Road, out near the County Government Center. By way of reminding Paul who he was, Dexter had casually mentioned that he used to date his daughter, Hallie, in high school. Paul had claimed to remember him, but Dexter was pretty sure he was just being polite.

"Where'd you hear this?"

"Howard Ellers was in the garage in New Richmond this morning. He said the medical examiner got called up to Summer's cabin. Took one look and requested a lab team."

"They found him at his cabin?" Evenson asked.

Grady nodded as he poured himself a cup of coffee.

"I think I remember that cabin," Dexter said. "Suicide, you're sure?"

Grady looked at him over the rim of his cup. "Ellers told me they found a note."

They were all quiet for a minute and then Dexter said, "I'm only a rookie, but do you think they need any help up there?"

Evenson shook his head. "His place is probably twenty-five miles north, Dex. Got nothing to do with Higgins Point. I'm pretty sure the Sheriff's going crazy trying to control the mob he's got out there already."

"Yeah." Dexter glanced at his unfinished report for Mrs. Daniels. "I guess Paul Summer is someone else's problem."

Three hundred miles south, in Madison, Wisconsin, DCI Agent Ann Summer stood in the chambers of Dane County District Judge Amos Bredner while he reviewed her search warrant application. She stared down at the top of the judge's head and for the hundredth time that morning thought about her father. This time she was ten, looking at the top of his head while he knelt on the dock in front of her, showing her how to bait her own hook.

Next to Ann stood her partner, Zack Rose, four inches shorter, and four years younger than Ann's thirty-six years. He was studying a framed 8 × 10 photograph hanging on the mahogany paneled wall of the judge's chamber, which showed Bredner looking cozy with Supreme Court Justice Anthony Scalia. When Bredner reached for a glass of water instead of his pen, the significance wasn't lost on either of them. He took a sip and then set both the glass and the paper on his desk.

"This Thomas Polter, he's the gang member who murdered the undercover cop two weeks ago?"

Ann nodded, and then remembered to add, "Allegedly."

Bredner took off his glasses, and leaned back. "Then we have a problem, because I want this piece of—I want this fellow in front of my bench, and this warrant isn't going to do it."

Ann and Zack both started to talk at once and then looked at each other. Zack stopped chewing his gum long enough to continue.

"Your Honor, we have an eyewitness on the warrant who places the gun in the apartment."

"Then why am I reading about someone else watching the suspect throw the weapon in question into Lake Monona?" The judge placed his glasses back on and consulted the application. "Apparently, it came to light during questioning in an unrelated case."

The glasses came back off and Bredner stared at them, eyebrows raised, waiting. Ann had known walking in that they were eventually going to be in this position.

"We were blindsided," she explained. "We stumbled across the information accidentally. The law says if it pertains, we have to include it."

"Don't quote the law to me." The judge narrowed his eyes at Ann. "Ever heard of the ACLU, Agent Summer?"

Ann could smell one of Bredner's lectures coming a mile away. Not bothering to answer, she distributed her weight evenly on her feet and relaxed her shoulders, waiting.

"Or any of a dozen other liberal, watchdog groups? There's no shortage of young, democratic lawyers out there eager to make a name for themselves by taking honest cops off the streets. What there is a shortage of, Agent Summer, is law and order on those streets. It's Polter's attorney's job to watch out for him. It's your job to put cop-killers like him in the deepest hole we can find."

Ann bit her lip and reminded herself to let him talk.

"*Technically*, the approval of a search warrant is based on probable cause; *technically* the reasons for must outweigh reasons against. And *technically*, as written, this warrant doesn't rise to that." Bredner leaned forward and lowered his voice, making his message to Ann personal. "Now, you're not new at this, and we both know you're allowed considerable latitude in deciding what information gets on a warrant application." The judge held up the piece of paper. "This mess has a built-in self-destruct in the form of the conflicting second statement. I want you to give closer consideration to the reliability of the source of this second statement."

Ann didn't have to look at her partner to know where he came down on the issue.

"I have no reason to question the reliability of the information, Your Honor."

"I would consider it a personal favor."

"Well, then we have a problem."

"You mean *you* have a problem."

"The interrogation made the statement a matter of police record. If we omit it, it'll just surface later and be used to nullify the warrant—we'd lose anything we found in the apartment."

"That's not necessarily a given, Agent Summer. Maybe Mr. Polter's attorney has a short attention span, or maybe he got his law degree from a diploma mill in the Bahamas. I want Polter under my gavel, and at the moment it looks like you're my biggest obstacle."

Bredner held the application out to her. Zack cleared his throat, but Ann shook her head. "I'm sorry, your Honor."

The judge took back the paper, looked at it for a moment, and then looked at Ann. When he spoke, his speech was slow and measured.

"Your misplaced dedication to the letter of the law does more harm than good to the interests of justice. You're not willing to submit the application without the statement, and I certainly can't sign it with the statement. If I did, and some defense attorney used the conflict to get the warrant nullified, I'd look as foolish as you do now." The judge slid the unsigned paper across the desk. "We're through here."

Outside of the judge's chambers, Zack threw a stick of gum into his mouth and said, "I must be losing it. For a minute, I actually thought you were gonna cave."

"We didn't have any other choice."

"Are you kidding? He almost ordered us to rewrite it."

"The statement's a matter of record." Ann hoped the note of finality in her voice would clue Zack to let it go. It didn't.

"Ann, you gotta loosen up and play the system, instead of letting the system play you. I told you to leave that second statement out; we both knew Bredner wouldn't sign it."

"There was a risk."

"Bredner's politics are a little to the right of Attila the Hun, we're never going to get a better shot than him. He offered a solution that stays within the system."

"Falsifying the application is staying within the system?"

"Not falsifying, we were just going to tweak it a little."

"And it doesn't bother you to see a judge try to 'tweak' the law like that?"

"Not if the end result is justice."

"It's the law that allows us the luxury of justice, Zack."

"That's a nice sentiment, but it belongs on a bumper sticker."

Ann didn't bother telling her partner that that 'sentiment' was chapter and verse of what she'd been taught by her father.

"Wait a minute." Zack stopped as they reached the door

that led out to the west parking lot. "Maybe we can do this without Bredner. How about if I put in a phony 911 call complaining about something at that address, and when a squad responds, we'll just happen to be in the vicinity? We'll go in with them and do a protective sweep of the premises, and if we happen to stumble across the gun, great."

"Zack, I want to get this guy too, but not that way."

Zack gave his short, unruly hair a vigorous rub. "Bad news is the enemy of promotions. Are you gonna tell Schifsky, or do I have to?"

Ann sighed. "I'll tell him."

They stepped out of the building into the heat and noise of the July afternoon in downtown Madison.

"By the way, any word from your dad?" Zack asked.

Ann had mentioned to Zack that her father had failed to show up at her apartment yesterday evening. She shook her head.

"Wasn't he supposed to drive down last night?"

Ann nodded. "I asked the Curran County Sheriff to send a car by his house in Higgins Point, but there was no sign of him."

"So now what?"

"He's got a cabin a little north of there. This morning I asked them to check it out. There's no reason he should be there, but I don't know where else to look."

"He's a cop, Ann. He knows how to take care of himself. Something probably just came up and he's slow getting back to you."

Ann returned his smile and tried to ignore the concern she read in her partner's voice. When they split up in the parking lot, she said, "Remember, Zack, no 911 calls."

She had several things on her plate for the day; she had to finish the report on the Maitlan murder, take a deposition from a key witness on the Danvers murder, and try and fit in a little racquetball after lunch. She walked quickly across the parking lot to her silver Dodge Stratus, but when she got in, she didn't start the engine. Instead, she sat in the heat thinking about the last, brief phone conversation she'd shared with her father. He'd mentioned something to her about needing her help, but he hadn't been specific. Now she was left with several questions. Why had he insisted on driving the three-hundred miles from Higgins Point down to Madison to talk in person? What was he involved in that was so important it couldn't wait until the weekend? And where was he now? Ann finally started her car, but hadn't left the parking lot when her cell phone rang.

Chapter Two

Muriel Evenson placed the script for Sheridan's *The School for Scandal*, into her bookcase beside the other plays and tossed the empty manila bank folder in her waste-basket. It was Wednesday already and the play was opening on Friday. She should be thinking about the rehearsal later that night, going over her lines, getting inside her character's head, but she couldn't stop worrying about the money. She walked through her apartment into the front room and stood looking out onto Vine Street from her second floor window. Though she'd only had this apartment for a year, Muriel had spent all of her nineteen years in Higgins Point, trying to figure out a way to leave. But now, with her departure about to become a reality, she looked down on the quiet street in the late afternoon colors and realized that she was actually going to miss the place. Not just the people, but the town; the tiny houses, the vacant lots, the rural quiet, the fourth of July parades with more people in them than watching them, the whole stupid, boring, backward, little hicksville that she had never been able to get out of fast enough.

When Muriel had gotten home after work, she'd seen Ardella, her landlady, in the backyard weeding her flowerbeds. If it weren't for the play rehearsal tonight, she'd be down there helping right now. Though her landlady knew a lot about gardening, and was happy to share her knowledge, Ardella was one of the few people that Muriel saw in the course of her day who liked to listen more than talk. Muriel couldn't tell her what she was up to, of course, but she was going to miss her company. The phone interrupted Muriel's thoughts.

"Hello."

"It's me. How are you feeling?"

"Oh, hi. I'm okay."

"I know I'll see you at rehearsal tonight, but I thought I'd call now to make sure you remembered our appointment tomorrow afternoon, you know, in St. Paul."

The twin cities of Minneapolis and St. Paul were only a forty-five minute drive to the west, across the Minnesota border. With a metro population of something over two million, 'the cities', as they were known, provided the people of western Wisconsin with anything they might need from a big city, including abortion clinics.

"Geoff, I don't know if I—"

"You promised me you'd go. At least hear what they have to say."

Muriel's hand went to her tummy. "I know I promised, but—"

"I'll be by to pick you up around two. In the meantime, study your lines. I know you're going to kill them on opening night."

"I guess."

"See you later."

"I love you," Muriel replied, but the line had gone dead.

The sound of a large car engine being gunned brought Muriel to the front window. A black Trans-Am had just pulled up in front of the house. She watched her best friend, Cara Lynn Grovsner, get out of the passenger side, and then Cara's boyfriend, Billy, slowly get out of the driver's seat. He paused, looking up and down the street, before shutting his door. Cara Lynn had called Muriel at work and told her they'd be stopping by. The scowl on Billy's face, and the oiliness of his stringy hair, lying over the collar of his leather jacket, were evident even from a distance, and for the thousandth time, Muriel wondered why Cara Lynn stayed with him.

There was no buzzer on the front door lock, so Muriel had to go down and let them in. When they were all back up in the front room, Billy hardly said anything before grabbing a kitchen chair and taking it into the hallway. Muriel watched him disappear through the door and then asked Cara Lynn if she wanted anything to drink. Cara Lynn shook her head.

"I'm sorry," she whispered, looking sheepish. They heard the scraping sound of the attic door being pushed aside.

"It's okay," Muriel said softly, though they both knew it wasn't. The presence of Billy Deal's drugs in her attic was something Muriel allowed only as a favor to Cara Lynn. If she didn't, Billy would make life hell for her best friend, though he generally did anyway. "I'll be gone before long, anyway."

Cara Lynn smiled, but a bruise on her cheek, a new one, marred the effect. Muriel had noticed it when they first walked in.

"Why do you stay with him, Cara? You can do better."

Ever since they'd met, Cara Lynn had always seemed to need someone to tell her what to do, and Billy Deal, while one of the worst, was only the latest. Muriel realized she shouldn't have said anything; it never did any good. The sad smile on her friend's face immediately made Muriel regret dragging up the worn-out topic again. Cara Lynn changed the topic for her.

"You're really going. God, I can't believe it."

"Neither can I."

"Do you have your plane ticket yet?"

Muriel shook her head. "I should have the money for it tonight though."

Cara Lynn looked around in the direction of the hallway, and lowered her voice.

"You're gonna be careful, right?"

"Sure, don't worry."

"You know when you're leaving?"

Muriel shrugged. "Geoff wants to leave right after the play run—about a week-and-a-half."

When Cara Lynn hesitated, Muriel already knew what she was going to say; it never varied.

"Are you sure you can trust him? What if you get out there and he meets someone else?"

"I'm sure we're both going to meet all kinds of people. But I love him, so I guess I trust him too."

Cara Lynn nodded, but Muriel knew her too well to believe she was convinced.

"How are you feeling? I mean—"

Muriel smiled. "Great, so far."

"Maybe you ought to just tell your parents, they'd help you out."

"Geoff and I are going to do this on our own. We'll be okay."

Cara Lynn smiled and took Muriel's hands in hers. "I can't believe you're actually going to Hollywood."

"I know."

"You're gonna do great. I just wish you didn't have to go."

"No one ever made it in Hollywood staying in Wisconsin."

"Guess not." Cara Lynn let go of Muriel's hands. "I gotta use the bathroom before we leave. I'll be right back."

After Cara Lynn was gone, Billy came in from the hallway carrying a small paper bag. Muriel noticed that he didn't bother to bring the chair back into the kitchen. When he saw that Cara Lynn was out of the room, he grinned and walked over to Muriel.

"Hey, babe, how's it goin'?"

Muriel crossed her arms. "Fine, Billy."

He tossed his bag on the sofa, then reached up and started to massage her neck. He lowered his voice to a soft purr.

"You look tense."

She pulled away, and for just a split second before he let her go, she could feel his grip begin to tighten. She knew he wasn't used to letting go until he was good and ready. She casually walked across the room and turned.

"When I leave town, you're going to have to move your drugs out of here, find a new place to hide 'em."

"Why you wanna go, anyway?" Even his grin looked oily. "If you let me handle things, you could do pretty good right here. You wanna act? I know some people in the cities who'd put you in a movie, give you a chance to do some real acting."

Muriel knew exactly what kind of 'movie' he had in mind, and the thought of it made her skin crawl, but she kept her answer to a simple, "No thanks."

He shrugged his shoulders. "Maybe after you're gone I'll make a deal with the landlady to keep my stuff here. Put her on the payroll."

Muriel gave him her most insincere smile, the one she'd used in *Long Hot Summer* to discourage Ben Quick. "Don't bother her, Billy."

His real nature surfaced in the flash in his eye before he caught himself and laughed. She knew he didn't take direct orders well. Among all the shady characters he dealt with, there had to be someone he was forced to listen to, but Muriel knew it wasn't a woman.

"Hey, take it easy, babe, you're leavin'. What you don't know, ain't gonna hurt you, right?" That grin again. "I'll take care of business when you're gone."

He just couldn't leave it alone. Muriel didn't think he would actually approach Ardella, but he just had to leave some doubt, anything to make him feel like he'd come out on top. She knew it was pointless to pursue the subject, and Cara Lynn chose that moment to walk back into the front room. She didn't seriously consider telling Cara Lynn about Billy's overtures to her; they were nothing new, and Cara Lynn already knew how Billy was.

"Thanks. Wanna go, Billy?"

"Yeah."

He picked his bag up from the sofa, walked to the door, and waited, forcing Cara Lynn to walk out in front of him. She paused at the door and said, "You gotta call me after you get out there. Let me know you're okay."

Muriel smiled and nodded, watching her turn and start down the stairs. When she looked at Billy he was staring at her, and he wasn't smiling.

"When you get back to Higgins Point, look me up, I'll get something goin' for you." He grinned suddenly and winked. When he left, he didn't bother closing the door.

After talking to Billy, Muriel felt the need for a shower. She looked at her watch, and decided that she had time for a bath before rehearsal. Her mom was a bath person and was always going on about how relaxing a hot bath was, and she needed to relax now. The play was almost set to open, she was still worried about the money, and on top of it all, her boyfriend, Geoffrey, hadn't exactly been acting like a doting expectant father lately.

She closed the apartment door and then walked into the bathroom and started running the water. While she removed her clothes, she thought about her parents. They'd always been there for her, always been supportive. She knew she was going to be homesick. She was going to miss things she used to think were a pain, like clothes shopping with her mom, who was constantly quizzing her about her boyfriend. She was even going to miss helping out her dad, the town mayor, in the family hardware store on Saturday afternoons. But as much as she hated to leave, she couldn't imagine staying in Higgins Point the rest of her life, wondering what might have happened if she'd tried it. She wasn't going to live her life without knowing.

At 10:30 AM on Wednesday, Ann Summer stared silently out the window of the limousine. The ride from the Franklin Funeral Home to Grace Lutheran Church was brief, but not brief enough. Her brother-in-law's voice droned on as the streets of Higgins Point passed by. She tried to tune him out as she gazed at the small anonymous homes with tidy yards full of crab grass, clotheslines, sheds and piles of firewood. She thought, *I don't belong here anymore*.

"Grief can do strange things, Ann." Ted, in an effort to grace both sisters with his wisdom, leaned forward in the back seat and spoke across his wife, Hallie. "It can affect your judgement."

"I appreciate your concern, Ted." Ann hoped her remark would quiet him. It didn't.

"It's during the grieving process that you need your perspective the most, to help you get past it."

Hallie patted her husband's knee. "Honey, maybe this isn't the time."

"I think she needs to hear this."

"Ted," Ann said, "He's not even in the ground yet."

The limousine stopped in front of the church and a slight breeze touched Ann's hair as the driver helped her and her sister out of the car. Emerging from behind the tinted windows, the sunlight seemed to erupt around them, reflecting off the limousine's chrome door handles. Ann thought the expressions of the people walking into the church seemed detached, and imagined she could sense the preoccupation with interrupted schedules that lurked behind the masks of concern.

At the church door they stepped from the heat and washed-out light of the late July morning into the cool interior, where three hundred people had gathered. Many were neighbors and friends of Paul Summer, but most were law enforcement officers, the majority of whom had never had the opportunity to meet her father.

Ann and Hallie sat beside one another at the front of the church and held hands, while Ann studied the smooth, lacquered grain of the pew. Pastor Lentz delivered a brief sermon and more than once Ann felt Hallie wince when she clenched her sister's hand too tightly. Among those who spoke after the pastor was her father's boss, Curran County Sheriff Moses Hicks. When his turn came, the large man moved ponderously down the aisle, taking his place behind the pulpit, which he loomed above like an adult trying to fit into a child's school desk. He related a few stories about their father, stories that contained an appropriate measure of humor, respect, and regret—and no reference to suicide.

During the service, Ann's senses drifted in and out of focus. At times she would be okay, and then she would suddenly realize that she had just missed the last several minutes. She tried to recall times when their father had seemed genuinely happy, but it gradually dawned on her that very few of those moments had occurred since their mother's death from cancer twenty-five years earlier.

When the church bells settled over the congregation at the conclusion of the service, six uniformed officers carried the casket out to the waiting hearse. Ann stood, gazing at the retreating group, envisioning the honor guard that should have been in attendance. Most law officers across the state considered suicide to be an occupational hazard and disagreed with the policy that denied them a formal departmental funeral. Ann couldn't fail to discern, in the many offered condolences at the back of the church, the tainted emotion of thinly disguised pity.

Outside, Ann, Hallie, and Ted formed a small group during the slow walk to the cemetery, which was located near the church grounds. After they'd begun walking, Ted lit a cigarette, and cleared his throat.

"It was a nice service."

"There should be a twenty-one gun salute at the grave," Ann said.

"I thought it was nice that so many people came," Hallie said softly.

They were quiet for a moment, and then Ann added, "And bagpipes."

Hallie had told Ann before she and her husband flew out from Seattle, that they were going to tap into some of Ted's vacation time and would be able to stay in Higgins Point for a little while to help sort through their father's things.

"When are you heading back to Madison, Ann?" Hallie asked.

"I'm driving back tonight."

Hallie and Ted both nodded lightly.

"But I'm coming back on Friday. I decided to take a leave of absence."

Hallie smiled. "That's great news."

"Is that the wisest thing to do right now?" Ted asked. "Don't they say it's best to stay busy, keep to some sort of routine when you're coping with a loss?"

"I've got something to keep me busy. Besides," Ann gestured toward her sister, "we're both dealing with a loss. Why all the concern for me? What about your wife?"

"Hallie accepts what happened."

"I have a friend who would tell you that blind acceptance is the enemy of logic," Ann replied, imagining what Zack would have to say.

Ted pulled up short, tossed his cigarette on the ground, and stepped on it.

"Hallie told me about your theory—that Paul was murdered. I have to tell you, as crazy as suicide seems, that's even crazier. I'm afraid you're going to have a tough time getting through this if you're not willing to accept the facts."

Ann had stopped also and now turned toward him. "What can you possibly say to me, Ted, to help me accept the idea that our father killed himself?"

"If he was murdered, wouldn't the authorities have come to that conclusion?" Ted looked back and forth between Ann and Hallie, appealing for reason. "With the technology they have today, how often does someone actually get away with covering up a murder?"

Ann started walking again. "You'd be surprised."

"Maybe Ann's right," Hallie reasoned, "there are all sorts of things on television about unsolved crimes."

"That's television, Hallie," the patience slipping from Ted's voice. "When someone dies on TV, they get up when the director yells 'cut'."

"I wasn't talking about TV dramas! I meant programs like *America's Most Wanted*."

"I'm afraid the whole thing's an attempt at denial," Ted said. "Suicide's hard to accept."

"So is murder," Ann replied.

Groups of people were leaving the path and making their way among the tombstones toward the lone open grave. The three of them strayed away from the others, and Ann paused next to a large monument and ran her hand over its smooth marble surface, warmed by the sun. She lived a six-hour drive from her father and only visited him once a year at Christmas. What kind of daughter does that? She was getting tired of the conversation, and decided to bring it to a head.

"Do you want to hear me say it? Okay, I'm in denial. I don't think our father had the slightest inclination toward suicide. And if I thought there was any chance at all it would do any good, I'd stop the burial right now and put his body on ice for forensics."

Hallie's expression was one of shock.

"All right. It's good to say what's on your mind," Ted glanced around, apparently concerned at the volume of Ann's voice. "Putting it right out in front like that is how you deal with it."

Ann stared at her brother-in-law. "The only way I see how to deal with this mess is to prove our father didn't pull that trigger and find the bastard who did."

Ted seemed to hesitate before he spoke. "What I see missing here is the element of acceptance, Ann."

Ann studied her brother-in-law for a moment and wondered if he actually intended to be humorous. Ted hurried to explain his remark.

"You've got to recognize that you're too close to things emotionally, and trust the authorities to sort it out."

"And you've got to stop starting sentences with 'you've got to'."

When Ted's only response was to sigh loudly, Ann turned to her sister.

"I think our father was murdered, and Ted believes the official script. What do you think?"

Hallie looked at Ann, her eyes wide and serious. "I don't know anything about police work."

"You know something about our father."

Hallie hesitated for a moment and then seemed to make up her mind. "You're my little sister, but you're also a cop, and I happen to know you're a good one. If you think there's something you could be doing, then I think you should do it."

When they continued walking, Ann felt better having vented her feelings; Ted was right about that. But when they got to the gravesite, there still wasn't a twenty-one gun salute.

Chapter Three

Somewhere, beyond conscious thought, Dexter Loomis heard the distant thunder, now grown to an almost continuous growl. Ever since he was a kid, the violence unleashed in thunderstorms had held a special fascination for him. He smelled the faint scent of ozone in the charged night air and sensed the drop in pressure that signaled the approach of rain. The lightning flashes were becoming more frequent and lit up Muriel Evenson's face as he brushed strands of auburn hair out of her eyes. His fingers traced a line across her cheek to the corner of her mouth where they paused, before drifting down the curve of her neck. There was no pulse, only an unnatural doughy quality in the rapidly cooling flesh, and he was suddenly aware of the smell of blood mixed in with the scent of her perfume.

She was lying on her back on the driveway pavement below the second-floor deck, a fan of hair across her face, wearing only panties and a partially opened, powder blue, satin bathrobe. A slipper clung to her right foot. The crown of her head was wreathed in dark crimson, and her arms were splayed at unnatural angles. Dexter's gaze followed a ribbon of blood a short distance, until it disappeared into a crack in the pavement, and he wondered how long it took blood to dry.

He had known Muriel and her parents, Mayor Dick Evenson and his wife, Inez, for more than twenty-five years. A vision of Muriel's laughing face flashed in front of him. She was just a kid, scaring the hell out of everybody, leaning out over the rail of Dexter's sailboat, and squealing every time the plunging bow washed her with spray. The span of years had purged Dexter's memory of imperfections; in his mind, Muriel's childhood was idyllic, and Muriel, perfect. But the memory spent itself quickly, and then he was once again kneeling in the humid July night, staring at the dead body of his friend's daughter.

It was Thursday night, and he was in the backyard of 621 Vine Street, roused from a sound sleep and summoned there a few minutes before midnight by Grady Penz. Grady had taken a portable halogen light stand from his EMS van and placed it on the driveway. It provided the only light in the backyard, and captured Dexter, huddled over Muriel on the pavement amid scattered pieces of the broken deck railing. The front of storm clouds moving in from the west had cloaked the backyard beyond Grady's light in near total darkness. Every time there was a lightning flash, it brought everything in close, giving the scene the intimacy of a stage.

"She fall off the deck?" Dexter asked, without taking his eyes off the body. When he didn't hear anything, he glanced at Grady, and followed his gaze up to the deck above, where splintered sections of wood still clung to the railing. A stupid question, his first.

Grady waved a mosquito away. "Looks like."

"Anyone call her folks yet?"

"I got Dick on the phone. Says her mother's spending the night with her sister in Cumberland. He's on his way over."

"So he knows?"

Grady nodded. "Couldn't let him just walk in on . . . this. Yeah, I told him."

Until tonight, Dexter's three months as a cop for Higgins Point had been mercifully routine, limited largely to campground patrols, traffic, and paperwork. He didn't really know what to say or do next, but for the moment his anxiety was swept away by gratitude that he didn't have to break this news to Dick. He stood up inhaling the night air deeply, and took a closer look at the wooden deck. It extended out over the backyard bordering the driveway on one side. It was on that side, on the driveway pavement, that Muriel now lay.

"Who found her?"

"Her landlady." Grady inclined his head back toward the detached garage about thirty feet away, at the edge of the light provided by his spotlight. An elderly woman in a pink housecoat knelt beside a large German shepherd. A wisp of smoke from her cigarette rose into the dark, while she petted the dog, which whimpered and growled in turn. Grady lowered his voice. "You know who that is? That's the lady who won the lottery and won't spend none of the money."

"You believe that story?"

"Don't you?"

Dexter ignored the question and walked over to the woman, who squinted up at him through a haze of cigarette smoke.

"How are you doing, Ardella?"

"I guess I'm okay, Dexter."

He offered a hand helping her to her feet. When she stood up, the German Shepherd crawled forward, as far as its leash, which Ardella had looped over the garage door handle, would allow. It lay with its head on the ground and its eyes fixed on Muriel's body, making small sounds. Ardella favored Dexter with a painful smile.

"It's nice to see you again. I read about your promotion to police chief in the paper."

Ardella Tophler was an old friend of Dexter's mother,

and he'd known her since he was just a kid, though he hadn't seen her since his mother passed away several years earlier. Her soft, slow manner of speech brought her back to him.

"Muriel lived upstairs?"

Ardella nodded. "She rents the apartment from me."

Dexter noticed Ardella's use of the present tense. "And you're the one who found her?"

"Uh huh, right where she is now—I touched her."

"I'm sorry?"

"When I found her, I touched her. I didn't know she'd already passed. I know from watching television that if someone's murdered you're not supposed to touch anything."

"No one's been murdered here, Ardella. This is just some kind of freak accident."

She knows as much about police procedure as I do, Dexter thought. The possibility, however unlikely, that this might actually be a crime scene sent a shock of adrenaline through his system.

Ardella stepped a little closer. "Did I cause this?"

"What do you mean?"

"It's my house, and if there's something wrong with the railing . . ."

"Ardella, you didn't do anything wrong." He walked over to where Muriel lay, and picked up one of the pieces of wood. It was a standard two-by-four painted dark brown.

"When was the deck built?"

"About twelve years ago. It was repainted three summers ago."

Dexter examined the splintered end for signs of decay and found none.

"It's so sad, Dexter. She was a lovely girl."

He laid the piece of wood back on the driveway next to Muriel. "How'd you find her?"

"It was Brando," she said, indicating the German Shepherd. "He started barking and woke me up. It's not like him at all."

"When was this?"

"Eleven-thirty."

"You're sure of the time?"

"Uh huh. I looked at my clock."

"Is this your dog?"

"He belongs to Muriel. He's really well trained. He never barks if Muriel's home, and when she's gone, Brando only barks if someone comes to the door. But this time he wouldn't stop."

"So you heard the dog barking."

"It seemed to come from out back here, so I walked around the house to take a look."

"And you found Muriel lying there, like that?"

Ardella looked over at the body and nodded.

"The dog was out back here, in the yard?"

"No, he was upstairs in the apartment. After I called 911, I went up and brought him down."

"So you've been upstairs?"

"Just to open the door for Brando, he came right out. I hope that's okay."

Dexter wasn't really sure whether it was okay or not. "No one else has been up there that you know of?"

"No."

"Is the door to her apartment unlocked?"

"I left it unlocked after I let Brando out."

"Was it unlocked when you first went in?"

"Yes."

"Thank you Ardella." Dexter turned toward Grady. "I'll be right back, I'm going upstairs."

"Take a look at something for me first."

Grady knelt down beside Muriel's body. When Dexter joined him, he directed the flashlight beam onto Muriel's face and leaned in. "You see anything unusual?"

Muriel's eyes were mercifully closed, and all Dexter saw

was the face of a young girl who could have been asleep. He had no idea what he was supposed to be looking for. When he didn't respond, Grady said, "In her cheeks. You see a flush in her cheeks?"

For a moment, Dexter tried to imagine a flush, but he couldn't be certain. If there was one, it was very faint.

"I don't see it," he said, finally, and looked at Grady. "Why? What's it mean?"

Grady shrugged and put the flashlight back in his pocket as he stood up. "I don't know, with this light, I'm probably wrong. Forget it."

Dexter looked down at Muriel's body and then back at Grady. "Keep an eye on things here. I'll be right back."

He walked around the house and entered the front door, which opened into a small foyer. To the left, a door led to Ardella's apartment, and straight ahead, stairs led up to Muriel's apartment. As he ascended the stairway, faded green carpeting muffled his footsteps. At the top of the landing he opened a dark brown wood door with glass panels and a white, opaque curtain, and stepped into Muriel's front room. A small glass chandelier hanging in the center of the room was already on. It was tarnished brass with several missing crystals, and its light, filtered through dusty bulbs, was a dull yellow.

The room appeared undisturbed. There was an overstuffed dark green sofa and matching chair, a mahogany end table with a white lace doily, and a brass floor lamp positioned behind the chair. A sleek-looking, black component stereo system sat on a green and gold antique trunk, and there were several plants around the room, including a neglected fichus in the corner, which looked to Dexter like it could use a little sunlight.

Ignoring the rest of the apartment for the moment, he walked through the kitchen to the deck, which was accessed through a sliding glass door. He flipped on the exterior light, slid the door open, and walked directly to the edge of the deck where the railing had broken away. The sight of Muriel's body captured in Grady's makeshift spotlight, made him feel like he was in a balcony looking down on a stage. For a moment he was sitting in the audience with Dick and Inez at a high school production of *Guys and Dolls*. Muriel's spirited portrayal of Salvation Army Sergeant Sarah Brown had made her a cast standout. Gazing down at her motionless figure now, Dexter could almost imagine her getting up and taking a bow.

Something seemed wrong about this accident. Dexter spent several minutes trying to put a name to what was bothering him, but all he could come up with was an obvious question: why was she out on the deck in her robe in the middle of the night? When he considered his own behavior, he had to admit that she could have been out there for any number of reasons.

He finally gave up and went back into the apartment, walking back through the front room and into the bedroom. Again, nothing seemed out of order. The bed was unmade, and there were a few articles of clothing strewn about the floor, but there was nothing that Dexter would characterize as signs of a struggle. The walls were covered with photographs of her with friends, some at parties, some skiing, several on stage, and one of her as a cheerleader. He noticed that her hair color varied from picture to picture.

He heard Grady calling his name from the backyard and hurried through the apartment and down the stairs. When he came around the side of the house, someone was bent over Muriel's body with his back to him. Suddenly, Dick Evenson's head swung around, his face was crumbling, and his glistening eyes were unfocused. He stood up gulping for air, with a vague, bewildered look on his face. His hands clenched and unclenched at his side.

"She's dead, Dex, she . . ."

His voice abandoned him, and his hand went to his mouth. Then, almost transparently, like a wisp of smoke, he slid back down until he knelt over his daughter again. He gently closed the robe over her exposed body and hovered over her for several minutes until his shoulders started shaking, and then Dexter stepped forward and helped him to his feet.

"Dick, I'm really sorry." The utter inadequacy of his statement made Dexter feel like an idiot.

"What happened?"

When Dick asked this, Dexter understood how his question must have sounded to Grady.

"Looks like she fell from the deck. Maybe she tripped or something."

"She tripped?"

With no answer to offer to his friend's question, Dexter disintegrated into nervous small talk. "Grady tells me Inez is at her sister's."

Evenson looked at him blankly for a moment, biting his lip, and then nodded.

"If you want me to, I can call her and tell her." When Dick didn't say anything for a moment, Dexter was afraid he was actually going to have to make the call, but then, to his immense relief, Dick shook his head.

"I'll talk to her."

Dexter motioned to Ardella. "Can you take Dick inside, let him use your phone to call his wife?"

Ardella stepped forward to help him, and the two of them walked away together, Evenson drifting down the driveway like a sailboat with no rudder. They had just reached the front of the house when Sheriff Moses Hicks came walking around Grady's EMS van, which was parked in the driveway. He stopped to talk to Evenson for a minute, placing his hand on the mayor's shoulder, and then turned and continued up the driveway. A shaggy-haired bear of a man, the Sheriff reminded Dexter of a tall, sloppy Orson Wells.

"Dexter. Grady." He nodded at both men.

Even though the sheriff had taken his time walking up the driveway, Dexter detected a slight wheeze in his voice.

"Evening, Moses."

Moses Hicks was a transplant from Kentucky, and though he'd lived in northern Wisconsin for ten years, he'd managed to maintain a heavy drawl in spite of a decade of hot dish. He turned his attention to the figure lying in the driveway.

"She's gone?"

"I'm afraid so." Dexter was annoyed at the slight southern drawl that seemed to infect his speech whenever he was around Moses.

The sheriff put his glasses on and went down to one knee next to the body and cradled Muriel's head in his large left hand. With his right hand he brushed some of the hair from her face, paused a moment, and then tilted her head forward until he could see the matted, bloody hair near the crown.

He gave a low whistle and eased her head back to the pavement, then stood up and removed his glasses.

"Was she dead when you got here?"

Grady nodded. "Tried to resuscitate, but she was gone."

Dexter knew that Moses had been a friend to Dick Evenson and his family for several years, and this wasn't particularly easy for him either. The Sheriff ran his hand over his face for a moment, glanced around at the broken sections of railing that littered the driveway, and then up at the deck. Finally he addressed Dexter.

"Must have leaned against the railing too hard, or maybe fell against it. This look like an accident to you?"

Dexter was unaccustomed to having his opinion solicited by the sheriff and answered the question before thinking it through.

"Seems to me there's something odd about this."

The sheriff's small brown eyes almost disappeared into the squint that dominated his face. "What's that?"

"I'm not really sure. Probably nothing."

Moses looked up again at the splintered railing on the deck, and shook his head slowly. "Maybe what feels strange to you is someone so young dyin'. It ain't natural."

"Yeah, maybe that's it."

The three men let an awkward moment of silence go by, and then the sheriff apparently felt it was okay to change the subject. "I hear you're the new police chief."

Dexter nodded. "Temporary."

"A lot of excitement for a new chief. Lewis Coffers left town, what, a couple of weeks ago?"

He nodded again.

"Where'd he retire to, Fiji, or some such place?"

"Boca Raton, Florida. He left a little unexpectedly, kind of put me on the spot."

There was another short pause, and then the sheriff glanced down at Muriel Evenson's body. "Anybody call the coroner yet?"

Grady leaned in. "Done. He's on his way."

Moses dug around in his pocket and came up with a tin of chewing tobacco. "Maybe I'll take a look around." He stuck a plug in his mouth and strolled into the backyard.

Dexter glanced toward the front of the house and saw a short man in rolled-up sleeves and suspenders walking quickly up the driveway. The note pad in his hand and the energetic look in his eyes suggested to Dexter that he was a reporter. Deciding to exercise some authority, he walked down the driveway to intercept him before he reached Muriel's body.

Dexter stepped in front of him. "Excuse me, I'm going to have to ask you to stay out in front of the house."

"Frank Kahler, Pioneer Press." The man extended a hand, which Dexter shook only because he would have felt uncomfortable ignoring it. "Don't think I know you."

Dexter tried his new title on for size. "Chief Loomis, Higgins Point Police."

Kahler scribbled on his pad. "Yeah, I heard Coffers pulled the plug, went to Hawaii or something."

"Boca Raton," Dexter replied automatically.

"Chief Loomis? Your name's not familiar. So what's your story?"

Dexter started to open his mouth and then realized that there wasn't anything he wanted to say on that subject.

"Coffers just left so you have to be new here. Where'd you come from?"

"This isn't about me," Dexter said.

"You had to come from somewhere. Where was your last job?"

"How'd you find out about this?"

"Police band. I was leaving Dick's Bar, over in Hudson. Happened to pick up the response to a 911 call. Got a dead woman back there? Homicide?" He craned his neck trying to see past Dexter, into the backyard.

"Nothing's been determined yet."

"Possible homicide," he said scribbling. "Alright, now we're getting somewhere. What was the cause of death? Any suspects?"

"Let's respect the family of the victi—deceased's right to privacy, okay?"

"Sure, but how about balancing it with the public's right to know?"

Sheriff Hicks walked up behind Dexter.

"Hey, Moses." Kahler wormed his way around Dexter. "Tell the chief, here, to let my people go."

"Well, Frank Kahler. Thought I heard your whiny little voice." Moses grinned and put a huge arm around the little man's shoulders and turned him around. "Guess you must be here to interview me about my run for reelection."

"Give me a break, Moses. If I hurry, I can still get something in the Friday edition."

"Frank, Frank, Frank," the Sheriff steered him toward the front of the house.

"And who's this Chief Loomis? Got no history. Got no clue."

"You hurt my feelings. Ain't you on board with my re-election?"

"Oh yeah, It's all I think about, Moses. Throw me a bone here, will ya?"

Walking next to each other, silhouetted against the head-lights from the EMS van, the two of them looked like a giant and a dwarf. Dexter could hear Hicks' fading voice as they walked away.

"It's an accident, Frank. That's how I want it to read. Do this for me, and I'll consider it a personal favor."

"Accident? What's with this place lately, first one of your investigators, and now this? You got bodies piling up like cordwood around here."

Dexter walked back up the driveway to where Grady was standing. "What the hell was that?"

Grady shrugged. "The press."

At 1:15 the County Coroner arrived and officially pronounced Muriel Evenson dead. After further examining her, he said he concurred with the finding of accidental death, and her body was removed to the Franklin Funeral Home on Croft Street. After Dexter had seen the last person leave, he said goodnight to Ardella, then got in his Jeep Cherokee and headed home. The numbing effect of the road passing under his headlights helped to force the image of Muriel Evenson's face from his mind for a while, but by the time he pulled into his driveway, and the first drops of the approaching storm were pattering across his windshield, she was back.

Chapter Four

On Friday morning, Ann Summer parked next to the Lorraine Building in downtown Madison, which housed the offices of the Division of Criminal Investigation. As an arm of the Wisconsin Department of Justice, the DCI had jurisdiction throughout the state, assisting city police and county sheriff's departments. Ann worked in homicide, and her cases generally took her to rural areas where someone had taken lethal exception to something someone else had done or said. When the local law enforcement wanted some assistance, they called the DCI. Ann seldom arrived at crime scenes before they had been trampled by well-meaning patrolmen, and her first glimpse of the victim was usually in the morgue.

She stepped out of her car and when she closed the door, the glint of sunlight on the door handle caught her eye, and suddenly it was a week earlier and she was staring at the polished bronze handles of her father's casket. *If you think there's something you could be doing, then I think you should do it.* Hallie's words were still with Ann as she walked across the parking lot to her meeting with her boss.

When she stepped off the elevator onto the fourth floor, everything in the office held a vivid clarity for her. Little things leapt at her; the chip in Jerry's Green Bay Packer mug, the piece of cardboard that Zack had taped up to deflect the air register above his desk, the faded ink stain on the carpet near the fax machine that resembled upper Michigan.

Ann walked directly to the door of the corner office, knocked lightly, and then entered. Seated at his desk, behind immaculately clean, silver-framed spectacles, was Director Marvin Schifsky. A view of the Wisconsin State Capitol Building over his right shoulder framed the director's tan face and white hair in a halo of morning sunlight, making him look like a dark cloud with a silver lining. Ann stood for a moment, waiting for him to finish reading something. He finally set the papers down and looked up.

"Ann, have a seat, please."

She closed the door and ignored the invitation to sit, instead straightening to her full five feet eight inches, against the pull of her shoulder holster. The shoulder holster, which violated a department policy mandating the use of hip holsters, was allowed in her case because of a bad back. She was aware of a distant tickle as a drop of sweat ran down the small of her back under her white cotton blouse and beige blazer.

"Once again, Ann, I'm sorry. I would have been at the funeral, but I couldn't get out of the damned governor's conference. I hope the flowers got there. I understand it was a—" He struggled for the right words, and finally settled for, "—a beautiful service."

Ann nodded.

"I think taking some personal time is an excellent idea, it'll give you a little time to sort things out."

"I appreciate the time off, Marvin." Ann could see that he knew what was on her mind, so she dropped the small talk. "Did you talk to—"

"After our conversation the other day," he said, cutting her off, "I had another talk with the Curran County D.A.

but with nothing new to bring to the table, he's not inclined to reopen the investigation."

Ann bit her lip and stared at the director, allowing his image to drift out of focus.

"Look, let it go, Ann. Try to think about something else for awhile."

She crossed her arms and scanned the plaques on the wall. "What did you have in mind? Because I'm fresh out of ideas."

"Ann—"

"It occurred to me the other day, Marvin, how ironic it is that the DCI's in the Wisconsin Department of Justice." She turned toward Schifsky. "Don't you think that's ironic?"

Schifsky's response was humorless and flat. "No, I don't see anything particularly 'ironic' about that."

"You don't? My father worked for the Curran County Sheriff's Department for thirty years—"

"Ann."

"Thirty damn years, Marvin, so where's his justice? After a lifetime of putting his life on the line for the law, where's the law when he needs it?"

"Ann, the sheriff's office did an investigation."

"We could have sent someone up there to assist."

"You know we can't just insert ourselves into an investigation. The sheriff said he had it covered; we weren't invited to the party—sorry, we weren't asked." Schifsky removed his glasses, laid them carefully on the desk, and leaned forward. "Ann, I know that you didn't see a lot of your father, living this far away from him. Isn't there even a remote possibility that you didn't know everything that was going on in his head? I think you mentioned once that he never remarried after your mother passed away."

Ann studied the light that was magnified through the lens of Schifsky's reading glasses on the desk and understood that her petition carried about as much weight as a letter to Santa. The simple fact was that her boss believed the investigation's findings. He knew how common cop suicides were, and he wasn't going to change his mind. She dug her fingernails into her palm and crossed her arms to conceal the gesture.

"I still haven't gotten a look at the final report."

"I put the request in, they said it was on the way. I don't know what the delay is."

"Seems a little unprofessional."

Ann knew her comment was the equivalent of elevator music and existed only in the vacuum left by the absence of something more meaningful. Schifsky seemed to struggle for a reply.

"I'll put in another request."

"Who's holding it up?"

"It's probably just something with the paperwork, maybe a clerk took a sick day. I'll call up there, see what I can do."

"Don't bother, I'll pick up a copy myself."

Schifsky studied Ann for a moment before he spoke. "You're going back up there?"

"I thought I mentioned that."

"No. No, I don't think you did." He paused. "We're both clear that you're on leave, right Ann?"

Ann didn't respond until she realized he was waiting for an acknowledgment. "Of course, Marvin." She didn't think he looked convinced. "My father left a house full of things for my sister and me to deal with. There's a lot to do."

Schifsky sighed in resignation. "I checked with Personnel. With the vacation time you've accrued, and the personal days, you've got three weeks of paid leave coming, take as much of that as you want."

"Thanks, Marvin."

"And that weapon," he indicated the Glock that he knew Ann carried under her blazer, "will find its way to the armory before you leave the building."

Schifsky put his glasses back on and began straightening his already orderly desk, and Ann recognized his usual signal that the meeting was over. "And by the way, I was just being polite earlier when I said this leave was a good idea. The truth is we're buried here, and I'm going to have to listen to Zack's whining about being overworked until you get back."

Ann worked to give him a smile before opening the door to leave, but then stopped, and turned back to face him. "Did you know my father received a departmental citation last month?"

"No, I wasn't aware of that."

"He went in the First Federal Savings in Hudson and walked smack into a robbery in progress. Some guy working alone was waving a gun around and had everyone in the bank lying on the floor. This guy was bending over the counter and didn't hear my dad when he came in. When he straightened up, he felt a gun pressed to the back of his head and heard a voice in his ear say 'Police—freeze and you may live through this'." Ann smiled. "He loved cop shows on TV. Anyway, he reached around and took the gun out of the guy's hand and stepped back. When the robber turned around, my dad was standing there with the guy's gun in one hand, and his Bic lighter in the other."

Schifsky had listened patiently to the story and now smiled at Ann. "He was a good cop Ann, you've got that."

"Yeah." Ann nodded. "He was a good cop. You know why he was in that bank in the first place?" She looked directly at Schifsky, who seemed caught off-guard by the question.

"Not a clue."

"He had an appointment to arrange a loan so he could buy a new bass boat." Ann knew her boss well and could tell from his expression that he was connecting the dots. "I know it's nothing that we can take to the D.A., Marvin, but it seems like odd behavior for someone who's supposed to be suicidal." Just before Ann pulled the door closed behind her, she glanced back and noticed that the sun was gone, and with it the director's silver lining.

Out in the office, Zack Rose was leaning against Ann's desk holding a cup of coffee in each hand and giving his chewing gum a thorough workout. He was wearing a cell phone earpiece, had a ring through his left eyebrow, and a smirk on his face. His short, punk-style haircut made him appear much younger than his thirty-two years.

"Knew that wouldn't take long," he extended a cup toward her.

Ann accepted the coffee without a word.

"Did you know coffee beans aren't really beans at all? They're seeds."

Ann knew better than to encourage him. She just watched her partner over the rim of her cup, while she took a sip.

"True beans are the seeds or pods of certain leguminous plants."

"Leguminous plants?"

"Uh, huh."

Neither of them spoke for a minute, and the silence had the quality of clearing the air. Finally, Zack lowered his voice and asked, "Now what?"

"My sister, Hallie, and her husband are going to stay with me at our father's house in Higgins Point for a week or so." She blew across her cup. "I'm heading back up there later this morning."

Zack nodded. "From what I saw of it during the funeral, Higgins Point's a nice quiet place, very pastoral."

"Yeah, it's been almost twenty years since I did anything but spend Christmas there."

"And you're staying at your father's house?"

Ann nodded.

Zack frowned for an instant. "That wasn't where . . ."

"No. He was found at his cabin."

Zack's smile returned. "Kick back time, huh? I suppose you're going to do a little fishing?

"Probably."

"Maybe some hunting?"

Ann looked at him. "Nothing's in season."

"Yeah, the great outdoors." He paused for a beat. "Ann, who do you think you're kidding? You start poking around up there, and you better be invisible, or the Schifmeister's gonna light you up and hang you out to dry."

Ann tried not to laugh but a snort escaped.

"Okay, I mixed my metaphors, but you get the idea."

"I can be invisible."

"What am I worried about? You could never trash the regulations anyway; it's not in your nature."

"Oh, and you know all about my nature?"

"Me and everybody else who ever worked with you. Think it through, Ann; rash action is the enemy of logic."

"Last week you told me that desperation was the enemy of logic."

"Desperation leads to rash action—which is the enemy of logic."

Ann kicked herself for the tenth time for buying him that desk calendar.

"Something's going on, Zack."

His eyebrows went up and his gaze settled on the floor. "Christ, Ann, they turned up nothing. I mean, I assume those were careful people looking into it, and—well, nothing."

She let her partner have the last word on the subject. But as she walked away from the Lorraine Building, Ann thought about his comment, and it occurred to her that maybe the people looking into her father's death weren't the only ones being careful.

While Ann was getting into her car in Madison, three hundred miles north, Dexter Loomis was sitting in his

Cherokee, staring across the street at Ardella Tophler's house. The aging two-story colonial was only a few blocks from his office, which wasn't surprising; Higgins Point was so small that anywhere was only a few blocks from anywhere else. He was groggy from lack of sleep. He'd been awake last night for hours, listening to the rain, while he tried to figure out what it was that bothered him about Muriel Evenson's 'accident'.

He finally got out of his Cherokee and walked across the street and around to the back of the house, where he stood staring down at what the rainstorm had left of the maroon stain on the driveway. He pictured Muriel lying motionless in the spotlight and remembered the faint fragrance of her perfume. Cigarette smoke invaded his subconscious before he actually realized Ardella was standing next to him.

"Hello, Dexter."

He jumped slightly and recovered. "Morning, Ardella."

She was wearing faded blue sweatpants with house slippers and a sleeveless flowered top. She held her cigarette in her mouth while rubbing her crossed arms as though she were chilled, though it was already eighty degrees and barely 10:00 in the morning.

"Thought I'd take another look around." Dexter intended to add something more, some sort of explanation, but realized, as soon as he began to formulate it, that he wasn't sure why he was there.

"I called the Evensons this morning," she said. "I told them how sorry I was—and I offered to take care of Brando for them."

"Brando? Oh, her dog." Dexter recalled that it was the German Shepherd's barking that had brought Ardella to the backyard where she'd found Muriel. He took a notepad and pen out of his khaki shirt pocket.

"What time did you say the dog started barking?"

"Eleven-thirty."

"Last night you said something about why this was suspicious. He didn't usually bark, or—"

"He only barked when Muriel was gone—" She tilted her head and peered at his notepad as she spoke. "—and someone came to the door."

"So you came out here because he kept on barking?"

"Uh huh, wouldn't stop."

Dexter scribbled this down. "Would you mind coming upstairs with me for a few minutes?"

Ardella seemed to think this over carefully before answering. "I guess I could."

Together they walked back around to the front of the house and up the carpeted stairs that led to Muriel's second floor apartment. Having been in the apartment for the first time in his life only a few hours earlier, Dexter's familiarity with the front room felt odd. Ardella picked up a photograph in a modern looking silver frame from the end table, and when Dexter looked at it over her shoulder, the smoke from her cigarette stung his eyes. In the picture, Muriel was on stage dressed in some sort of Victorian costume with several other actors. They were smiling and holding hands, apparently taking a curtain call.

"She loved acting and I believe she was pretty good—I know she could sing. That fellow on the far left," she indicated a slightly older man in a sport coat, "that's her boyfriend. He teaches drama at the college. His name is Padgett, Geoffrey Padgett."

"Her boyfriend's an actor and her teacher?" Feeling a little like an actor himself, Dexter wrote this information down. "Can they do that now, date their students?"

Ardella shrugged. "He used to come around more often than he has lately."

"You were her landlady. Did you know Muriel well? Did you talk much?"

"Oh yes. She was very friendly, and she liked to help me in the garden."

"Anyone else come around to see her?"

"Well, her friend Cara Lynn was over a lot. I think they were pretty good friends. And then there was that young hoodlum friend of Cara Lynn's, Billy something. He used to come over too, sometimes by himself."

Dexter was writing, and without looking up he asked, "Billy, huh? And he struck you as a hoodlum?"

"Well, it's not my place to judge, and Lord knows I'll never get used to young men with earrings, but the times when I saw him coming in or out he just seemed so . . ."

"So what?"

"Well, menacing."

Dexter paused. "He ever do anything specific, anything you can point to?"

"Not really. I probably shouldn't have said anything."

Ardella set the photograph back on the table, and as they walked into the bedroom she said, "She worked at the bank, you know."

"Which one?"

"First National, I think, on Delphi Street."

He walked over to Muriel's dresser. Its top contained several tiny glass figurines and random pieces of jewelry arrayed on a lace doily along with more photographs in a variety of frames. The aroma from a small bottle of perfume brought Muriel's memory into sudden focus. On the floor beside the dresser was a small blue nylon knapsack. He picked it up and looked inside. There was a notebook, a macroeconomics textbook, a speech textbook, several books of collected plays, and a dog-eared script of *Macbeth*. He set the knapsack down. The wastebasket next to her dresser was empty except for a manila folder. He plucked it out and looked at the tab on the side, it read *First Nat. Bank.*

"This the bank she worked at?"

Ardella craned her neck to look at the folder. "That's it."

"I don't suppose you know anyone who was bothering

her? You know, someone obvious, who'd make this whole thing easy?"

"I thought you said it was an accident?"

"Let's pretend it wasn't for a minute." He dropped the folder back into the wastebasket.

"Well, she seemed to have a lot of friends, but I don't recall her having any problems with anyone." Ardella's eyes welled up and she paused for a moment. "I'm sorry, it's just . . . how could this happen to her? She was such a nice girl. If it wasn't an accident, who would do this?"

Dexter led her out of the bedroom, searching for something insightful to say, but finally gave up.

"Can you remember anything else, anything unusual about last night?"

Ardella was using one cigarette to light another, which he noticed was unfiltered.

"No." She hesitated, and then said, "Wait, you know it seems like I heard a car starting about the time I came outside. I believe I did."

They were walking through the kitchen toward the back deck.

"Which direction?"

"I'm sorry, I couldn't really tell."

"On this street?"

Ardella only shrugged her shoulders. Dexter wrote this down and then slid the glass door open and stepped out onto the deck. He walked over to the side above the driveway and peered over the edge at the pavement, where a faded ribbon of dried blood formed a crooked line. He examined the splintered end of the railing that remained attached to the deck but saw no evidence of rotting that could explain a weakening in the wood.

Ardella stood back by the door with her arms crossed and held her cigarette near her mouth. "The sheriff said she must have tripped and fallen against the railing."

Dexter walked across the deck to the opposite side from

the driveway, where the railing was still undamaged. He leaned against it applying a little weight, gauging the resistance. He leaned a little harder, and then bumped the railing with his hip. There was a tiny bark from the nailed joints, but it seemed solid.

Ardella lowered her cigarette. "Dexter, you be careful."

Then he stepped back, raised his foot, and kicked the rail, which gave a sharp cry of complaint but otherwise remained intact. Ardella seemed too shocked to say anything, her cigarette hung forgotten at her side. Dexter kicked a little harder and the railing shuddered and moved a little. Finally he reared back and kicked violently, and the railing splintered and fell onto the lawn below. He looked over the edge of the deck studying the broken pieces lying on the grass, and suddenly realized what had seemed odd to him about the scene the night before. He looked over at Ardella, who was staring at him with her mouth open.

"I'll pay to have the railing repaired."

Ardella brought her cigarette up to her mouth without taking her eyes off of Dexter.

Chapter Five

On Friday afternoon, Ann pulled her Stratus into the driveway of her father's home in Higgins Point. The dirt driveway ran for a hundred and fifty feet through a stand of blue spruce and Norway pines and was covered with needles and cones. At the end of the driveway sat the familiar two-story home. The white aluminum siding was slightly yellowed along the foundation, and there was a prominent dent next to the garage door where, at the age of eleven, Ann had hurled an errant high hard one. That was the year she had been determined to play baseball with the boys, before eventually discovering guns and fishing rods. That was also the year that her mother had died.

The garage door was up and there was a rental car parked inside. Hallie and Ted were in the house, and Hallie was undoubtedly fixing dinner. If she was living and breathing, her sister was cooking. Ann sat in her car, stared at the front door, and thought about staying here. She hadn't actually lived in the house for nineteen years, and Hallie had been away even longer. Their bedrooms were on the second floor, and their father had kept them unchanged since the girls left home. Looking around at the house and yard, Ann suddenly realized what seemed strange to her; she wasn't accustomed to being here without everything covered with snow. She couldn't remember the last time that she'd been up here during the summer. No, that wasn't true, she had been up here fishing with her father four years ago, the same summer she'd transferred into homicide.

Ann finally got out of her car and pulled two suitcases out of the trunk. One habit she'd never managed to pick up from her father was his knack for packing light. She stepped up onto the porch and opened the front door, letting it swing wide. Leaving her bags in the doorway, she stepped inside and inhaled the smell of the house, surveying the small front room. The arm of her father's overstuffed chair, a comfortably frayed, brown monstrosity, still held an empty coffee cup. Back issues of *Guns 'N Ammo* and *Field and Stream* lay on the ottoman, and a two-week-old newspaper lay on the floor next to the chair. Ann heard the refrigerator go on in the kitchen and thought, *the house doesn't even know he's gone.*

Hallie came out of the kitchen wiping her hands on a dishtowel. When she saw Ann, she smiled.

"Thought I heard a car. Hey, little sister, glad to see you."

"Hey, big sister. You guys get settled in okay?"

Hallie sighed and looked around. "Oh, yeah." Then her faced cracked a little and she stepped over to Ann. Then they were in each other's arms, both of them crying softly, discretely avoiding eye contact. After a minute they released one another and shared the dishtowel to wipe their eyes.

"I really am glad you're here." Hallie laughed a little nervously. "Ted and I spent last night here and it felt kind of creepy."

Ann smiled. "Ted's not that creepy."

Hallie laughed and punched her sister's shoulder. "That's not what I meant. It's like I'm afraid to touch anything, you know?"

"Actually, for the time being, how about if we don't touch anything we don't have to?"

Hallie smiled quizzically and then the smile melted away. "You're serious? You mean because of evidence?"

Ann touched Hallie's shoulder. "Just until I can take a good look around, okay?"

Hallie nodded.

"Where's Ted?"

"He's upstairs taking a nap."

Ann went over and closed the front door and picked up her bags.

"I hope you don't mind," Hallie said, "we took dad's room—you know, because of the double bed."

"That's fine, it makes sense."

She hiked up the stairs to her bedroom, pausing when she reached the upstairs hallway. Her father's bedroom was off to her left, cast in soft shade, curtains drawn. She could hear Ted's faint snoring. She set the suitcases down again and studied the framed photographs that covered the walls, and for the hundredth time recalled the last phone conversation she'd had with her father. "Annie," he'd said simply, "it's your old man. There's something I need your help with." Whatever was on his mind had been important enough for him to insist on a face-to-face meeting. He had planned to make the drive from Higgins Point down to Ann's apartment in Madison on the following day, but he never arrived. It was later determined that he had died within hours of hanging up the phone.

Ann forced the thoughts away. She took a deep breath, picked up her bags, and carried them into her bedroom.

Crouching behind bushes near the corner of his cottage, Dexter gripped the rifle and stared out into his backyard. His house sat on an acre of land a few miles north of Higgins Point, and had been left to him by his aunt Myra when she passed away two years earlier. There was a neighbor on one side, and nothing but dirt road on the other, and trees everywhere. The front yard was tiny like a postage stamp, which was fine with Dexter, who didn't see any point to spending a lot of time and energy maintaining a big yard. The back yard, though large, was mostly restored to original prairie, and was a riot of wildflowers. Inheriting the cottage had eventually allowed Dexter to retire from his county engineering job. He'd hoped that part-time employment as a town cop would provide enough pocket money to avoid eating up his savings. The job had been a low-stress diversion, and a way to stay involved with the community—until recently.

He heard footsteps on the gravel driveway behind him and glanced back to see Grady Penz approaching.

"Get down!"

Grady hesitated, looking around until a gesture from Dexter sent him dropping to the ground. He scuttled forward.

"Don't worry. When a white lunatic with a gun says 'get down,' I'm gettin' down."

Dexter rolled his eyes. "Knock it off, he'll hear you."

"Who'll hear me?" Grady leaned forward on his hands and knees like a pointer, peering through the bushes. "What am I lookin' at?"

Dexter sighted down the barrel. "By the birdfeeder."

Across the backyard, tinged in a soft pink glow from the setting sun, a squirrel rested on the ground eating birdseed.

"Nothin' there but a squirrel." Grady studied the gun in Dexter's hands. "Dexter, you don't own a twenty-two."

"I borrowed it from Steve, next door."

"And you gonna shoot that squirrel?"

"He plants himself up there on that feeder every day. I'm going broke paying for birdseed. I figure it's his turn to pay."

"That's 'cause your feeder is what they call an attractive nuisance."

"A what?"

"It means he can't resist, so it's your fault."

Dexter looked at Grady. "I thought it through, okay? It's easier to kill him than to explain to the city that I need a raise to pay for birdseed."

"He's not on your feeder, he's sittin' on the ground."

"So what?"

"Can't shoot him if he's not on the feeder."

Dexter lowered the rifle and looked at Grady. "Is there some rule about this that I'm not aware of?"

"Karma."

"Excuse me?"

"Karma. Means what goes around, comes around."

Dexter looked at the squirrel. "So if I shoot him—"

"Someday, somebody gonna shoot you."

Dexter felt a headache coming on. "You're just full of useful information today. What do you want anyway?"

Grady turned away from the squirrel and sat on the grass, leaning against the house.

"I want to talk about the Evenson girl."

Dexter was glad to hear that. "So do I." He set the rifle down and sat next to Grady.

"Maybe you ought to go first," Grady said.

Dexter drew a slow breath. "I went back over to her apartment this morning and took a look at the railing she was supposed to have fallen through."

"Supposed to?"

"I don't think someone Muriel's size could have broken the railing just tripping and falling against it."

"Think she was pushed?"

Dexter shook his head. "It took a while for me to figure out that what was bothering me last night. It was the way the railing was tangled up with her legs. However she ended up on the ground, I think it's possible that the railing came down after."

"Meanin' somebody knocked the railing down?"

"After they threw her off the deck, to make it look like an accident."

It felt strange to Dexter to say it out loud like that. Neither man spoke for a minute until Dexter finally asked, "What did you want to talk about?"

"I thought I saw a flush in her cheeks. Wasn't sure, 'cause of the poor light."

"Yeah, you mentioned something about that last night. I didn't see it, but what would it mean?"

"It could have been caused by hemorrhaging around the face."

"Why would she hemorrhage?"

"If she was strangled or smothered."

The words took a few seconds to sink in. "You think it's possible?"

"If it was there, it was faint, but yeah, it's possible."

"If we have an autopsy done, the medical examiner should be able to tell, right?"

"That's why I'm here."

"Autopsies don't happen automatically, do they?" Dexter asked.

"No, only if there's a question about the death."

"Well, it sounds like we both have questions about her death."

Suddenly a short man in suspenders came walking up Dexter's driveway taking quick, energetic steps, and Dexter recognized the reporter and his notepad from the previous evening.

"Howdy, Chief."

"Hello, Mr—ah."

"Kahler. Frank Kahler, Pioneer Press."

"That's right. This is Grady Penz."

Grady stood up next to Dexter and nodded.

He scribbled down Grady's name. "You were there last night. I've seen you around before. You're an EMT, right?"

Grady nodded again. "New Richmond Medical Center."

"Grady was the first one on the scene last night," Dexter explained. "So what brings you out here, Mr. Kahler?"

"Call me Frank, okay? Nothing much, just the Evenson girl's murder."

In spite of Dexter's suspicion that it was indeed murder, his instinct was to deny it until he had something concrete to point to. "Nothing's been established that—"

Grady placed a restraining hand on Dexter's arm. "It was an accident, Frank, like the sheriff said."

"C'mon. I talked to the coroner who brought her in. He doesn't think the head injury could have killed her."

Dexter wasn't sure what to say. "You talked to the coroner?"

"Yeah! Are you surprised?"

"It was an accident," was Dexter's only response.

Kahler took a second while he put a skeptical expression on his face. "Look, here's how it works. I collect everybody's version of the facts, mash 'em all together, and write a story. You know, so the public is informed about what their police force is doing to serve and protect them."

"Then go write your story," Dexter replied.

"Ah, but if you won't talk to me, then I can only write what other people tell me, and nobody gets to hear your version."

Dexter shook his head. "As far as we know, she fell against the railing somehow and went over."

"Now we're getting somewhere; specifics." Kahler scribbled on his pad. "Any theories about what would cause her to hit the railing hard enough to break it?"

"Maybe she tripped. We're still looking into that."

Kahler looked up, and Grady winced.

"Oh, you're looking into it. So, there is an investigation? Thought you said it was an accident? Want to adjust that statement?"

"Why don't you lay off the man?" Grady asked.

"Okay, let's switch topics. How come Higgins Point's

entire one-man police force is sitting around on his can Friday afternoon, instead of looking for answers to this 'accident'?"

Dexter almost blurted out that Sheriff Hicks also thought that it was an accident but caught himself in time. Instead he ad-libbed a statement that he thought sounded official, like the ones he'd heard on television. "We don't have any evidence at this time that points to foul play."

"Foul play?" Kahler grinned at Grady. "Is he kidding?" He looked back at Dexter. "So you're going to dummy up on me, huh? A one man 'blue wall'? What do you think this is about, anyway, Chief?"

"I know what this is about," Dexter said. "This is about a sleazy reporter trying to find something sensational to fill up his column."

"No, it isn't," Kahler replied. "This is about a dead nineteen-year-old girl. If you can't get anything else right, at least try and remember that."

"Hey, you're talking to the Chief of Police," Grady reminded him.

"Thanks for your time, Chief."

After they'd watched Kahler walk back down the driveway to his car, Grady shook his head. "Sleazy reporter?"

"I guess I could have handled that better."

Grady shrugged. "Maybe, seein' how he might be right about it being murder, but he was gettin' out of line."

Dexter picked up the .22. "Something just told me to keep things under wraps for the time being; in case we're wrong." Dexter glanced into the backyard and noticed that the squirrel was now up on the feeder.

"Probably a good idea," Grady said, "in case we're wrong."

Dexter thought about the alternative possibility. "You know, I hope to hell we are wrong about this."

He crouched down and eased the barrel of the rifle through the bushes.

"Leave that rifle alone. Don't be temptin' your Karma."

Hanging by his hind legs, the squirrel swung athletically from the suspended feeder cramming birdseed into his mouth.

Dexter drew a bead. "Relax, he's got to be at least sixty feet away," he said as he squeezed the trigger. "If I hit him, it'd be a miracle."

An hour later, after Dexter had deposited the victim of his 'miracle shot' into a hastily prepared shallow grave in the corner of his lot, he returned the .22 to Steve and promised himself he would never shoot another unarmed animal. Then he put in a call to Sheriff Hicks to try and convince him of the need for an autopsy on Muriel Evenson. He was told the sheriff was in a meeting, so his next call was to the Franklin Funeral Home. He got Elliot, the oldest son in the family business, on the line and asked if they had done anything to Muriel's body yet.

"That was a terrible thing—someone so young." Elliot's speech was precise and soothing. "In spite of what you may believe, no matter how long one is in the business, it's impossible not to feel a measure of genuine grief when someone so young is taken."

Dexter wasn't sure if he should bother to clarify that he'd never believed otherwise. So he just waited for Elliot to continue.

"She was brought in a little after 1:00 AM this morning. We did the arterial embalming immediately."

"The reason I ask," Dexter said, "is we want to have an autopsy performed, and I wanted to catch you before it was too late."

"Arterial embalming doesn't interfere with an autopsy," Elliot explained. "Everything's still intact, we just replaced the blood."

"So we can still go ahead?"

"Certainly, but the visitation was to be this Sunday. The

service will have to be rescheduled, and we'll want to do that as soon as possible. May I ask when the autopsy is scheduled?"

Dexter paused. "I'll have to get back to you on that."

His last call was to Dick Evenson. It was barely fifteen hours since they'd both stood over his daughter's body, and it wasn't an easy call to make. When Evenson answered the phone, his voice sounded distant. Dexter asked him how his wife, Inez, was holding up.

"As well as can be expected, I guess. The pastor's here now. They're in the front room."

Dexter had no idea how to say what he had to say, so he just blurted it out. "Dick, I want to have an autopsy done on Muriel."

The line was quiet for a moment. "Autopsies are for . . . I thought you said this was an accident?"

"I know I said that last night, but it's turning out now that there may be some question." Saying this to Muriel's father based on pure speculation gave Dexter the queasy feeling of stepping out over a long drop.

Evenson's voice gained power. "Are you telling me that somebody did this to her?"

"I'm telling you that we don't know, Dick, but an autopsy would help answer the question."

"But who would possibly—"

"I want you to give that question some thought. Let me know if you think of anyone who might have a reason . . . I don't know, maybe somebody in her crowd." This was met with silence.

"Dick, you there?"

"I'm just wondering what I'm going to tell Inez."

"Maybe you shouldn't tell her anything until we know more. There may be nothing to this."

"Is that what you think, Dex, that there's nothing to it?"

Dexter paused a little longer than he intended. "I'm going to have to get back to you on that."

Chapter Six

The ceiling fans mingled the greasy-sweet aromas of Saturday breakfast while Ann sat at the counter of Janet's Café, finished the last of her bacon and eggs, and studied the front page of the *St. Paul Pioneer Press*. One of only two breakfast spots in Higgins Point, Janet's was where she and her father usually ate during her visits. It was a comfortable place, from the cloth-covered stools, to the small blackboard that displayed the day's specials, to the conversation of the customers, most of whom knew one another.

In the half-hour that she'd been sitting there, Ann had recognized and said hello to several people. Among them, Cliff Helstedt, a retired friend of her father's who used to work in robbery for the county sheriff's office, and Linda Bursch, a fellow graduate of Higgins Point High, who was getting a coffee to-go on her way to a house showing for Edina Realty. The surprise had been a tidy-looking lady with deep-set, peaceful eyes, perhaps sixty-five years old.

"You're Annie Summer, aren't you?" she'd asked. "Do you remember me? I'm Claire Schultz."

When Ann pleaded ignorance, the woman revealed that she had known Ann's mother many years earlier. She told Ann she was sorry about her father, and they spoke for several minutes. When Claire left the restaurant, Ann marveled at how she could have recognized Ann after so many years, and for just a moment, she wished that she'd never left Higgins Point.

Ann went back to her newspaper, and when she paused for a sip of coffee, she shifted her gaze to the large window that opened onto Main Street. A man was walking across the street toward Janet's with a stride so distinctively ungainly that she recognized him from his walk before she could fully discern his features. He was tall and slender with unruly black hair that looked as if it hadn't been combed since she'd last seen him almost twenty years earlier. Dexter Loomis was coming to Janet's for breakfast.

He entered the restaurant, nodded at a couple of people, and was about to sit down when he happened to glance at Ann. A look of surprise scrambled his features, but by the time he stood before her, a smile had bloomed on his face.

"Annie Summer!"

"Dexter Loomis!" Ann replied, mimicking his cadence.

"Well, son of a gun, it's still Summer, isn't it?"

Ann noticed his glance at her ring finger and squeezed her eyes in disapproval.

"It must have been your tact that Hallie found so charming." She let her smile slip through. "And yes, it is still Summer."

He took the seat next to her at the counter, ordered coffee, and then turned and looked at Ann so closely that she was caught off guard by a sudden concern for her appearance.

"So what happened to the tomboy I used to know?" Dexter's expression clouded, and his hand went to his forehead. "Oh, what an idiot. Look, I'm sorry about your father."

"Thank you," Ann said quietly, studying the counter in front of her.

"I went to the funeral, but I pretty much stayed out of

the way. I talked to Hallie for a minute, but I don't think you noticed me."

"She said she saw you."

"I suppose you're in town to take care of your father's affairs."

Ann nodded. "Hallie and her husband, Ted, are staying with me at dad's place."

"Any idea how long you're going to be around?"

"That depends on how long it takes to clear things up."

Dexter nodded. "Yeah, probably a lot to go through. Wow, what's it been now, eighteen years since you left?"

"Nineteen."

"Been in Madison all that time?"

"Well, I usually manage to get back here for Christmas."

A cup of coffee appeared before Dexter, placed there by a waitress who was already on to other stops.

"Funny I haven't run into you before now."

"Hallie mentioned that you were some sort of engineer," Ann said.

"Yeah, was, civil. I put in sixteen years with the county, but I'm, uh, retired."

Ann took another look at him. "Wait a minute, you're only four years older than me." She took her time reacquainting herself with the lines of Dexter's face. As a kid, she'd had a crush on him and had always resented being told to get lost. She used to accept movie money from them and then hang around spying on Dexter and her sister.

"I thought it made more sense to retire when I could still enjoy it." He grinned and veered the conversation back toward her. "You're a local legend, Annie. Everyone around here knows what happened to you. Division of Criminal Investigation in Madison, right?"

"Uh, huh."

Dexter raised his coffee cup. "Here's to a serious cop. So what's the worst part about working for the DCI?"

Ann didn't hesitate. "That's easy. Not being able to have a dog."

"How about the best part of your job?"

Ann thought for a minute. "I guess the autonomy. I'm away from the Madison office and on my own a lot of the time. That and when I manage to get a result, it feels great."

"A 'result' being a collar?"

"Yeah. It makes a difference to me when I see the family of a victim get some closure."

"Victims? What area do you work in?"

"Narcotics originally, then white collar crime, and for the last four years, I've been in homicide."

Dexter's eyes narrowed. "You investigate murders?"

"We call them death investigations. Yes, I do." Before Ann had a chance to add anything, a man wearing the neon orange vest commonly seen around road construction sites appeared at Dexter's side and slapped him on the back.

"What do ya say, Mr. *Police Chief*?"

Dexter glanced up and then smiled. "Hey, Daryl."

Ann watched Dexter look around the room until he located the table with the other orange vests and waved. He apparently knew that these guys didn't travel alone.

"Ann Summer, Mr. Daryl Hains."

Ann nodded. "How you doing, Daryl?"

"Better now that I got someone to fix my tickets for me." He winked at Ann and grinned, and with a flourish, produced a small, white paper bag, which he presented to Dexter. "Dex, me and the guys thought you could use this."

Dexter opened the bag and withdrew a powder sugar doughnut. Hoots could be heard across the café from the direction of the table of orange vests. He took a bite.

"Tell the guys," he said, wiping the powder from his mouth and raising his voice, "that I prefer mine nutty."

More hoots, and Ann noticed a few people from other tables joining in. Daryl shook Dexter's hand and wished him good luck and then retreated to the breakfast waiting back at his table. Ann studied Dexter for a moment.

"*Police Chief*?"

Dexter took another bite of the doughnut. "Well, there's a very boring story there actually." He held the bag of doughnuts toward her. "Want one?"

She shook her head. "I thought you said you were retired?"

"I retired from engineering. Sixteen years with the county was enough municipal red tape for me. I took a job working for Lewis Coffers, and now I have all different red tape. Lewis was our Police Chief. He needed help with campground patrols, traffic duty, that kind of thing. I just do it to keep busy. It's not supposed to be a big deal."

"But *Chief*?"

"About three months ago, just after I hired on, they took Lewis to the hospital with a heart attack. Only it wasn't a heart attack, it turned out to be more like—severe indigestion."

"Indigestion?"

Dexter nodded. "His secret barbecue sauce. But the time he spent in the hospital started him thinking, so when he spotted a cut-rate airfare in the paper, he realized that he'd never really been anywhere and decided to fly down to Boca Raton. That's down in Florida, just above Miami on the Atlantic side."

"I know where Boca Raton is," Ann said.

Dexter took a bite of his doughnut. "Anyway, he must have liked what he saw because a few weeks after he came back, he quit. Moved down there for good about three weeks ago, and then last week our mayor, Dick Evenson, appointed me police chief until they could line up someone permanent."

"You've been chief of police for a week?"

Dexter's eyebrows went up. "I like to think I bring a fresh point of view to the job."

"I take it you used to work with Daryl?"

"Yeah, I've known some of those guys for a long time. They do surveying for the county, which means they're all certifiable."

"Let's see if I understand this. You spent sixteen years as a county engineer and have only been in law enforcement for three months?"

He took a slow breath and let it out. "I'm enrolled in the required law enforcement classes, so I'm legal under Wisconsin law."

"You're legal." Ann was just realizing that his blue jeans and khaki shirt constituted some sort of uniform. "Are you on-duty now?"

"Hey, are we cops ever really off-duty?" Dexter asked, smiling.

"Didn't they give you some sort of badge?"

Dexter glanced down at his shirt. "I must have left it on the dresser."

"Where's your gun?"

"In the Cherokee."

"You shouldn't leave it in your vehicle, Dexter. You should keep it on your person."

"I guess they didn't get to that part in the class yet." Dexter reached into his shirt pocket and produced several bullets. "It's okay, it's not loaded."

Ann took one of the bullets and studied it. "Congratulations on your antique. I didn't think anyone still carried a .38 revolver." She had the feeling she was in an episode of *The Andy Griffith Show*. "Oh, and these go in the gun, not in the pocket."

"That's what I thought too, until I read somewhere that the number one cause of accidents involving firearms is loaded guns—and don't you have any hobbies?"

"Hobbies?"

"Anything we can talk about to change the subject. What have you been doing for the past two decades?"

Ann laughed. "Well, I like to hunt and fish and rock climb, and I'm a sucker for a good target range."

Dexter thought about this. "I like to paint." he said, and then added, "watercolors mostly—usually while I'm scaling live volcanoes."

Dexter's smile removed years from his face and reminded Ann of the boy who used to walk her older sister home from school.

A thought occurred to Ann. "Were you the police chief a week ago, when my father was—when he died?"

"That was a quick change of subject. Fact is, I heard about your father the same morning I was promoted."

"Did you have anything to do with the investigation into his death?"

Dexter shook his head. "Just campgrounds and traffic, like I said. Sheriff Hicks handled it."

"Were you close enough to the investigation to have an opinion about it?"

"No, but even if I was, I'm not really qualified enough to have an opinion about it."

"And Lewis Coffers was in Florida?"

"Yeah. He was gone before it happened. My understanding was that your father—that his death was a suicide."

Ann ignored the statement and began hunting through her purse for her wallet. "So, Dexter, now that we're fellow members of the fraternal order of law enforcement officers, is police work turning out to be what you expected?"

"It's okay, I guess—except when I have to associate with the criminal element."

"The criminal element, huh?" Ann laid some money on the counter, and Dexter pushed it back toward her with a wink.

"It's on me, Annie, welcome back."

"Thank you, Dexter. Hallie always said, in spite of everything else, you were a gentleman."

"In spite of everything else? Everything else what?"

Ann stood up and smiled. "It's been nice seeing you again, Dexter Loomis."

"If you're going to be in town for a while, can I call you?"

"Do that."

He took another doughnut out of the bag, and studied it for a moment. When Ann started to turn toward the door he said, "Tell me something, Annie."

She paused. "If I can."

"I'm a trained engineer, so when I approach an engineering problem, my reasoning is fairly reliable, but I'm not a trained lawman. I guess what I'm getting at is, when you're on a case, how do you know when you're on the right track?"

The serious tone in his voice caused Ann to consider her reply carefully.

"This is where I'm supposed to mention the value of course work and experience, but the truth is that nothing's ever a lock. If you're talking about the physical aspects of a crime there are guidelines to help; you follow the evidence and see where it leads. But if you're talking about the human elements of a crime, the emotions, and the factors that establish motive, then things aren't always so direct." A thought occurred to Ann. "Dexter, if you knew anything about my father's death, or had any suspicions, you'd tell me, right?"

"This isn't about your father, Annie. I'm sorry if I gave you that impression. It has to do with something else."

"Sure, my mistake." The quick denial and Dexter's expression of mild embarrassment leveled Ann's brief hope of learning something about her father's death.

"I know what you're thinking," Dexter said, "how much crime can there be in this one-horse town, anyway?"

Ann looked into his face, and surprised herself with a small, but genuine laugh. "Now that you mention it." She walked to the door and turned. "I thought you said you didn't like associating with the criminal element, Dexter?"

He smiled. "I don't, but I guess sooner or later we all have to do things we don't want to do."

"Sooner or later," Ann said, as she pushed the door open.

Sheriff Moses Hicks' two-story home in Candle, Wisconsin, sat on half-a-dozen rural acres. The expansive lawn, graced with a variety of gardens and shrubs, had the unmistakable appearance of professionally maintained grounds, which is exactly what they were. The house itself was colonial in style and must have had at least five bedrooms. Dexter had only been inside on one occasion, but he knew there was a huge foyer with a sweeping, curved staircase to the second floor. The triple garage doors were closed, but Dexter knew that behind the doors sat Margie's Lexus, the sheriff's black Hummer, and a vintage sky blue '59 Corvette. Given how much money a county sheriff earned, Dexter figured that Moses must have brought his money with him when he came up from Kentucky.

The sheriff's official county car was parked out in the circular drive where Dexter left his Cherokee. He walked around the house to the backyard, where Moses was standing in front of a large gas grill, looking like sausage casing in his shorts and T-shirt. His wife sat at a picnic table a few feet away with a bottle of Bud Light and a pack of cigarettes in front of her. Behind them, out in the middle of the yard, was a large built-in pool with a bathhouse and sauna next to it. The water in the pool sparkled blue in the bright sun.

"Well, Dexter Loomis!"

"Afternoon, Moses." Dexter shook the sheriff's hand, which was wet and cold from holding his beer bottle, and nodded to his wife. "Hello, Margie."

She smiled. "Well, if it isn't Higgins Point's new chief. Tell me, how is Lewis doin'? I heard he moved down to the Florida Keys. Haven't heard a word from him since he left."

"No." Moses waved his tongs. "He's down in Baton Rouge, isn't that right?"

"Boca Raton, actually," Dexter explained.

"Hey, Marge, why don't you run inside and grab a beer for the Chief here? Can I burn a little meat for ya? Got plenty."

"No, thanks anyway."

Margie smiled and walked inside, and Moses spent a moment turning over chicken breasts and laying a fresh coating of sauce. Both men allowed a brief silence to pass, until Moses finally spoke.

"So what can I do for you, young man?"

Dexter didn't want to prolong the sensation of being a little dog yapping at a big dog, so he came right out with it. "I want to talk about having an autopsy done on Muriel Evenson's body."

Moses closed the hood of the grill and set his tongs down. "That was a sad thing, Dexter, a real sad thing. I know how you feel."

"Do you?"

"Sure I do—frustrated and angry. You think if you can find someone to blame, then it won't seem so frustratin'. Nothin' satisfies like revenge." He picked up his beer and raised it to his lips, watching Dexter, while he drank. "They talked about it at a seminar I went to once, in Chicago. It's all got to do with stress levels and such."

"It's frustrating all right, but this isn't about me and my stress levels. Grady and I were talking and he thinks there might be a possibility she was strangled."

The Sheriff lowered the bottle slowly. "Grady said that?"

"Says there might have been some kind of hemorrhaging in her face."

"Grady ain't no medical examiner, and I don't recall seeing anything in her face."

"Well, he's actually not real sure, the light in the backyard was pretty bad. But Frank Kahler claims the coroner doesn't think the head injury by itself would have caused death."

"When did you talk to Kahler?"

"He stopped by my house yesterday. I'm afraid things got a little contentious."

The Sheriff snorted. "With him they always do. Just got to know how to handle him, that's all."

"There's something else. The way Muriel was lying in the driveway, I noticed that a piece of the railing was kind of tangled up with her legs."

Moses regarded Dexter for a moment in silence, apparently content to wait for him to continue.

"If someone kicked out the railing after she was already on the ground, it might have looked like that."

"Kicked out the railing? That'd be murder."

Dexter nodded, and Moses thought for a minute before he spoke.

"Dexter, I believe you're seeing intrigue where there ain't nothin' but tragedy."

"You don't think an autopsy would help clear things up?"

"What I think is that you're actin' like a shave-tail right out of the police academy, except you never went to no academy."

"What about the coroner?"

"Let's let the medical examiner decide. It's his job."

Dexter hadn't anticipated getting shot down so completely. He didn't say anything, but the look on his face must have conveyed his frustration because the sheriff added, "Nothin' personal here, Dexter, just a little disagreement. Better get used to it if you're gonna work in law enforcement."

Margie came out of the house carrying Dexter's beer.

"Sorry to take so long, but here's your beer, Mr. Police Chief."

Dexter accepted the cold bottle and sat down next to Margie, at the picnic table. Moses proceeded to explain the more humorous points of running dogs on a hunt, while Dexter drank his beer and tried to laugh in the right places.

Chapter Seven

Ann held the empty rifle case in her left hand and watched through the bulletproof glass as the desk officer spoke briefly into her phone. She was a pleasant looking, middle-aged woman, and though she wore the crisp brown uniform and star of the Curran County Sheriff's Department, and was legally deputized, she carried no sidearm. Her job was to wrestle with paperwork rather than felons. Heavy tortoise-shell glasses dominated her face, and her auburn hair was tied back in a tidy knot, contributing to her well-scrubbed appearance. When Ann had presented herself at the front desk, she'd been surprised to find that the officer-on-duty seemed to know her, until the offered condolences led her to realize that this woman had attended her father's funeral. She hung up her phone and turned to Ann, speaking through perforations in the glass.

"He's bringing the property up from Evidence."

Ann smiled and nodded, and then turned away to examine the pale, beige block walls of the corridor. The 'property' was her father's belongings that had been removed from his cabin during the investigation into his death. Ann brought the empty rifle case with her because she knew they probably wouldn't release her father's Winchester to her if she couldn't carry it away legally. She turned back to the window and spoke through the perforations.

"What about the report?"

"I'm checking the disposition now," the officer said without looking up. After a few more minutes she rose to her feet.

"Okay, records show the case has been closed; I'll run you a copy."

Before the desk officer returned with the report, a box arrived, delivered by a young deputy whose expression said he'd either known Inspector Paul Summer or known of him. He set the box on the floor of the office, laid the rifle on top, and gave Ann a brief, self-conscious nod before turning to leave.

Ann stared at her father's Winchester and thought about running into Dexter Loomis at Janet's. She stared at the rifle and wondered what she would have ended up doing with her life if she had elected to spend it in Higgins Point. She stared at the rifle and tried to complete a mental inventory of her rock climbing gear. She stared at the rifle and tried to think about anything in the world but her father's last moments on earth.

She snapped out of her trance when the desk officer returned with the report. Although she hadn't yet seen the final report, Ann knew that an investigator named Bob Tilsen had led the query into her father's death. She asked if she could speak with him for a couple of minutes. The desk officer picked up her phone, spoke quietly for three seconds, and then put it down and smiled at Ann.

"He'll be right out."

Thirty seconds later, Bob Tilsen opened the hall door. He was medium height, with a sandy colored crew cut and wore a plaid sports jacket. Ann recalled his face. He was one of the scores of police officers she'd met for the first and only time at her father's funeral. He smiled at her when they shook hands.

"Can I help you, Miss Summer?"

"I wonder if we could talk for a minute somewhere in private?"

"Of course, let's go in my office."

Tilsen held the hall door open, and as Ann passed the desk officer's door, she tossed the canvas gun case she had been carrying on top of the box containing her father's effects. Tilsen led her down the hall to his office, where he sat down behind his desk and gestured for Ann to have a seat also. Looking at him, surrounded by his photographs and mementos, Ann felt like she was standing before a featureless brick wall, and just on the other side, only inches away, was something she desperately needed. She dropped the preliminaries.

"You worked with my father. You knew him." Ann sat down on the edge of the chair.

"Yeah, I knew Paul pretty good."

"And you supervised the investigation into his death?"

"I was one of the people looking at it."

Tilsen apparently didn't feel chatty, and his unembellished answers offered little access to a conversation. Ann decided to try a direct approach.

"What sort of cases was my father working on when he died?"

"I can't really say offhand, but as a professional courtesy I'll make his case files available to you if you want."

"That'll help, but how about work he may have been doing that was off the record?"

"Off the record?"

Ann felt her speech quicken in spite of herself. "I know that from time to time my father worked off the record. If someone knew something about what he was involved in but was reluctant to come forward, a motive for his murder could get overlooked."

"Motive for what?" The investigator paused, and then seemed to understand. "You're questioning the suicide."

"The hole in that suicide theory is big enough to drive a truck through. I'm convinced there's legitimate doubt in—"

"You may be convinced, but the medical examiner's findings were conclusive." Tilsen's eyes narrowed. "And I don't recall seeing the words 'theory' or 'doubt' in the report."

"Look at the weapon he was supposed to have used," Ann said, "a Winchester 308 that hadn't been fired in ten years."

"That weapon may not have been fired in ten years, but it was sure enough fired last week. Ballistics established that a bullet from that rifle was the direct cause of death."

"Most cop suicides use their service revolvers."

Tilsen dismissed her observation with a shrug.

"Did the report contain anything about the call he made to me the night he died? He told me he had something he wanted to talk about."

"It's not unreasonable to believe that a man who's suicidal might have wanted to talk to his daughter about what was on his mind."

"Why does everybody keep insisting he was suicidal? He wanted my help—" Ann fought to bring her voice under control. "He wanted my help with something, but it didn't have anything to do with his mental health. It was something specific, I could hear it in his voice."

"Our understanding is that it was a sixty second phone call, and you were the only one who heard it."

"Right, I was the only one who heard it, so I'm the only one in a position to judge."

Tilsen lowered his head and took a deep breath. "Don't you think maybe you're a little too close to Paul to be objective?"

"These things warrant a closer look."

"What *things*? There's nothing to look into." Tilsen held up his hand, ticking the points off on well-manicured fingers. "We've got an absence of any physical evidence that points to a homicide, we've got a phone call to you that no one else heard, we've got a medical examiner and a district attorney who are in agreement on the finding of suicide—"

"And we've got unexplained activity just prior to death, activity that needs to come under a hard light."

Tilsen's fingers, which had paused during Ann's interruption, now continued their count. "And we've got a note."

"Oh right. The note where he calls me 'Ann,' but my father never called me 'Ann' in his life, it was always 'Annie'."

Tilsen shook his head. "I've heard of people misspelling the names of their spouses on suicide notes. The handwriting was verified by an expert."

Ann peered into the investigator's eyes trying to figure out just how close her father and Tilsen had actually been, but said nothing.

"Do you have anything else, anything at all to support what you're saying?" Ann still said nothing. "It's too thin, Miss Summer, it's too circumstantial. There's just nothing to work with."

Ann looked out the office window at the perfect July day, and wondered what the hell she ever thought she was going to accomplish with this conversation. If she couldn't think this through a little better, she should never have approached Tilsen in the first place. Maybe he was right, maybe she *was* too emotionally involved. Her surrender must have been evident on her face.

"I'm sorry," he said, "I really am."

After having to work to get him to discuss the case at all, suddenly Ann couldn't stand to hear his voice. She bit her lip, focusing herself, and extended her hand.

"I'm sorry about the imposition. Thank you for your time."

He seemed to hesitate before shaking hands. He looked

like he wanted to say something more, but finally just said, "No problem."

Ann walked slowly through the hall to the front desk, where the box and the rifle were still waiting for her. While Ann was still inside the office, the desk officer dug around in her drawer for a minute and came up with a small "Receipt of Property" form. She filled it out and handed it to Ann for her signature. Ann signed and returned the form and the officer.

"Don't forget this," she said, handing the report to Ann.

"Thanks," was all Ann could manage. She set the report on top of the box and picked up the rifle. She placed it in the case, and as she drew the zipper closed, she noticed an oily, graphite-like residue on the wooden stock, and realized that it was the remnants of the fingerprint dusting powder left behind after the gun had been wiped off. A closer examination verified traces of the powder in the crevasses of the rifle's mechanism as well. Damn stuff never goes away, she thought to herself.

Dexter sat in his office on Third Street and stared at the green, rectangular patches, slightly darker than the rest of the wall, where Chief Coffers' pictures had hung. It being Sunday, he was the only person in the building, and the only sound in the room was the muted tapping of his pencil on the desk blotter. He absentmindedly beat out the rhythm to 'Hotel California' by the Eagles without realizing the song had been playing on his car radio when he drove in that morning.

He was trying to divide his attention between routine paperwork and his notes on Muriel Evenson's 'accident,' but the paperwork was suffering. Without warning, his thoughts veered to Ann Summer. The feelings he'd experienced at seeing her at Janet's on Saturday morning had definitely caught him by surprise. During the time in high school when he'd dated her sister Hallie, Ann had just been the skinny kid sister, someone to pay to get lost. At Paul Summer's funeral, Dexter had kept a respectful distance, speaking only with Hallie briefly, to offer his condolences. He hadn't spoken to Ann at all. But talking to her at breakfast yesterday had brought back to him her green eyes and generous smile, and suddenly Dick Evenson was standing in front of Dexter's desk.

The mayor's tan failed to mask the stress and fatigue he was experiencing. Dexter could tell he hadn't slept. Normally well spoken, the mayor fumbled for the right words as he bent to a task for which he clearly had no real enthusiasm.

"Do you still think there's a chance my daughter was murdered?"

Dexter thought about the question for a minute under Evenson's unwavering stare.

"Yes," he said, finally.

"Well, I've been thinking about what you asked, about could I think of anyone who would hurt her?"

Dexter leaned forward and waited.

"I was trying to think who might actually have a reason to do it, and I couldn't come up with a single person. I mean, I don't know all the people in her crowd, but c'mon, a nineteen-year-old girl with enemies?" He paused, drawing in air like it was water.

"Anyway, then all of a sudden it came to me—Nick Lundholm."

"You think Nick Lundholm murdered Muriel?" Even though they were alone in his office, Dexter still found himself whispering the question.

"He made a lot of noise after the accident, Dex, he made threats."

The accident, to which the mayor referred, had involved Muriel Evenson driving a car involved in a traffic accident that took the life of Lundholm's only daughter, Vickie. Dexter couldn't recall Lundholm ever actually threatening

Muriel, but looking into his friend's eyes, he wasn't about to split hairs just at the moment.

"He just lost his daughter, Dick. He didn't know what he was saying."

The lack of sleep had Evenson's eyes blinking rapidly. "He talked around, a lot of people heard him. Saying how Muriel got special treatment."

"That happened last summer, almost a year ago. After all this time, you think he'd do something like this?"

Evenson seemed to falter. "I guess I don't want to believe he could."

The wall clock ticked on, filling the silence. It fell to Dexter to finally say something.

"Dick, I'll have a talk with him, okay?"

"Yeah." Evenson got up slowly and walked to the door. He paused and started to say something more, but then turned and just let himself out.

When he was gone, Dexter sat back in his chair and rubbed his face vigorously. When he took his hands away, he was staring at the phone. Ann had said she was staying at her father's house while she was in town. He reached into his desk drawer for his phone book.

Chapter Eight

The only thing more surprising to Dexter than his impulse to invite Ann Summer sailing, was the readiness with which she accepted his invitation. By 2:00 that afternoon, they were climbing down the rocky bank of the dike along old Highway 12, in Hudson, several miles down river from Higgins Point. Dexter's weathered dinghy waited at the base of the dike, hull to the sky and chained to a tree a few feet above the waves of the St. Croix River. It was a short trip out to his twenty-five foot sailboat, moored in the middle of the buoy field, a hundred feet offshore. Soon they were motoring away, with Ann tending the tiller, while Dexter went forward to set the main and foresails.

Once the sails were raised, Dexter returned to the cockpit and sat beside Ann. He killed the motor and took control of the tiller, glancing at the wind indicator atop the mast. The breeze was stiff out of the south and felt good on his face. He adjusted their heading and trimmed the sails, bringing them in a bit, and the boat responded by heeling over nicely. When he glanced down, Dexter marveled at how preposterous his large, bony knees appeared beside Ann's tan, athletic looking legs, and when she happened to look away, he found an excuse to lean in towards her, inhaling her scent. Gulls wheeled above, their squeals mingling with the tinging of the halyards on the aluminum mast, and the soft friction of the water rushing along the hull. Ann held her medium length, dark brown hair against the wind and looked at Dexter through sunglasses.

"Where did you get such an interesting name for your boat, 'Serendib'?"

"It's from a Persian tale called 'The Three Princes of Serendib,' something to do with an island that can only be found if you're not looking for it. It's supposed to be the origin of the word serendipity."

"A happy accident."

"Yeah, like running into you at Janet's yesterday." As he looked at her, he wished that she weren't wearing sunglasses. "If we come about now, we can have a nice long tack across the river."

"Can I do something?"

"Sure, when I tell you to, release the jib sheet, and mind your head when the boom swings around."

"Great! What's the jib sheet?" Dexter pointed to a line attached to the starboard cleat that controlled the foresail or jib, and Ann nodded.

"Ready about!" There was no response from Ann.

"Say 'ready'."

"Ready?"

Dexter pushed the tiller over hard, and the four-thousand pound boat veered, sweeping across the wind line on its way to a starboard tack. The sails, which had been silent and full until then, luffed suddenly, flapping noisily in the headwind. As the bow crossed the wind line, the boom swung over, snapping tight against its sheet, bringing the boat over to heel on its new course. Their world tilted in the other direction, and then the filled sails were silent once again. Dexter trimmed the sails to the new heading and secured the jib sheet at the port cleat. The entire maneuver had taken only seconds, and now they were sailing smoothly toward the opposite shore a mile away. Dexter looked at Ann, unable to conceal how pleased he was with himself.

Ann matched his gaze for a moment with a straight face and finally said, "Oh please!" They both laughed.

They spent the next couple of hours crisscrossing the river and getting reacquainted. When Ann revealed a fondness for blues music, Chicago style, not country, Dexter realized how little he really knew about Hallie's sister. The temperature soared above ninety, and when they were near the middle of the river, he asked Ann if she would like to go swimming.

"I thought you'd never ask," she said. "How do we do this, do we anchor at a beach?"

"No, the water's clearer out in the middle and the river's wide enough here, so the current's pretty slow. I'll drop the sails, and we'll just let the boat drift."

Ann disappeared into the cabin for a few minutes and emerged wearing a one-piece, blue swimsuit. Dexter had come on board wearing his swimsuit, as he generally did on hot days, so he was ready to go. He hung the aluminum ladder off the side of the boat and threw out the swim rope, and for a while, they swam around the drifting boat and enjoyed the cool current of the St. Croix River.

When he'd finally had enough, Dexter climbed back on board and toweled off. Ann was still in the water, and he enjoyed watching her as she dove and surfaced repeatedly, playing with the current. He sat on the cabin roof and leaned against the aluminum mast, allowing his mind to drift back to Muriel Evenson. He guessed that Ann probably realized that he had an ulterior motive for inviting her to go sailing, but it didn't matter. As an engineer, he'd been trained to use whatever resources were available.

His thoughts were interrupted by the realization that he was still waiting for Ann to surface from her last dive. He peered into the dark water looking for any flicker of movement below the surface. More time passed, and still no sign.

He called out to her, but there was no response. Becoming more concerned, he moved to the other side of the boat, hoping that she was over there, but again found nothing.

The depth gauge in the cockpit told him that they were in forty-five feet of water, and his mind began going through all the things that could be happening to her at that moment. He knew that without any clue as to where to search, it would be foolish to simply jump in the water and start thrashing around, yet he was rapidly approaching an all-out panic that cried out for some sort of action, no matter how futile. He climbed on top of the cabin so he could scan completely around the boat, but still saw nothing. He called her name again. It had been at least two minutes since he had seen her on the surface. Then a white form slowly began to appear about thirty feet off the starboard side of the boat. Gradually, the shifting form became Ann, and then she was treading water and smiling at him.

It was clear from her unconcerned smile, and the way she began a languid backstroke parallel to the boat, that she hadn't meant to worry him. He said nothing at the moment, but after she finally did climb back on board, and he was putting the ladder away, he casually mentioned the 'scare' she'd given him. Ann seemed genuinely surprised and apologized for any worry she may have caused. Dexter handed her a towel, and as she wrapped herself in it, she mentioned that she had always loved swimming under water, and had excelled at it as a kid.

"Sometimes I drove my father crazy," she said.

They put up the sails and were soon under way again. While they were settling into the cockpit it seemed to Dexter like a good time to take a chance on a new subject.

"When I saw you in Janet's yesterday, you asked me what I thought about police work," he said.

"Yes. As I recall, you said it was a great gig, except for the criminal element."

"Well, it was a great gig—until Thursday."

"What happened on Thursday?"

"Local girl, a girl that I watched grow up, died."

"Who was she? Do I know the family?"

Dexter had to think for a minute. "I'll bet you do, her name was Muriel Evenson."

"Evenson. The name sounds familiar."

"Her father's Dick Evenson, our mayor."

Dexter watched the light go on. "He ran the hardware store!"

"Still does."

"He sold me my first .22 rifle. God, how long ago was that? His daughter died?"

Dexter glanced at the wind indicator. "Uh huh."

"How old was she? She must have been just a kid."

"Nineteen."

"How'd it happen?"

"She fell from her second floor deck, landed on the driveway. We thought it was an accident, but Grady, he's the EMT who responded, he said there may be evidence pointing to murder."

Ann stood up and stepped down into the cabin. "Think I'll get a soda. Do you want anything?"

"Thanks, I'll have a Coke."

She stepped back up into the cockpit and handed him a can, and then looked directly at him. "Is that why you invited me sailing?"

"Well, I—" Dexter felt his face redden. "Okay, you got me. I admit I didn't lure you out here to seduce you."

Ann smiled, "Oh, damn." She cracked open her soda and sat down next to him.

"Falling from a second story isn't generally fatal, maybe the EMT is onto something. What kind of evidence?"

Dexter hoped her professional curiosity was getting the better of her. "Some kind of hemorrhaging in the face that could indicate strangulation." Then he added, "I feel like a bug stuck in amber, Annie, I should be doing something, but handing out traffic tickets isn't going to cut it, and so far I'm not trained for much else."

Ann didn't respond. For a while they listened to the water rushing along the hull, while Dexter studied the gentle bump midway up her nose.

"She used to sit where you're sitting now," he said. "She loved to tease us by holding onto the side stay and leaning as far out over the water as she could, used to drive Dick crazy. When she got older, she liked to hang onto the swim rope and tow behind the boat; by then she could swim like a fish."

"If she was strangled, it'll show up in the autopsy."

Dexter grimaced. "That's what Grady said. Moses, er, Sheriff Hicks, knows the family and feels bad about it, but he's convinced it was an accident. Says I'm acting like a rookie, which, of course, is exactly what I am." The sudden flapping of the sails told Dexter that he had neglected to watch the wind line. He corrected their course slightly.

"Where did this happen? I mean the actual residence where she was found?"

"At her apartment on Vine Street."

"Is Vine Street in the town of Higgins Point? I mean inside the jurisdiction of the town?"

Dexter nodded "Yeah, it is."

"Then what's the county sheriff's opinion got to do with anything?"

"What do you mean?"

"If it happened in your town, you've got a say in things, Chief."

Dexter looked at her. "So I can order an autopsy?"

"Of course."

"I didn't know that." Dexter was actually feeling slightly dizzy from embarrassment.

"Sheriff Hicks does. I would go so far as to say that as police chief, if you have legitimate concerns about this death, and you *don't* do anything about it, you're being derelict."

Dexter swallowed, and the look on his face must have conveyed the depth of his concern.

"I'll tell you what, Dexter, I was planning on talking to the sheriff anyway. I'll stop in to see him in the morning and let him know that you're going forward with an investigation into the Evenson girl's death. Whether he thinks it was an accident or not, he's not going to tell *me* I'm acting like a rookie. Meanwhile, you call the medical examiner in Ramsey County—they cover this area of Wisconsin—and request an autopsy; he'll schedule it."

"That's it?"

"Just keep the D.A. in the loop, and get ready for a blizzard of paperwork."

"I don't know anything about investigating a murder, Annie."

"You're a college-educated engineer, Dexter; how much intelligence do you think it takes?"

Dexter couldn't believe he was hearing this. "I'm an engineer, not a lawman! What about training? I wouldn't know what to look for. What if I miss something?"

"Oh, you'd be surprised at what a trained lawman can miss."

Dexter just looked at her like she was crazy, unable to think of a thing to say. Finally, Ann smiled.

"I'm having a little fun with you, Dexter, I apologize. Look, Higgins Point is such a small town, that if the autopsy points to homicide, your district attorney is certain to request help from our office."

"The DCI?"

Ann nodded.

Dexter grinned. "Hey, maybe they'd assign you."

"I'm on leave."

"But whoever they sent would handle things?"

Ann paused. "Yeah, they'd handle it."

They spent another hour on the water before heading back to the buoy, but as though by some silent mutual consent, they kept the remaining conversation on a more social level. Dexter was grateful that Ann was willing to provide some much-needed advice in the matter of Muriel Evenson. And he was enjoying getting to know her after all these years, really for the first time, but he couldn't shake the feeling that her faith in law enforcement was shaded by a tinge of doubt. The fact that she asked him if he knew anything about her father's death when they met at Janet's yesterday, told him that there might be some issues that had been settled legally that weren't so settled in Ann's mind. Dexter was certain that Ann had concerns about her father's death.

An hour after Ann returned from sailing with Dexter, she sat in the kitchen, staring at the cardboard box that lay on the floor in the corner. Hallie stood at the counter, chopping vegetables and humming to herself. In the two days since they had moved back into their father's house, Ann, Hallie, and Ted had completed a thorough search of the premises, though Ann understood that they were retracing steps already taken by others. The house had appeared undisturbed, but that just meant that the sheriff's investigators had been careful not to trash the place during their own search. In the end, all of their efforts had yielded nothing. Only the box remained unexamined. It had been sitting there since she'd brought it home that morning from the sheriff's department. Not looking forward to it but unable to put it off any longer, she decided it was time to go through its contents.

She asked Hallie if she wanted to see the effects too. Without saying a word, Hallie picked up her cup of coffee, walked across the kitchen, and sat down at the table beside Ann. They started by reading the report, which bore the signature of Investigator Robert Tilsen at the bottom. Death had resulted from a single gunshot wound to the chest. Checks for gunpowder residue on her father's hands, and fingerprints on the gun had been inconclusive. Nothing surprising there. What caught Ann's eye, however, was the mention of a glass of Bailey's Irish Cream that was found on the desk where the suicide was supposed to have taken place. That sent Ann into the box where she dug, hesitatingly at first, past their father's bloody clothing. Then she pulled out and set aside an envelope containing the contents of his pockets and a plastic bag containing the suicide note. Hallie's expression was stoical as she watched Ann silently. Finally, Ann found both the glass and the bottle of Bailey's. She held the glass to her nose and was able to identify for herself, the unmistakable smell of Irish Cream in the dried residue on the inside.

Hallie's curiosity finally surfaced. "Is there something special about the Bailey's?"

Ann looked at the report again. "It says that the only prints found in the study belonged to dad, including the ones on the bottle of Bailey's."

"Yeah?"

"I remember handling this bottle myself last December when I was here for Christmas."

Her father was well aware of Ann's fondness for Bailey's and had developed the habit of treating Ann to a glass whenever she came for a visit. Over the years it had become a sort of minor ritual; they would visit the cabin, do a little ice fishing, and then he would bring out the bottle. After the drink, the bottle would be returned to the cupboard where it would remain undisturbed until her next visit on the following Christmas. It remained undisturbed because her father never touched the stuff, not a drop, couldn't stand it. The whole thing was strictly a gesture of affection toward his daughter.

"If you handled it, why aren't your prints on it?" Hallie asked.

"Maybe somebody else handled it since then, and they wiped it clean. You knew that dad didn't drink Bailey's, right?"

Hallie nodded. "Neither do I. It was something between you two."

Ann indicated the glass in her hand. "If dad didn't drink Bailey's, how likely was it that he would have poured himself some Irish Cream as his last earthly gesture before taking his own life?"

Hallie looked from Ann to the bottle and back at Ann, but said nothing.

Ann dropped the glass back into the box and brought out the 'suicide' note, still encased in a clear plastic baggie. She had seen the text of the note in the preliminary report, but now she opened the baggie and held the actual note in her hand. The paper was greasy to the touch with smudges of black fingerprint powder on its white surface, and Ann recognized the handwriting, which had supposedly been verified by an expert as her father's. She laid the note on the table between them so they could both read it, just as Ted walked into the kitchen. When he saw what they were doing, he paused.

"That has to be tough." He reached out and took Hallie's offered hand. "Is that the note?"

Ann nodded. "That's it."

The three of them read it together in silence. The contents were brief.

Dear Ann and Hallie,

I'm sorry, I should have been more of a father to you both, you deserved better. I hope you can forgive me. It's time for me to be with your mother.

Love, Dad

The words in the note meant nothing to Ann; the sentiments expressed in the writing sounded like canned music. She looked at her sister. "Think it's real?"

Ted didn't pick up on the fact that Ann had intended her question for Hallie and gave his own opinion. "Why wouldn't it be? You told us that the preliminary report said the handwriting had been verified as being Paul's."

"I know he wrote it, Ted, that's not what I asked," Ann said. "I asked if it was real; did he mean it?"

"Why would he write it if he didn't mean it?"

"Certain circumstances."

"What circumstances?" A hint of sarcasm was beginning to creep into Ted's speech, and it was starting to annoy Ann.

"Very specific circumstances. The same circumstances that would cause you to write those words."

Ted smiled uneasily. "Under what circumstance would I ever write those words."

"Well, let's see, Ted," Ann said. "If I held a gun to your head and told you to write those words or I'd blow your brains all over the kitchen, you'd probably write them. Wouldn't you?"

Ted didn't answer, only scowled at Ann, who ignored him and turned to her sister. "So do you think the note's real?"

Hallie hesitated, and her eyes were moist when she finally shook her head.

"Neither do I." Ann dropped the note back into the box.

Completely out of ideas and with nothing left to examine, Ann left the two of them in the kitchen and walked into the front room. She sat in her father's beat up old chair and thought to herself, it isn't his chair anymore, it's ours now. She began thumbing through an old *Field and Stream* magazine, examining an ad for a shotgun, when a thought occurred to her. She went back into the kitchen and pulled out the bottle of Bailey's Irish Cream. Every year her father had given her a drink at Christmas. Let's have a drink to him now, she thought.

She told Hallie and Ted what she proposed and asked if

they wanted a drink too. They both declined. She got a glass out of the cupboard and poured herself a measure of the thick chocolate liqueur before thinking that she'd like it chilled over ice. Her father's refrigerator had an automatic icemaker, which kept the ice-cube container full. She opened the freezer door and, without meaning to, thrust her hand into the ice container too deeply, displacing several cubes, which clattered to the floor. Ann didn't notice the mess, however, because she was looking at the plastic bag that she had pulled out from under the ice cubes. It was heavy and cold, and contained a gun.

The weapon was a 9 mm Luger with an evidence card wired to the finger guard. Handling the plastic bag carefully, Ann laid the gun on the kitchen table so they could read what was written on the card. The information it contained was typical: a description of the gun, and the St. Paul address where it had been found, along with the time and date. The victim was listed as someone named Casper Bottom, but the suspect line was left blank. They all stared at the gun. Hallie wondered aloud what something like this was doing in their father's freezer, but Ann wondered why it wasn't in the county evidence locker.

Chapter Nine

On Monday morning, Ann stood in front of the same bulletproof window at the County Government Center that she had stood in front of on Sunday, talking to the same officer. This time she asked to speak with Sheriff Moses Hicks and was told he would be right out. Ann had left the Luger behind at her father's house. She wasn't exactly sure why she had decided not to tell the sheriff about it, but her intuition told her to wait. Perhaps it was because she didn't know why her father hadn't turned the gun in himself. Plus, she was almost certain that the gun had something to do with his wanting to see her just before he died. In any case, she felt there were enough unanswered questions for her to err on the side of caution.

Sheriff Hicks opened the door and extended a large hand to Ann. As he wrapped his hand around hers, Ann noticed a tattoo containing the word 'VIETNAM' on his wrist, peeking out below his shirt cuff, and was almost overcome by his lime scented aftershave. She followed behind his large, lumbering frame as he led her through the halls, back to his office, where he asked her to have a seat.

"Miss Summer, I want to tell you again how sorry I am about Paul. We're sure gonna miss him around here."

"Thank you, Sheriff. I appreciate your speaking at his service."

Hicks nodded slightly and looked down at his desk and then back at Ann. "How long you gonna be in town, if you don't mind my askin'?"

"I don't mind at all, but it's hard to say how things are going to go, you know, trying to straighten out my father's affairs." Ann glanced around the sheriff's office and was surprised by how bare his walls were. There was almost nothing to break up the expanse of the beige painted concrete block walls; no photographs, diplomas, citations, no artwork, not even a calendar.

"You on some kind of administrative leave?" he asked.

"Yes, that and some vacation time. I know you're probably busy, Sheriff, so I'll get right to the point. I have two things I'd like to discuss. The first concerns the circumstances surrounding my father's death."

Hicks smiled. "Yeah, Bob mentioned he talked to you yesterday. Said you're questioning the suicide ruling. That right?"

"I afraid it is." Ann's gaze was absolutely level while she said this.

"Schifsky, he's the director down at the Madison office, ain't he? He send you up here?"

"No, this is strictly unofficial. I'll be honest with you, If my boss knew I was talking to you about this, I'd be in trouble. I know it's unusual, but I thought since we're both professionals, and it involves my father, maybe you'd be willing to look the other way, while I satisfy myself that things are in order."

"You want to take an unofficial look into Paul's death?"

Ann nodded.

"You ain't goin' after Tilsen, cause you think he was derelict, huh?"

"Absolutely not."

Hicks stared at her for a minute, ran his tongue over his lips, and then seemed to make up his mind. "Probably won't do no harm. Do we both agree that investigating Paul's death and investigating my officers are two different things?"

"Certainly."

"Okay. Out of professional courtesy, you can poke around if you want. I'll even make Paul's current cases available to you if you want, and I won't call your boss."

"I appreciate it, Sheriff."

Hicks held up a finger. "But if I get the notion for even a second that you're lookin' harder at Bob Tilsen than at Paul's death, I'm gonna send you back to Madison with a nasty note pinned to your shirt. Fair enough?"

Ann smiled. "More than fair, Sheriff."

"You can call me Moses if you want to. Up to you. Now what's the second thing you had?"

Ann cleared her throat. "Chief Loomis is going forward with an investigation of Muriel Evenson's death. He knew I was coming in to see you this morning and asked me to let you know."

Hicks squinted at Ann and then raised his eyebrows. "It's Loomis' town, and it's the town's money. I'll assist in any way I can."

"I'm sure he'll be glad to hear you said that, Sheriff."

The Luger that Tilsen's people had overlooked in Ann's father's freezer was the obvious key to tracking down his killer. The evidence card attached to the trigger guard listed Casper Bottom as the victim but no suspect. Her father's possession of the gun all but guaranteed that he had been investigating Bottom's murder, though it wasn't one of his official cases. On the record or off, it didn't matter; whoever killed Bottom was in her father's crosshairs and had a prime motive to kill him.

It was late Monday morning when Ann walked into the

Tenth Ave. station of the St. Paul Police. She asked the desk officer sitting behind bulletproof glass what officer was assigned to the Casper Bottom homicide. She was given the name, Detective Joe Perry. She asked to speak with him, and a few minutes later he appeared and let her through the door into the hall that led to his office. When they reached his office, he sat down behind his desk which, at the moment, was covered with a Subway sandwich and soft drink. He waved her into a seat.

"You're Agent Summer?"

Ann nodded. "I can come back after lunch."

He shrugged. "If you don't mind me eating while we talk, it's all right with me."

Detective Perry had more hair above his lip than on his head and piercing brown eyes that gave Ann the feeling that she'd been summed up quite competently. When he spoke, his voice had soft tones that suggested calm and reason. "You said on the phone you had something for me on the Casper Bottom thing."

"I said I had a question about Casper Bottom that you might be able to help me with."

Perry's eyebrows turned doubtful. "A question?"

"Is that investigation going anywhere?"

He picked up his sandwich. "That your question?'

Ann smiled. "No, that was small talk." When Perry didn't respond, Ann asked, "Was Casper Bottom involved in drug trafficking?"

Perry set his sandwich back down and leaned back in his chair. He studied Ann for a moment while he sucked his teeth. "I think you said on the phone that you're with the DCI, Madison office."

"Yes."

"Don't think you showed me any ID."

Ann produced her badge.

"You're out of your jurisdiction."

Ann smiled. She had known she would end up in this position. "Only a few miles."

Perry hesitated, but then apparently decided the question was harmless. "Was Bottom 'involved' in drugs? The guys in Narcotics tell me he was 'involved' up to his eyeballs. Apparently, he ran with a gang that was operating meth labs in Minnesota and Wisconsin."

"Wisconsin?"

Perry nodded. "They were branching out. I guess it's just like any other business in America today; it's all about hostile takeovers."

"Any idea who killed him?"

Perry shook his head. "Lot of possibilities, but nothing solid yet." He took a moment to look Ann over. "Summer, why does that name sound familiar?"

"My father was Paul Summer, investigator with the Curran County Sheriff's Department." Ann watched his two-part reaction; first, the realization that her father was the officer in Wisconsin who had died recently, followed by the recollection that it was suicide.

"Yeah, I heard about that. I'm sorry."

Ann nodded. "I think whoever killed Bottom, may have also murdered my father."

"I thought he was a suicide." When Ann didn't say anything, he said, "What makes you think that? Did you talk to him before he died. Did he tell you something?"

"He didn't have time to tell me anything," Ann said truthfully, and then said, "Okay, here's my question. Was Paul working with your department off-the-record?"

Perry shook his head. "No, I'd know it if he was."

"I have a favor to ask."

"Just one?"

"Can you give me the name of anybody who was close to Casper Bottom, someone involved in his activities?"

Perry studied his sandwich for a moment, while his tongue moved around the inside of his mouth. He looked at his filing cabinet and then at Ann. "You know, there's a couple of guys in this department who knew your father. Neither one of 'em thinks the suicide made sense." He got up from his chair and walked over to the cabinet. "One name?"

Perry's words washed over Ann like a cooling balm; other professionals agreed with her. She barely heard his question. Then she said, 'Just one name."

"You find anything, you keep me in the loop, right?"

"Count on it," Ann said to her new best friend.

Chapter Ten

When Dick Evenson brought up Nick Lundholm's name as a possible suspect, Dexter had immediately understood what he meant. A year earlier, Lundholm had lost his daughter, Vickie, in a traffic accident. It happened late on a Wednesday night. Vickie and two of her girlfriends had been driving back from a party in River Falls when their car ran off Highway 35 and smashed into a tree. Both Muriel, who was driving and wearing a seat belt, and the girl in the back seat who had been asleep at the time, escaped with minor injuries. Vickie, however, who was in the passenger seat, wasn't wearing a seat belt and went through the windshield. She died at the scene.

When Chief Lewis Coffers got to the scene, Muriel explained that a deer had jumped in front of her car. When she swerved to miss it, she lost control. She had apparently been successful in avoiding the deer because there was no carcass to back up her story. And since the third girl had been asleep, she had no opinion in the matter. Muriel's word was good enough for everyone concerned with the exception of one man, Nick Lundholm. Vickie's father had been devastated. He became convinced that alcohol was involved and that Muriel had been drunk when she ran off the road. Chief Coffers never bothered to check Muriel's blood-alcohol level because she didn't exhibit any symptoms, but Lundholm claimed it was because Muriel was the mayor's daughter. The way he saw things, the mayor's daughter was responsible for his daughter's death. He shot off his mouth around town about the special treatment Muriel got, but few people listened to him. They were sympathetic to his loss, but they weren't inclined to doubt Muriel's honesty. Eventually, Lundholm shut up about the matter and was seen less and less around town. When he appeared at all, he spoke to few people.

Dick Evenson's notion of revenge as a motive for murdering a nineteen-year-old girl struck Dexter as more in keeping with some made-for-TV movie than with reality, though he did have to admit that he saw stranger things in Chuck Sheppard's *News of the Weird* column, all the time.

It was late morning when Dexter pulled up in front of Lundholm's house on Beech Street. Looking at his house gave him the first inkling of just how completely Lundholm had retreated from society since the accident. The shrubs that fronted the pale green wood-framed house were overgrown and surrounded by weeds that were infested with scraps of paper snatched from the wind. Discarded toys and debris from neighborhood kids were strewn about the lawn, which clearly hadn't seen a mower in months.

A porch swing that had obviously weathered the previous winter outdoors swung gently from rusting chains in the light breeze. As Dexter stepped up to the door, a closer look at the swing revealed a mosaic of cobwebs. He rang the bell but couldn't be sure if it worked, so he knocked on the door. Presently, the door opened, and a face emerged on the other side of the screen. Nick Lundholm was medium height with receding dark hair and glasses. Veins stood out in relief on his forehead, his mouth was a flat line drawn across a three day beard, and a cigarette dangled from his right hand.

"Nick Lundholm?"

"Yeah?"

"I'm Officer Loomis with the Higgins Point Police." Dexter chose to leave the word 'chief' out of things.

"Yeah?" He registered no change in expression, merely a slow blink behind his spectacles.

"Mr. Lundholm, I wonder if I could come in for a minute and talk to you?"

He grunted something that Dexter couldn't catch, but as he walked away he nudged the screen door open a few inches. Dexter eased inside and was immediately hit with the sickly sweet smell of whisky. The front room looked like someone was recovering from a lingering illness. Newspapers lay discarded on the floor, remnants of past meals littered most surfaces, and cigarette butts lay in small puddles of alcohol on the coffee table. The curtains were drawn, and a single floor lamp, which leaned crookedly in the corner, cast the room in a yellowish light. Judge Judy was dispensing judicial wisdom from the television in the corner.

"Have a seat."

After the chilly reception on the porch, the invitation caught Dexter slightly off-guard. He pushed some papers out of the way and sat on the couch.

"Mr. Lundholm, I apologize for bringing up painful memories. I'll get right to the point. I understand that about a year ago—" Dexter hesitated, then felt himself flush as he realized that he had forgotten the daughter's name, "your daughter died in a car accident."

Lundholm's head swung around and he narrowed his eyes at Dexter, but said nothing, allowing the silence to punctuate the awkwardness of Dexter's statement.

"The thing is that at the time of the, ah, accident, people heard you say things—make threats toward Muriel Evenson, the girl who was driving the car your daughter was in."

Lundholm shifted in his chair, and took an unhurried drag on his cigarette. When he spoke, it was very quietly.

"Her name's Vickie."

"Uh, Vickie, I'm sorry."

"I suppose I did say some things, after it came clear what they were up to."

"What were they up to?"

"I don't care if these city hall types want to screw each other over liquor licenses, but my daughter was killed, damn it! And the one who was driving, she's let go without so much as a blood test."

"Muriel Evenson was murdered on Thursday night." Dexter had decided to go ahead and use the word 'murder' so he could gauge Lundholm's reaction. At first, he didn't seem to know what expression to put on his face, but to his credit he didn't smile. As the news began to sink in, Dexter thought that the look of surprise was genuine.

"I guess I'm sorry for that," he said finally. He took another drag on his cigarette and looked like he was going to add something, but then chose to say no more.

"You hadn't heard?"

"I don't get out a lot these days."

"First thing most people would ask is how it happened," Dexter said, *unless they already knew*.

"What difference does it make how? You stop by just to tell me this?"

"No, it's police business. I want to ask you a question."

Lundholm leaned back and picked a fleck of tobacco off his tongue. "What question would that be?"

"Where were you on Thursday night?"

Lundholm's eyes narrowed. "Who told you to ask that? Evenson tell you to ask that?"

"Mr. Lundholm—"

"You tell Evenson to go screw himself!"

"Several people heard you saying some pretty rough things after the accident."

"First, he pulls strings so his daughter don't have to pay for what she done, and now he wants to blame me for her murder. For Chrissakes!"

"So, where were you?"

"Thursday night?"

"Late, after eleven."

"Where I am most nights, passed out right here."

"Alone?"

"Sorry, no witnesses," he said sarcastically.

"What about your wife?"

"She's staying with her sister."

They looked at one another for a moment while Dexter worked to suppress the anger he felt at himself; just what the hell did he expect him to say? Finally, shaking his head, he rose to leave. "Sorry to have bothered you, Mr. Lundholm."

Lundholm's eyes followed Dexter to the door while he remained seated, saying nothing. When Dexter was halfway through the door he stopped and turned around. Lundholm was leaning over, his arm outstretched for a bottle of Jim Beam on the coffee table.

"Mr. Lundholm, I know it's not possible to forget what happened to your daughter, but maybe you should give some thought to talking to someone about—things."

In response, Lundholm gathered in the bottle and took a pull, and his eyes never left Dexter's.

When Dexter got back out to his office, he opened the door to the sound of laughter. Phyllis Beiderman, the town clerk who divided her time between Dexter and the mayor, and who was easily the most terminally serious person Dexter had ever encountered, was wiping tears of laughter from her eyes. Frank Kahler stood at the counter, smiling. When he saw Dexter, his smile broadened.

"Hey, Chief, long time no see."

Dexter looked back and forth between Kahler and Phyllis, astounded at what his clerk's face looked like when contorted in laughter.

"Frank is so funny," she said, fighting for breath. "He knows so many jokes."

"Hello, Mr. Kahler. I guess you've already met Phyllis."

"Yes indeed, I have, and call me Frank, okay?"

Dexter walked around behind the counter, putting himself on the 'official' side, and leaving Kahler on the 'public' side. He tossed his car keys on his desk and turned to face Kahler. "Okay, 'Frank'," he said, trying it out. "I guess I should apologize for calling you 'sleazy' the other day."

"Not necessary, but thanks. I was a little harder on you than I should have been too. I mean what with you being new at this."

Dexter smiled. "I can guess why you're here."

"When I smell a story, I stay on the scent."

"What makes you think there's a story here?"

"I smell something. For instance, why were you just over talking to Nick Lundholm?"

"Who told you I was?"

Phyllis suddenly grabbed her purse off her desk. "Dexter, I've got to run over to the—to the ah—to the Driver's License Bureau. I'll be back later." She dashed for the door and was gone before Dexter had a chance to point out that the Driver's License Bureau wasn't open on Mondays.

"A little bird told me."

"Right, a little bird named Phyllis. So, what's up?"

"I talked to your mayor this morning."

"Christ, Frank, the man just lost his daughter. Why don't you leave him alone?"

"He's got some kind of crackpot idea that Nick Lundholm murdered his daughter."

"Dick's pretty tore up. I don't think there's any real substance to his suspicions."

"Then why did you go over to Lundholm's place? What did you ask him?"

Dexter shrugged. "Nothing much. Dick wanted me to talk to him, so I talked to him. That's all."

"I bet you asked him where he was last Thursday night."

Dexter didn't say anything.

"So where was he?"

Dexter sighed in resignation. "He was home alone, but you can't go printing things like that in the paper."

"Why not? It's the truth."

"It makes him look guilty without any evidence."

"It's your job to find the evidence, Chief."

"Don't remind me," Dexter muttered.

"What was that?"

"Printing hunches in the paper is only going to make them look legitimate, and then you're doing a disservice to everyone involved, not just Nick Lundholm."

"Like who? You?"

"Yeah, me. And Sheriff Hicks, and the other law enforcement people who are looking for answers to this thing. When you print lies in the paper, it destroys the public's trust in us."

Kahler laughed.

"You think that's funny?"

"Hilarious. You're concerned for your public image."

"Of course I am, I'm a public official."

"Let me tell you about the integrity of public official number one, Sheriff Hicks."

"Moses. What about him?"

"The best way I can put it is to borrow an old saying: he's so crooked, that when they bury him, they're going to have to screw him into the ground."

Dexter started to laugh and then caught himself. "That's exactly what I'm talking about here, Frank, rumors. Unsupported garbage."

Kahler smiled at Dexter. "You're brand new on the scene, Chief. You may have lived in Higgins Point all your life, but you've only been working in the city government for a few months. What makes you think my garbage is unsupported?"

"I don't see you printing it in your paper."

"Maybe that's because I'm careful about choosing my battles."

"Or maybe it's because there's nothing to print."

Kahler thought for a minute. "Ever been to the sheriff's house?"

"Yeah, I was out there on Saturday."

"That's a nice pool he's got, isn't it?"

"Sure, what about it?"

"Two years ago, a nineteen-year-old kid robbed the Holiday Gas Station on Coulee Road in Hudson. He wore a ski mask and fired his gun into the ceiling to scare everyone. He took some money and managed to get away without killing anybody, but three days later he got stopped for speeding and the police found a gun in his car. They matched the gun to the bullet in the ceiling and charged him with armed robbery. Since he was wearing a ski mask, nobody could identify him, so the gun was the only thing tying him to the crime."

"Is there a point to all this?" Dexter asked.

"Couple of weeks before the trial date, the gun disappeared. Gone. Without the gun they had no case, and the kid walked."

"Are you going to try and tell me that the sheriff took the gun out of his own evidence locker?"

Kahler shrugged. "Maybe he did, maybe he didn't. Along with everybody else, I don't know what happened to the gun. But I do know this: that nineteen-year-old kid's father was the same contractor who put in the sheriff's swimming pool six months later."

Dexter felt uncomfortable, and he knew why: he found Kahler's story too easy to believe. His silence must have tipped Kahler to his doubts.

"No big thing, Chief, just a story is all. So Lundholm

was at home alone on Thursday night. Okay, I'll sit on it. To tell the truth, and I always tell the truth, I don't like him for a suspect anyway."

While Dexter was at his office going three rounds with Frank Kahler, Ann and Hallie were twenty-five miles north, pulling up beside their father's cabin. Ann turned off the engine and they sat in the car for several minutes, staring out into the yard, studying the weeds growing around the rusted swing set. When they finally got out of the car, Ann looked down at the dirt and gravel area where they had parked and realized she was looking at several sets of tire tracks—clearly the remnants of the police vehicles that had been there.

"I wonder if anybody thought to make imprints of the car tire tracks before the posse rode in and destroyed them?"

"Is that something they'd normally do?" Hallie asked.

Ann nodded. "Only if they thought it was a homicide."

"Maybe they did it here."

"I doubt it; the sheriff didn't think this was a crime scene."

The cabin was folded in the silent shade of close pines, with the band of yellow police tape stretched across the entry yielding the only clue to what waited within. Ann had intended to go directly to the front door but instead circled around behind the cabin. Together they walked across the back lawn to the path that led down to the lake. As they approached the entrance to the path, Ann stopped next to a rotted out tree stump at the edge of the lawn.

"Let's take a look at the lake," Hallie said, walking ahead onto the path.

Ann stared at the old stump and remembered the summer when she was seven years old. The stump had still been hard and flat then, and she had set up a lemonade stand on its surface. It happened to be a weekend when no friends dropped by the cabin, so her only customers were the vacationers next door and her family. Hallie, she recalled, drank all she wanted but refused to pay anything. Her father must have had at least six glasses, making horrible faces after every gulp, pretending it was too sour. Ann always knew that it was her mother who was quietly coaxing her father to buy more lemonade, but she smiled now as she remembered how delighted she had been to see an adult acting goofy just for her.

She moved past the stump, onto the path, and her shoes crunched over small twigs that littered the trail that she knew so well from her childhood. A few moments later, she paused near an oak tree that was perhaps twenty feet from the path. It was huge and old and had outlived her mother, and now her father, and it would likely outlive both Hallie and herself.

Suddenly, Ann was eleven years old, and it was the summer that her mother died. No secret had been made of the fact that her mother was sick; the illness was far too advanced to disguise. Both daughters had been told that she had cancer. On the occasions when they had talked about it as a family, their parents had spoken in only the most optimistic terms, taking care to avoid crushing the hope within Ann and Hallie. Though Ann was in the fifth grade and knew perfectly well that cancer was something that could kill you, the emotional reality of the disease remained a blind spot in her heart.

It was late in the morning, and Ann had been standing behind that same oak tree intently watching a large beetle crawling over the tree roots, in and out of the patches of sunlight, when she heard her parents on the path walking back to the cabin from the lake. They had no idea she was there. Ann heard her mother ask to stop for a minute, saying she felt tired. And then suddenly, before Ann had a chance to show herself, her mother was in tears. She wept in her husband's arms and spoke of not being around to see the girls grow up. Ann's shock at witnessing such wrenching adult emotions firsthand was washed away by the devastating realization that her mother wasn't going to get better; she was going to die, and not even Ann's father, could help her.

Ann had remained behind the giant tree holding her breath, terrified that she would be discovered, until her mother finally calmed herself and they continued on to the cabin. Ann immediately went in search of her older sister. When she found her and told her what she had learned, Hallie tried to be tactful but failed to conceal that she already understood how serious their mother's illness was. The loneliness of being the only one in the family excluded from the awful truth was a feeling that Ann could still summon at will to this very day. She glanced down the path in the direction that Hallie had walked. The lake was still far enough away so that the trees hid it from view, but she could smell it, and hear it, and that was enough.

Ann turned and walked back to the car where she got her father's Winchester out of the back seat, and then went to the front door. Just as she tore the yellow police tape from the door, Hallie came around the side of the cabin.

"Guess it's time, huh?" Hallie said as she joined Ann on the porch.

"Hallie, this isn't going to be easy, for either of us. I haven't seen the room yet, so I don't know how bad it is, but, well, I just wanted to warn you."

She pushed the door open, alert for unpleasant odors, but found only the faint mustiness of a house that's been closed up for months at a time. The front door opened to the main room of the cabin with a tiny kitchen at the far end, separated by a counter. Ann looked around slowly at the familiar walls covered with decades of bric-a-brac. Several old, framed black-and-white photographs hung crooked beside antique snowshoes made of wood and leather. On the mantel above the fireplace sat her father's collection of hats, each one covered with fishing flies, tied by him over the years. A thick, worn, braided rug covered most of the floor, and a faded old Indian blanket masked the tears in the old sofa's upholstery.

As they crossed the main room, Ann set the rifle on the table and then opened the door to the left of the kitchen, which led into the cabin's only bedroom. It was a small, tidy room containing a bed, a nightstand, and a dresser. At the other end of the bedroom, another door opened onto a small stone patio behind the cabin. The curtains at the window were closed and the room was dark.

Hallie had stopped at the kitchen counter. "Is that the room?" she asked.

"No, it was in his study."

Ann stared at the bottom drawer of the dresser where she knew her father kept his guilty secret—knitting needles and dozens of rolls of yarn. Reds, blues, yellows—her father loved the bright colors. Once when his buddies had stumbled across a partially finished scarf that he'd accidentally left lying on the kitchen counter, he'd told them it belonged to Ann. In a phone call to her that night he told her about it, and they'd both laughed, but Ann didn't miss the unspoken petition in her father's voice to go along with it and keep his secret. Now that the sheriff's investigators have been through the place, Ann thought, it's not a secret anymore. When she walked away, she left the door open.

Back in the main room, Ann walked through the kitchen, took her sister's hand, and together they paused outside of the door that led to their father's office. It was there that he used to tie his flies and load his own cartridges, while listening to ballgames on the radio. The door was partially open. Ann squeezed Hallie's hand, let it go, took a deep breath, and walked in. She heard an audible gasp from behind her. Until now she had kept her emotions in check, but the sight that met her eyes brought everything tumbling out. The sisters put their arms around each other and stood there for a minute.

They'd found him in this room; his body sprawled across the floor beside the fallen chair. His scarred wooden desk was spattered with a mixture of fingerprint dusting powder, and blood. There was so much blood! Until this moment, Ann had managed to avoid thinking about what she would find, but now reality swarmed in on her with a vengeance. A fine crimson spray colored the wall next to the desk, and the simple wooden chair lying on its back on the bare floor was also spattered with blood. Ann's understanding was that their father had been sitting at the desk when the rifle had discharged into his chest.

Ann gently let her sister go and bent over the chair, examining the splintered hole in its back through which the bullet had passed. Then she stepped around the large section of dried blood on the floor and examined the small hole dug into the wall where technicians had removed the fatal bullet. That bullet would currently be found in an envelope in the evidence room at the Curran County Sheriff's Office.

Hallie went back out into the main room and Ann began a search of the desk drawers. She didn't really expect to find anything important; it was more out of a need to perform some familiar activity than anything else. After several minutes, she noticed that her movements were becoming clumsy and confused. She finally abandoned her search and walked back out into the main room where Hallie was sitting on the couch, staring at the Winchester lying on the table. As Ann approached, Hallie looked up at her.

"Why did you bring that thing here?" she asked, indicating the rifle.

"I thought it should go back up over the fireplace. I thought it belonged here."

"We should destroy it."

Sounds like she's talking about a horse, Ann thought, and then said, "It's only a rifle."

"Right, guns don't kill people, people do."

"I thought keeping it here would remind me, because I don't want to forget. I don't ever want to forget. But if you can't live with that, I'll get rid of it."

Hallie looked away. "I don't care."

On the wall that faced the sofa was the fireplace mantel that held her father's hats. Above the mantel was an empty space on the wall, where the 308 Winchester had rested until nine days ago, when it had been taken down and used one last time. Ann had intended to put the Winchester back up on the wall as some sort of defiant gesture, the significance of which she didn't really understand herself. But now seeing how Hallie felt, she was unable to do it. When they walked out of the cabin, she left the rifle lying on the table.

Chapter Eleven

Early Tuesday morning, wearing bluejeans and a Milwaukee Brewers T-shirt, Ann walked down her father's driveway under the canopy of evergreens and turned west toward the center of town. The houses she passed were a collection of one-story, aluminum-sided ramblers, nondescript frame houses, and prefabs, each one carefully maintained, and each one unique. As she walked, she tried to convince herself that the houses looked familiar, reciting the names of the neighbors she could remember from her childhood. She recalled quite a few names, but by the time she'd walked a block, her recognition was spotty. She managed to identify the home of Dr. Lamott, her dentist, and Jerry Willis, the paperboy on whom she'd had a crush in the tenth grade. After walking for half-an-hour, she finally admitted to herself that she was actually looking for Dexter Loomis' office, and twenty minutes later, she found the Village Government Center on Cherry Street.

When she entered, she was standing in a small reception area at one end of a long room. Behind a wooden counter was a secretary's desk. Dexter Loomis and another man, a tall black man, were in the near corner, bent over an electric coffeepot, discussing something in the hushed tones of surgeons conferring over a fallen world leader. Several feet away, a middle-aged woman stood watching with apparent concern. Dexter held the coffeepot's electric cord in his hand while the other man poked at the frayed strands, as though it was a snake they didn't want to startle.

Dexter looked up and did a double take. "Annie, good morning!"

"Hi."

"Grady Penz, meet Annie Summer, an old friend of mine."

Grady straightened up for his introduction and didn't stop until he'd reached six foot five inches. Between Dexter at six foot three and Grady, the two men seemed to fill up the room.

"Hello." Grady's voice had a deep, velvety tranquility to it.

"Hi." When Ann shook his hand, she sensed a gentle strength.

"Grady's an EMT," Dexter explained, "works out of New Richmond, but he tends to bother us in his spare time. And this is Phyllis Beiderman, she was Lewis Coffers' secretary, but now she belongs to me. My own personal minion dedicated to fulfilling my every wish, no matter how sordid. Right, Phyllis?"

Phyllis rushed forward, sweeping the coffeepot, along with its damaged cord, into the safety of her arms, then turned and smiled at Ann.

"It's nice to meet you."

"Likewise," Ann said.

As soon as her reply was out, Phyllis' smile was replaced by a grimace of determination. She dodged around the counter past Ann and paused at the door only long enough to turn and explain. "We used to have a microwave, until these two tried to repair it."

Dexter turned to Grady. "This is Paul Summer's daughter, the one I took out on the boat. She moved down to Madison after college, but she's back visiting the area."

This elicited a slow nod. Dexter raised his eyebrows slightly and lowered his voice, "Homicide detective."

"That a fact?" Ann felt Grady, fine-tune his gaze. "Well, then, I am glad to meet you." He seemed to hesitate for a moment and then added, "I'm sorry about your father."

"Thank you," Ann said. "Hallie and I went out to his cabin yesterday."

"I haven't been out there," Dexter said, "but I heard about it. It must have been tough."

Ann nodded. "I've been all over murder scenes for the last four years, but this one even got to me."

"It involvin' your father, and all," Grady offered.

"Yeah, but even without that, there was so much blood."

"Grady, did I ever tell you how my dad used to fly in a B-17 in World War II?"

"You never told me nothin' about your dad at all, Dex," Grady said.

"He was a radio man and waist gunner. Used to tell me how sometimes a plane would take a hit on a mission, and there'd be a terrible mess. Like if, for example, the ball turret guy got killed, the crews would have to wash out the remains. But the thing he told me was they never made the crewmen clean out their own planes, because they flew with the guy, and they knew him. So the crews were always assigned to clean out each other's planes."

"I think I see where you're goin' with this," Grady said. "I'll volunteer to help."

Dexter turned to Ann. "Annie, Grady and I'll go up to your father's cabin and clean out the room where he was found for you. We'll take care of it tomorrow morning, okay?"

Ann seemed a little taken aback. "I was just taking a walk around town this morning, and I thought I'd drop by to thank you for the boat ride on Sunday, Dexter."

"Pleasure was all mine. Maybe we can do it again some time?"

"Sure, that would be nice. But I didn't expect you guys to offer to do this for me."

"I know, but we will, okay?"

She looked back and forth between them. "Thank you."

This was followed by an awkward silence while Ann's gaze drifted to the top of Dexter's desk, where a book lay open. She craned her head around trying to identify it.

"*Autopsy Technique*. Let me guess, you're an amateur pathologist in your spare time."

"When I'm not busy associating with the criminal element." Dexter picked up the book. "Grady and I were trying to zero in on a symptom he may have identified on Muriel Evenson's face the night of her death."

"You're talking about the hemorrhaging that you mentioned on Sunday?"

Dexter turned to Grady. "You saw it, you tell her."

Grady hesitated for just a second. "I thought I saw a flush in her cheeks. Not sure what you call it, but I've seen it before. I think it could mean she was strangled."

"Petechiae," Ann said.

Both men looked at her. Dexter tried it. "Pet—"

"PE-TEE-KEE-AH," she repeated phonetically. "The flushed appearance is caused by hemorrhaging, brought on by a lack of oxygen." Ann looked at Grady. "You saw this?"

"I think so. Hard to be sure given the light we had."

"How long have you been an EMT, Grady?"

"Eight years in Chicago, and four years here."

Ann turned to Dexter. "Did you schedule an autopsy?"

"After we talked on Sunday, I called the medical examiner and he scheduled one for later this morning, in fact." Dexter tossed the book back on the desk. "We were just doing a little homework. You think we're on to something?"

"Sounds like Grady knows what he's talking about. It's possible the girl could have been murdered."

Dexter shook his head. "I read about this stuff in the paper, but I still can't believe it's happened here, in a town like Higgins Point."

"The larger cities have their own homicide investigators. They don't need help from the DCI," Ann said, "so I spend all my time in small towns like this, and believe me, they keep me busy."

"We were just going to head over to Muriel's apartment to look around, maybe you'd like to come along?"

Ann wasn't assigned to the case, but investigating her father's death already had her butt hanging so far out over the edge, she decided it couldn't possibly do any more harm. "Sure, I'll take a look."

"Great." Dexter grabbed his car keys off the desk and Ann followed him to the door.

"Back to that crazy, rich lady's house again," Grady said, as he closed the door behind them.

Muriel Evenson's apartment on Vine Street was only six blocks away, and five minutes later they were walking up the stairs. After Ann learned that there hadn't been a lab team up there yet, she cautioned them to avoid disturbing anything. The three of them worked their way through the rooms with Ann reviewing Dexter's notes as they went. She checked the windows but could find no signs of a forced entry. Eventually, they ended up out on the deck where Dexter explained why he thought Muriel hadn't simply tripped and fallen against the railing.

"So you broke the other railing yourself."

"I conducted what engineers refer to as a destructive test, to find out what it takes to break it."

"And what did it take?"

"A lot more force than a girl Muriel's size would generate just stumbling and falling into it."

Ann leaned over the edge of the deck and studied the

rust colored bloodstains on the driveway. "Anybody take any photos?"

Dexter looked sheepish. "No pictures. Sorry, we thought it was an accident."

"Okay, let's see if we can piece together a possible scenario."

Ann and Dexter left Grady out on the deck and went back into the apartment. Standing near the front entry, they could see both the front door at the bottom of the stairs and the door leading into Muriel's bedroom.

"The bed appears to have been slept in." Ann checked Dexter's notes. "The landlady heard the dog start barking around 11:30 Thursday night, right?"

"That's right."

"By the way, why did Grady refer to the landlady as 'that crazy, rich woman?' Is she crazy? I mean can we trust her story?"

Dexter smiled. "No, Ardella's not crazy."

"Then why'd he call her that?"

"Grady Penz is one of those people who's capable of believing everything he hears."

Ann couldn't help but ask. "And what has he heard?"

Dexter paused, apparently composing the explanation in his head before beginning.

"Ardella and my mother were good friends all their lives. About four years ago, I got a phone call from Ardella. She called me because my mother wasn't home, and she needed a ride into St. Paul. Ardella was sure she had a winning lottery ticket and needed to go claim the prize."

"A big winner?"

"Over a million."

Ann gave a low whistle. "Visions of Tahiti just passed before my eyes."

"Boca Raton," Dexter said automatically. "Anyway, I was happy to help out, but I was a little skeptical; I knew something about Ardella that almost no one else in Higgins Point knew."

"This sounds like a soap opera. What did you know?"

Dexter ignored the question. "Ardella refused to let me see the ticket. She left a message on my mother's phone telling her about it, and then the two of us made the drive into St. Paul. Sure enough, when we got to the store where she'd bought the ticket, it was no good. The numbers were backward."

Ann crinkled her brow for a second. "Backward? So what you knew about Ardella was that she was—"

"Dyslexic," Dexter said, "and extremely embarrassed about the whole thing. In fact she made me promise never to tell anyone the truth. But while we were driving into the cities, my mother came home, got the message, and played Paul Revere, spreading the good news all over town by phone."

"So Ardella never won any money?"

"No, none. But everyone in town thought she did. To this day, Ardella is highly admired in the community for maintaining her modest lifestyle in spite of her wealth."

"Did your mother know?"

"Uh huh. Took the secret to her grave."

"And you haven't even told Grady."

"I promised Ardella I wouldn't."

"But you told me, why?"

Dexter looked at Ann for a minute. "I'm not sure, maybe because you don't live here anymore, or because you have an honest face. Or maybe you just charmed it out of me. But we can trust Ardella if she said the dog barked at eleven-thirty."

"What if she misread her clock?"

Dexter smiled. "That occurred to me too. Her bedside clock isn't digital, I checked."

"Right." Ann oriented her thoughts back to the matter at hand. "So, sometime before eleven-thirty, Muriel arrived home, undressed, and went to bed. Someone, let's assume for now it was a male, came to the front door, so she put on her robe and slippers, and went down. One way or another, he talked his way inside. She closed the door when they went up, but left it unlocked. Her dog was in the apartment, what's its name again?"

"Brando."

"And I think you said that Brando is a German Shepherd, right?"

"Uh huh. He goes about eighty pounds."

Ann walked across the front room and through the kitchen, stopping at the glass door.

"The dog's big enough to be a problem, so the intruder gets Muriel out onto the balcony where he can shut the door on him." Behind Ann, on the other side of the glass, Grady appeared to be examining the deck. "Once out there, he could have struck Muriel over the head with something and dazed her enough so she could be dragged to the edge of the deck and thrown over. Then he kicked out the railing to make it look like an accident. If we assume it was at that point that the dog started barking, it pinpoints the time of the assault at eleven-thirty. The murderer couldn't go back into the apartment because of the dog, so he lowered himself down from the balcony. He checked the victim and discovered she was still breathing, so hoping to make it look like she died in the fall, he strangled her, resulting in the hemorrhaging that Grady observed."

"So we're looking for someone she knew," Dexter said.

"That's where I'd start. And it'll be someone with the physical ability, the opportunity, and, most importantly, the motive."

"Ardella said she heard a car starting in the distance, but couldn't tell which direction it came from."

Ann slid the glass door open and walked out onto the deck. She looked out across the houses beyond the back fence. The trees were waving in the warm breeze of the

July morning. She imagined the murderer trying to think this through beforehand. The sound of the starting car had been distant. If the murderer parked on the next street or down the block, then he knew beforehand that he didn't want to be seen. That would make it less likely that it was a spur of the moment thing, which might rule out a lover's spat. If it were planned, he would have brought his weapon with him, concealing it as he entered her apartment, but did he anticipate the dog forcing him to do it out on the deck? Maybe he knew the victim, but not well enough to know she had a dog.

Grady was kneeling down, examining the area where the deck met the siding of the house. His face was inches from the surface of the wood planks. "Might have somethin' here," he announced. "Looks like blood."

Ann and Dexter squatted down and looked where he indicated. Dexter saw a tiny but unmistakable spray of maroon droplets.

"More up here," Grady said, pointing at the surface of the siding.

"This must have come from the blow to her head." Dexter looked at Ann. "Looks like you nailed it."

"My guess would be that the killer went over the back fence to the next street," Ann said. "But we should talk to the neighbors in both directions to see if anyone noticed a strange car parked on their street around that time."

"In the movies they always check phone records," Dexter said. "Should I check hers?"

"I knew you had a flair for this."

"It really teed me off when they yanked *Murder She Wrote*."

An idea occurred to Ann. She walked back through the apartment examining the framed photos. She collected only the ones that had been taken in the apartment, apparently during parties. There were four of them, three hanging on walls, and one on Muriel's dresser. She gathered them up and one by one positioned herself in the apartment so she was looking at the same view as the photo. In the last picture, she found something. The shot was directed at the rear of the apartment through the dining room. The camera had captured Muriel and three of her friends, arms linked in mid-kick, in what looked like a spontaneous chorus line. Off to the side was a small, dark cherry table with a replica of the *Statue of David* on it. The statue was about twelve inches high, and as Ann viewed the room in front of her, the table was there, but not the statue. She pointed out the missing statue to Dexter. The dark cherry showed up dust readily and when they examined the top of the table, they found a faint, dust-free circle marking the former position of the statue.

"We may have found the murder weapon," Ann said. "Let's hold on to this photo, for forensics. You mentioned that Muriel had a boyfriend, right?"

"Yeah," Dexter flipped through his note pad. "The drama teacher at a local community college. Ardella said his name was Geoffrey Padgett."

"We'll talk to him, and we'll talk to Muriel's girlfriends, her employer, and anyone else we can find."

Dexter glanced down at his notepad again. "According to Ardella, her best friend was Cara Lynn Grovsner. I've seen her around. She's a waitress at Janet's Café."

"As good a place as any to start."

Dexter's features rearranged themselves into a quiet smile. "You're going to help?"

"I guess I am."

He shook his head. "I can't believe that there could actually be a reason for someone doing this."

"When we find the motive, it'll wind up making perfect sense to someone."

"What if it's a random act, you know, some drifter or something?"

"Then it's going to get more complicated. But those murders aren't too common—they're just the ones you read about in the papers."

"So it's a matter of motive."

Ann nodded. "We have to look for anything out of the ordinary, a change in her behavior recently, maybe someone new in her life."

"Why do I get the feeling that's not as simple as it sounds?"

"If I've made it sound simple, I didn't mean to."

"By the way, Muriel's father, who happens to be my boss, wanted me to question Nick Lundholm based on an incident that happened a year ago." Dexter briefly told her about the accident and the perceived miscarriage of justice.

"Sounds like a load of horse manure to me," Grady said, when he heard the story.

"It seems far-fetched to me too," Dexter said, "but I promised Dick, so I stopped by Lundholm's yesterday, and talked to him for a few minutes."

"What'd you ask him?"

"I asked him where he was Thursday night."

"And?"

"He said he was home alone, drunk. No alibi."

"Think he did it?"

Dexter thought the question over. "His daughter's death knocked him flat, he's a mess—but I think he was genuinely surprised to hear about Muriel."

Ann just nodded her head.

"I still want to talk with Mrs. Lundholm," Dexter said. "If I do that, then at least I can look Dick Evenson in the eye."

"When is the autopsy scheduled?"

"Ten-thirty, interested in going?"

"I'll go, but in an unofficial capacity."

Dexter looked at his watch. "We probably have time to talk to the waitress first, if you're interested."

"Sure."

Dexter consulted his notepad again. "I've got one other name at this point. Ardella mentioned that Cara Lynn has a boyfriend who used to go up to Muriel's apartment, someone named Billy."

"Put him on our list too," Ann said.

After the three of them had left the apartment and were about to get back into Dexter's Cherokee, Ann put her hand on his arm.

"You know that conversation we had on your boat on Sunday?"

Dexter grinned. "Yeah."

"I have a question for you."

"Okay."

"If the results of this autopsy are what we expect, how important is it to you to find the Evenson girl's killer?"

"Is that a trick question? There's no other option."

"Then if I were you, I'd keep an eye on this investigation."

"I thought you said the pros would handle it."

"A lot of people will try to help, and maybe they'll get results, but don't abandon your own instincts."

"Now I'm confused."

"I'm just saying that sometimes if you want something done right, you have to do it yourself."

Dexter spent a few seconds processing this information. "While that is, of course, a time honored platitude, it doesn't sound like chapter and verse from any law enforcement manual."

"Do you want to follow the law, or bring Muriel's killer to justice?"

"Can't we do both?"

Ann hesitated. "I used to think so. But if it's important to you to solve this case, don't depend on them being the same thing."

"I guess I won't."

After they'd gotten into the Cherokee, Dexter paused before he turned the key. "I have a question for you. If I take you to the autopsy, does that count as a second date?"

Chapter Twelve

Janet's Café after the morning rush was almost empty. Ann and Dexter walked in, and without really thinking about it, Ann took the same counter stool that she'd had on Saturday when she'd run into Dexter. She glanced around, and for the first time noticed a watercolor painting on the wall. The painting, which was done in luxurious earth tones, showed a silver-flecked stream running off into the distance through a stand of trees. Two figures, one small and one large, stood beside the stream, holding fishing poles. The painting brought back the memory of uncounted hours spent beside her father with a fishing rod.

When Ann and Hallie lost their mother to cancer, their father's response was to buy them a puppy and learn how to cook, and though he never actually avoided talking about their mother, he seldom brought her up in conversation. It wasn't until three months after her mother was gone that Ann chanced upon her father one night in his study. His shoulders were shaking, and as she watched silently from the doorway she realized that a towel was silencing his sobs. For the first time, Ann realized that while it was true she had lost her mother, it was also true that her father had lost his wife. From that day forward, Ann made it her business to be his constant companion.

The thought passed through Ann's mind that perhaps her father actually could take his own life, and the immediate payment was a stab of guilt. Though she had concrete reasons for rejecting the possibility, when the pain faded, the suspicion lingered.

Ann was interrupted in her thoughts when a waitress appeared before them with a glass of water and a menu. Her dull blond hair was pulled back, with wisps trailing down her neck. Her face, while pleasant, just missed being pretty. Her nose was a little large and her eyebrows, which were too rounded, sat above smallish pale eyes. Ann noticed a cut on her lower lip, which had not yet healed.

"We serve breakfast till eleven," she said with a mechanical smile and started to walk away.

"Are you Cara Lynn Grovsner?" Ann asked.

The girl turned and looked at Ann and then Dexter, carefully. Ann reminded herself that at the beginning of these things everyone looks both innocent and guilty.

"Yes," she finally replied.

Dexter looked at Ann, silently cueing her to take the lead. "I'm Special Agent Summer, and this is Police Chief Loomis. We're looking into the circumstances surrounding the death of Muriel Evenson, and we'd like a few minutes of your time."

When Cara Lynn didn't say anything, Ann continued. "I understand you were a good friend of hers."

"I thought she died in an accident?"

"We're looking into that," Dexter said.

Cara Lynn hesitated and glanced back at the kitchen, and then sat down on the stool next to Ann. "I guess I can take a few minutes."

"Thank you. How long did you know Muriel?"

"We met in, like, the sixth grade."

"Let's see, she was nineteen, so you knew each other for about seven years?"

"I guess." Cara Lynn's expression changed, and Ann guessed it was her use of past tense.

"Good friends all that time?"

Cara Lynn just nodded.

"What was she like?"

Cara Lynn thought for a moment. "She was serious," she said finally, as though just realizing that fact herself.

"Serious about what?"

"Well, we used to talk about stuff we wanted to do, ya know, like get out of this hole," she glanced around her, "find Mr. Right, get a decent job, but Muriel had, like, real dreams. I mean she always knew she wanted to be an actress."

"I understand she was taking acting lessons at a community college?"

"That's what I mean, she went after what she wanted."

"Why didn't you take acting lessons with her?"

Cara Lynn smiled sheepishly. "This diner's more my speed."

"I'm told she was dating someone named Geoffrey Padgett," Ann said, "her drama teacher at her college."

"Yeah, she was going to go to Los Angeles with him, to study acting."

"I haven't been in college for a while, but isn't it frowned upon for a teacher to date one of his students?"

Cara Lynn shrugged.

"What can you tell me about their relationship?"

"Not much, but it seemed a little cooler lately."

"Cooler?"

"Like he's got something better to do, ya know. I didn't say anything to Muriel, but I never really trusted him. I mean, lots of girls go to that college, and I hear his class is pretty popular."

"Did you spend much time up in Muriel's apartment?" Ann asked.

"Some, but lately she's been getting busier with her classes and the acting."

Ann threw in the next question as casually as she could, looking down at her pad.

"You go around with a guy named Billy something, right?"

There was a slight hesitation while Cara Lynn's gaze shot sideways for just an instant. "Yeah, Billy something." The seriousness in her voice caused Ann to pause.

"He have a last name?"

"Deal. Billy Deal."

"Did Billy Deal go up to her place with you?"

"Once in a while," she replied cautiously.

"Did you happen to notice Muriel hanging around with anyone new lately?"

"No."

"When did you see Muriel last?"

Cara Lynn's eyes filled and after a moment she replied, "Thursday. Me and Billy stopped by her place for a few minutes after work." She reached in her apron pocket and pulled out a tissue and blew her nose. "Excuse me."

Dexter leaned forward. "This last Thursday, the day she died?"

Cara Lynn shifted her gaze to Dexter. "Yeah, in the afternoon, before her rehearsal." She glanced back at the kitchen. "Guess I should get back."

"Just one last question," Ann said. "Can you think of anyone who would have a reason for doing this to Muriel?"

Cara Lynn paused. "Doing what? The papers said it was an accident."

Ann understood that this was her answer. "Thanks for your time, you've been very helpful."

Ann placed some money on the counter for coffee they'd never gotten around to ordering, and stood up, addressing Cara Lynn before she could get away.

"By the way, Miss Grovsner, what happened to your lip?"

Cara Lynn's hand went up to her mouth involuntarily.

"I walked into a door. Pretty dumb, huh?"

"Oh, I don't know," Ann replied, "seems like I'm always running into things myself."

A nervous laugh from Cara Lynn accompanied Ann and Dexter to the door. They stepped outside under the shade of Janet's green and white striped awning and stood on the sidewalk surveying the street. The restaurant reminded Ann of her father, but there were so many other memories mixed in. She could see the town water tower several blocks away, standing blue and white above the buildings and trees. She looked at it silhouetted against the sky and remembered one night many years ago when she was in the seventh grade. She had climbed the tower with a boy from school and while sitting beside one another on the catwalk, their legs dangling in the air, had received her first kiss. Her mother had been gone for two years by that time, and she never mentioned it to her father. But when she told her girlfriends at school about it, the camaraderie she experienced amid the giggling surprised her—and lasted a lot longer than the boy did.

Ann happened to glance to her left, through the window, into the restaurant. Cara Lynn was walking back toward the kitchen when a figure in a corner booth gestured to her. Through the window, Ann could see that he had long greasy hair and a sparse moustache. He wore a black leather jacket, though there was no motorcycle parked outside, and Ann saw the glint of an earring. When Cara Lynn got close enough, he reached up and took her arm, pulling her into the booth across from him. By this time, he had Dexter's attention as well.

Their conversation seemed to consist of him talking and her shaking her head. His expression was a permanent scowl. Suddenly, Cara Lynn leaned forward and spoke low to him. For a few seconds his expression didn't change, and Cara Lynn turned and glanced at the kitchen. Then he grabbed her jaw in his hand, peering at her closely. His face showed no apparent emotion, but Ann thought she saw tears welling up in Cara Lynn's small eyes. They remained frozen like that for several seconds, framed by the anonymous activity around them. Finally, just as Dexter started to move toward the door to reenter the restaurant, he suddenly released Cara Lynn. She rose and hurried away, and he settled down to finish his coffee. Ann was sure they had just met Billy Deal.

All autopsies for the region of western Wisconsin near the twin cities are done at the Ramsey County Medical Center in St. Paul, Minnesota. The room in which this particular autopsy was to be performed was located in the basement, and the centerpiece of the room, inert under the cold, industrial lights, was the stainless steel table that held Muriel Evenson's naked body. A variety of exotic-looking machines were arrayed around the room, but for Dexter, the focus was pretty much the stainless steel table. He couldn't quite bring himself to look at it, but he couldn't completely look away either.

Dr. DeMott, a man of perhaps fifty with thinning hair and strong looking hands, was the resident pathologist performing the autopsy. He introduced himself to Ann and Dexter and then introduced his technician, a thin young man with stringy hair, simply as Eugene. Dexter thought Eugene looked a little pale. They were all wearing blue caps, gowns and masks. Dr. DeMott and Eugene also wore goggles.

The autopsy room had stainless steel furnishings and a hard tile floor. It was larger, brighter, and, thanks to a constantly humming air conditioner, colder than Dexter had expected. What surprised him the most was the lack of any particularly foul odors. He had come prepared to encounter at least a strong scent of formaldehyde.

"This isn't so bad," Dexter said, to no one in particular.

"Excuse me?" Dr. DeMott said.

"The smell," Dexter glanced around, "it isn't as bad as I expected."

DeMott smiled. "You're right," he said, gesturing toward Muriel's body. "This one's still pretty fresh." Dexter immediately regretted opening his mouth.

They briefed the doctor on the findings at the crime scene and showed him the photo of the Statue of David as the possible weapon. Then, Dexter casually began wandering around the examination room, gradually putting as much distance as he could between himself and the table. But when Dr. DeMott and Eugene became involved in a spirited discussion, his curiosity got the better of him, and he drifted in closer to pick up on the conversation. He was surprised to discover that the subject of their debate was whether to listen to the Twins game on the radio or put on a CD. Apparently, Eugene was a baseball fan, but Dr. DeMott was holding out for Grieg's *Peer Gynt*.

"Grieg's depressing," was Eugene's comment on the matter.

"And the Twins aren't?"

Dr. DeMott eventually prevailed, but only after Eugene made him promise not to hum along. With this issue resolved, Dr. DeMott turned on the microphone clipped to his gown, picked up Muriel's chart, and began reciting her basic statistics. The thinly eerie opening strains of *Peer Gynt* crept in around the doctor's precise, detached voice, and the autopsy was under way.

Dexter watched for a while, thinking perhaps it wasn't going to be so bad. Then the gross body examination was complete and, under the watchful eye of Dr. DeMott, Eugene picked up a scalpel and made a shocking incision across Muriel's chest from shoulder to shoulder, followed by a second one from that incision, down the center of her torso, to her pudendum. Dexter nimbly retreated to the far corner of the room, where he remained, taking deep breaths and developing an appreciation for Grieg.

Sometime later, Dexter was studying the contents of a medical cabinet and making up names for the strange devices, while he half-listened to the droning voice of Dr. DeMott, as he extracted, examined, and weighed the various organs of the cadaver that was previously his friend's daughter. Suddenly the cadence of the recitation was interrupted.

"Hmm."

Dexter glanced across the room at the doctor poised above the body. Ann, who had taken a seat along the wall, got up and stepped closer.

"Something?" Her voice was slightly muffled behind her cotton mask.

"Hmm," Dr. DeMott said again.

Dexter walked over to the table, taking care to keep his eyes on the doctor and off the body.

"Hmm what?" he asked.

Dr. DeMott looked up and in his recitation monotone said simply, "Fetus."

Three hours after the first incision, with the biting whine of the saw that had removed the top of Muriel's skull still ringing in Dexter's head, they stepped into Dr. DeMott's office. Sheriff Hicks was waiting for them.

"Miss Summer, I'm surprised to see you here."

"She's here at my invitation, Moses," Dexter said.

The sheriff nodded as Dr. DeMott seated himself behind his desk and began studying his notes, seemingly oblivious of the others in his office. They all sat down to wait, and after several minutes Dexter finally had to ask.

"You're telling us she was pregnant?"

Dr. DeMott looked up and nodded.

"Cause of death?" Ann asked.

"Asphyxiation, you were right about that. The brain exhibited clear evidence of petechiae. I didn't see anything on the neck indicating strangulation, but I did find evidence of trauma around the nose and mouth. It looks like she was probably smothered, possibly while unconscious. It's my opinion that the injuries to her head weren't fatal, but they certainly could have knocked her out."

Sheriff Hicks leaned forward in his chair. "Then this was a homicide?"

Dr. DeMott nodded.

"I looked at her out on her driveway and couldn't see anything, least not anything pointin' to murder."

Dr. DeMott laid his notes aside. "That's understandable. There was a large area of impact on her skull consistent with striking the driveway pavement that was clearly caused by the fall. But after I got her in here under the lights and cleaned her up, I found a less obvious localized injury. It looks like the result of bludgeoning by some object, such as a pipe, or quite possibly the statue in the photo you showed me."

For several seconds, the only sound in the office was the creaking of Dr. DeMott's leather chair. Dexter glanced at Ann and recalled the blood they'd found on the deck and her theory that Muriel had been knocked out and then thrown off.

"Anything under the fingernails?" Ann asked.

"The residue was bagged for the lab." Dr. DeMott rubbed his hand over his face, "I didn't see anything that looked like tissue, but you never know."

"Any sign of sexual assault?" Dexter asked.

"Nothing obvious. My guess is that the lab tests will come back negative."

"When will the results be ready?" Ann asked.

"Oh, they'll start coming back in two or three days, but

it'll take longer for some things. The brain won't be ready to section for another two weeks."

"But it's your opinion we have a homicide here?" Sheriff Hicks asked again.

Dr. DeMott placed his notes in a manila folder and closed it. "There's no doubt."

Ann stood up. "Thank you, Dr. DeMott." After the three of them had made their way down to the parking lot, Sheriff Hicks stopped Dexter.

"Dex, I want to say something."

"Moses, I'm sure there were better ways for me to handle this."

Sheriff Hicks put a large hand on Dexter's shoulder bringing an abrupt halt to Dexter's explanation. "If you'd listened to me, we'd have likely buried her and never known." He shook his head. "Christ almighty, I must be gettin' old."

"So now what?" Dexter asked anyone who cared to answer.

"I'll send a lab team over to her apartment," Sheriff Hicks replied. "Been a few days, but we might still be able to pick up something. You folks been talkin' to anyone yet?"

"Yeah," Dexter said, "one of her friends, a local waitress named Cara Lynn Grovsner."

"Anything look promising?"

Ann and Dexter both shook their heads. "Too early to tell," Ann said. "The fact that she was pregnant throws another wrinkle into it."

Sheriff Hicks studied the ground and spat. "Yeah, well, we'll see what we can do. I'll have a preliminary report on the crime scene brought around to your office soon as I can." He looked at Dexter and winked. "Good work, Chief." Then he turned to Ann. "Miss Summer, anything come up on that other thing you were lookin' into?"

"I visited the cabin yesterday, that's all. Nothing so far."

"Well, you let me know if anything surfaces, or if there's anything I can do to help out; one lawman to another, you hear?"

"I hear, Sheriff."

After he walked away, Dexter turned to Ann. "What was he talking about?"

"My father. He knows I'm looking into his death."

"You are? You know, when we talked on my boat I got the impression that there wasn't much else on your mind."

Ann smiled. "You were right."

"So tell me, how does that work again, the procedure for requesting help from the DCI?"

"Don't you trust the local law enforcement?"

"Considering *I'm* the local law enforcement—not entirely."

Ann smiled. "Call your district attorney and have him fax a request to Madison. I'll call my office and see if Marvin can assign Zack to the case. If he can, he'll be up here in the morning."

"Zack? Who's Zack?"

"Zack Rose, he's my partner. Don't worry, he's a pussycat."

Chapter Thirteen

Lakeview Community College was located in Minnesota on eighty acres of land, about a mile from the western shore of the St. Croix River. No lake was visible from the Lakeview campus. The college consisted of several identical buildings situated around a central grassy area, with stone benches and rows of featureless, immature trees. The buildings had tall, thin windows, which rose the full three-story height of the buildings and were separated by sections of stone façade. They were pointed at the top, giving them a modern, yet gothic appearance that seemed out of place. The overall effect was exacerbated by persistent rumors around campus that the architect was well-known as a designer of mausoleums.

It was mid-afternoon when Ann and Dexter stopped at the main office and were directed to the building in which Geoffrey Padgett's faculty office was located. They walked down a fluorescent-lit corridor with masonry block walls painted beige and adorned with occasional corkboards and display cases and a floor that was tiled in a light green geometric pattern that made Dexter dizzy. The overall effect was that of a sterile, modern high school.

When they reached Padgett's office, his door was open and he was seated at his desk, reading. Thick brown hair curled around his ears and over his high forehead, which was creased in concentration. A first glance would leave the impression that he was perhaps twenty-five years old, but after a closer look, Dexter realized that he was probably pushing forty. Before Padgett looked up and saw them, Dexter could have sworn he saw his lips moving.

Padgett seemed slightly irritated at being interrupted, until Ann and Dexter produced identification and explained who they were, and then his face took on a serious cast and he invited them to sit down. The room was tiny and they had to borrow one chair from an adjacent office. Dexter opened his notebook, content to assume the role of observer while Ann took the lead.

"Mr. Padgett, I'm sure you're aware of the recent death of one of your students, Miss Muriel Evenson?"

Padgett seemed mildly surprised to be questioned by Ann rather than Dexter. "Of course, it was a terrible accident, tragic."

"It wasn't an accident."

He looked from Ann to Dexter with impossibly blue eyes. "I don't understand."

"She was murdered," Ann stated simply.

"Oh my God. Do you have any idea who may be responsible?"

"Let's just say that so far no one's come forward with any first act confessions. I understand that you and Muriel Evenson were seeing one another."

Padgett lowered his voice. "Yes, of course, that's why you're here."

"How long would you say you've known her?"

"Almost a year. She enrolled in one of my acting classes." Almost to himself, he added, "She had such talent."

"Mr. Padgett, were you aware that at the time of her death, Muriel Evenson was pregnant?"

"Pregnant?"

Padgett's hesitation cued Dexter that a decision was being made.

"You didn't know?" Ann asked.

"No, I knew."

"Was it your child?"

Padgett hesitated again, because this was placing his teaching position in jeopardy, Dexter assumed.

"It wouldn't be hard to establish your relationship with the victim," Ann pointed out.

"Yes," he said, finally. "The child was mine."

Ann leaned forward and looked at him closely. "You seem to be taking the death of both your girlfriend and your unborn child with remarkable poise, Mr. Padgett."

At that point Padgett's façade seemed to crack. His face lost its expression and he looked down at the floor and mumbled. "Don't be misled by the fact that I'm in the theatre; I don't always feel it's appropriate to give release to my emotions."

"Don't worry," Ann said, "we'll try our best not to be misled."

"How did you feel about her pregnancy?" Dexter asked. "I mean did it bother you at all?"

Padgett's head snapped up. "Bother me? What do you mean, 'bother me'?"

"Were you looking forward to having a baby?"

Padgett exhaled his anger and answered softly. "Of course."

Dexter had the impression that Padgett's concern was manufactured for their benefit.

"Have you noticed anyone unusual or suspicious hanging around Muriel's classes lately?" Ann asked. "Anyone who seemed to be paying particular attention to Muriel?"

Padgett allowed himself a humorless smile. "Quite a few of our drama students are what you would probably call unusual, and Muriel was certainly popular. But no, if I understand what you're asking, I don't recall seeing anyone particularly suspicious."

"Anything strange about her behavior lately?"

"Nothing comes to mind. I really wish I could be of more help."

When Padgett turned his head slightly, the angle was just right and Dexter saw the unmistakable edge of a contact lens in his eye. Tinted contacts! No wonder his eyes are bluer than Paul Newman's—he's wearing tinted contacts. Padgett seemed to be staring at Ann.

"Excuse me," he said, peering at her face as though he were appraising a rare gem. "I don't mean to pry, but have you ever worked in the theatre?"

"Me? No, never." Ann smiled. "Well, one play in high school, in my senior year."

"The reason I ask is that the combination of your facial bone structure and green eyes is really quite striking. I was sure that somewhere along the way, an enterprising director must have tried to lure you onto the stage."

"Mr. Padgett—"

"My guess is that you were quite good. What production was it, if I may ask?"

Ann sighed. "*Our Town*, and I threw up."

Padgett leaned back in his chair. "Oh. How unfortunate."

"That's what my father in the front row thought too. Mr. Padgett, we just have a couple more questions, and we can get this behind us. Could you tell me where you were on Thursday night?"

"At rehearsal, as was Muriel."

"And after rehearsal?"

"I went home—alone."

"I see, and what time did the rehearsal end?"

"I believe we finally packed it in around ten-thirty. Possibly a few minutes later."

"Was that when Muriel left, ten-thirty?"

"Give or take a few minutes, yes."

"So that was the last time you saw her on the night she was murdered?"

Suddenly, a pretty face with curly blond hair appeared around the corner of the door and threw a blinding smile at Padgett.

"Oh, sorry! I was just checking on tonight." In response to his obvious confusion she added, "The rehearsal?"

Although seemingly impossible, her smile actually brightened up a level as she beamed it at Ann and Dexter. "Sorry to interrupt," she sang.

"There's, ah, no rehearsal tonight, Bridget," Padgett said with a cardboard smile.

"But Geoff—Mr. Padgett," she glanced at Ann and Dexter, "you were going to help me with my scenes, remember?" Dexter recognized elements of both petulance and urgency in her delivery, which could not be characterized as subtle, and was impressed by her passion, if not her acting technique.

"Well, come back a little later and we'll see what we can arrange, all right?"

With a parting smile Bridget disappeared and the briefest flash of embarrassment on Padgett's face removed any doubt in Dexter's mind about what he intended to arrange later.

"Is she in a play that you're putting on now?" Ann asked.

"Yes, she is."

"Was Muriel in that play?"

"Bridgett was Muriel's understudy actually."

"What play is it?" Ann asked.

"Macbeth," Dexter said suddenly, recalling the script he'd found in Muriel's knapsack.

They both looked at him. "Yes, that's right," Padgett said slowly. "How did you know?"

"I know many things," Dexter said, hoping they wouldn't ask him to prove it.

Ann was smiling as she rose and thanked Padgett for his

time. Padgett said that he would certainly let them know if he thought of anything that might be of help.

As they crossed the parking lot to their car, Dexter was at a loss for some way to work it into the conversation naturally and finally just blurted it out.

"I wonder if those contact lenses were for a performance?"

"What contact lenses?"

"You want to give me a break? You mean you didn't notice them? And what was all that garbage about your bone structure?"

"Garbage?"

"I didn't mean . . ."

"You think my bone structure is garbage?"

"No, of course I—"

"I was in a play once. What's wrong with that?"

"Nothing. I mean—" It suddenly occurred to Dexter what he must sound like.

Ann smiled. "Did you think I was buying what he was selling?"

"Well, I . . ." Dexter felt his face redden.

"Dexter, you're going to have to give me a little more credit than that; I'm not the twelve-year-old girl you used to know."

He unlocked her door and as he walked around to his, he said, "I heard that."

When Ann and Dexter got back to Higgins Point, they went to the First National Bank on Delphi Street to talk with Muriel's supervisor at work. Tom Manning was a thin man of about thirty-five who wore silver wire-rim glasses. He was all quick movements, with a high-pitched voice that Ann personally found a bit whiny. His eyes carried the bags of someone who stared at a computer screen all day, and he had a bad case of the sniffles. He apologized twice during the interview for having a cold. Apparently, Manning had already heard a rumor through some customer at the bank that Muriel Evenson had been murdered. Ann wasn't surprised; she knew what small towns were like and assumed that Ardella Tophler was probably busy spreading the word.

"It's, ah, it's terrible," he said, removing his glasses to clean them. "She was—" he exhaled on the lenses, "she was—" he polished them carefully with a white handkerchief, "ah, such a—" he placed the glasses back on his face blinking, "nice person."

"Mr. Manning, approximately how long did Muriel work with you?" Ann asked.

"About a year-and-a-half. I was the one who hired her."

"I see. What sort of relationship did you have with her?"

Manning drew back in alarm, "I, we had no relationship."

"No, Mr. Manning," Ann said quickly, "I'm talking about your working relationship."

"Oh, of course. She assisted with the paperwork for the loans we process."

"Did you work fairly closely? I mean did you see one another much during a typical day?"

"It varied, but typically we saw a lot of each other." Ann thought that for some reason this admission seemed difficult for him.

"Do you know of anyone she might have been seeing, anyone coming around the bank?"

"Just her boyfriend."

"Muriel's boyfriend visited her here at the bank? Are you talking about Geoffrey Padgett, a teacher over at Lakeview?"

"Yes, that's his name. He came by occasionally."

"Had everything been okay with her at work recently? Nothing out of the ordinary, nothing strange?" Ann asked.

"Strange? No. Well, she had been arguing on the phone quite a bit lately."

"Do you know who she was arguing with?"

"It sounded to me like she was fighting with her boyfriend." He straightened his posture and looked from Ann to Dexter. "Is he a suspect?"

"Any idea what they were fighting about?" Ann asked.

"I couldn't say, but there were a few times when she certainly seemed upset. She went home early after one call. It looked to me as though she'd been crying."

"How recent was that?"

"Maybe two weeks ago."

"And you have no idea what upset her?"

"No, she didn't confide in me. Sorry."

"Was Muriel a good employee?" Ann asked.

"Good? You mean did she know her job?"

"Did she ever give you any trouble, ever come in late or hung over? Did she seem stable to you?"

"Oh, absolutely. Never had any trouble with her," he said between sniffles. "She was a good employee, a hard worker. It's a real shame."

Ann looked at Dexter and he shrugged, indicating that he had nothing to ask.

"Well, you've been very helpful, Mr. Manning," Ann said, rising. "If anything occurs to you, anything that you think may be helpful in our investigation, please let us know."

"There is one other matter, related really," Manning said suddenly. Ann and Dexter stood waiting while he plucked a tissue from the box on his desk, and blew his nose. He took a quick peek at it before tossing it into his wastebasket.

"There are a few loan files that Muriel had taken home to work on before she, before she died." He glanced from Ann to Dexter and back quickly. "It's just that I, we, the bank, need those files, so I was wondering if it would be okay for me to pick them up?"

"I don't think any files—" Dexter stopped when he felt Ann's hand on his arm.

"I'm afraid that would be out of the question, Mr. Manning," Ann said crisply.

"I didn't think there would be any harm," Manning said. "I mean I can't imagine that a few loan files had anything to do with her death."

"Probably true, but we still can't allow any contamination of the crime scene until we're through, and that would certainly extend to removing any materials."

Manning just looked at Ann; her response allowed no room for discussion. Outside the bank, after they were in the Cherokee, Dexter made an observation.

"We didn't find any bank files in Muriel's apartment."

"I know."

"But you let Manning think we did."

"I know."

Dexter squinted at her. "Is this some kind of cop thing, where you don't tell certain people certain things and then it leads you to the killer?"

Ann smiled. "Yeah, it's a cop thing."

Chapter Fourteen

After Dexter dropped Ann off at her father's house, he placed a call to the district attorney and related the results of the autopsy to him. The D.A. agreed to send an immediate request for assistance to Madison. With that out of the way, Dexter's thoughts returned to Nick Lundholm. He knew it probably didn't rate this much attention, but his tendency developed over years of engineering was to tie things up neatly, and he couldn't seem to completely eliminate Lundholm from consideration quite yet. He decided to drive over to the New Richmond Medical Center, where Vickie Lundholm had been brought in DOA. If he could talk to someone who actually witnessed what happened in the emergency room that night, maybe that would put his doubts to rest. He was almost out the door when he got tangled up with Grady, who was walking in carrying a newspaper.

"Grady, I'm heading over to New Richmond Medical. Come on with me."

"I just got off work there, Dex. You're askin' me, do I want to go back to work?"

"Quit your caterwauling, and get in the Cherokee."

"First, you got to read this article."

"In the Cherokee."

"It's about you."

"You can read it to me in the Cherokee."

Once they were on the road, Grady unfolded the newspaper. "This was in yesterday's Pioneer Press," he explained.

"Don't tell me. Frank Kahler."

Grady grinned. "Why don't I let his sparkling prose speak for itself? This is in the Wisconsin section."

"Tragedy struck the tiny town of Higgins Point, Wisconsin late Thursday night when the body of Muriel Evenson was found on the driveway outside her apartment at 621 Vine Street. Muriel was the nineteen-year-old daughter of Mayor Dick Evenson and his wife, Inez. Why don't I just cut to the interesting stuff?

"In spite of questions raised by the coroner at the scene, Police Chief Dexter Loomis had originally claimed that 'no foul play' has taken place."

"That was before we had the autopsy," Dexter complained.

"I love that, 'no foul play,'" Grady said. "Here's some more."

"Drawing on all of his three months of police experience, Chief Loomis says he is pursuing suspects, including one very unlikely person, who shall go unnamed at this time, because if I printed it, Chief Loomis might be laughed out of town."

"Are you 'pursuing suspects,' Dex? I saved the best one for last."

"Given what I have seen of the quality of police work on this case, which is the first murder case in Higgins Point in more than a hundred years, this may be the best candidate for America's Most Wanted since Jimmy Hoffa disappeared."

Dexter was silent when Grady finished reading. His first impulse was to scream at the paper and throw both it and Grady out of the Cherokee. But his second impulse prevailed; he agreed. Frank Kahler had pretty much summed up how Dexter himself felt about his efforts. Grady must have sensed Dexter's frame of mind, because he folded the paper, and said "Hey man, I thought you'd get a laugh out of it. It don't mean nothin', Dex."

They were both silent for the rest of the ride. When they arrived at the Medical Center, it was late afternoon, and except for the receptionist, the area was deserted and quiet. Grady introduced Dexter to the young girl behind the counter whose tan was so deep it had to be artificial. The police files indicated that the date of the accident was July 24th. Dexter explained that he needed to know who had been on-duty that night. When the receptionist spoke, her voice was a husky whisper.

"I don't think we're supposed to release patient information without some sort of court order." The tone in her voice was apologetic.

"I'm not after any information about a patient," Dexter explained. "I only want to know what hospital personnel were working."

She hesitated, obviously wanting to be helpful. Finally she said, "You need the Medical Records Department. Follow me."

She disappeared for a moment and then reappeared around the corner in the waiting area and led him down a beige hallway to a plain looking door with MEDICAL RECORDS printed on it in businesslike block letters. She pushed the door open and turned on the light, motioning for them to follow her in. Once inside, the young lady disappeared again and then popped out behind the records counter.

"Can I help you? She smiled innocently.

"Do you have a twin sister who works in the reception area?" They both laughed.

"Yeah, you can help," Grady pointed out. "You can get a shotgun for Dex, cause he's on a wild goose chase."

"You know the accident I'm talking about?" Dexter asked, ignoring Grady.

She nodded and typed something into a computer terminal on the counter, which brought up some sort of menu. She typed in Vickie's name, and in a few seconds, the computer responded with a screen full of information.

"It was a Wednesday night, she was brought in at twelve-thirty AM," she announced, reading from the screen. "Attending physician was Dr. Phyllis Skadahl. She's the one who pronounced her DOA."

Dexter wrote the information down. "Can we find out who else might have been there besides the doctor?"

She thought for a moment and then cleared the computer screen and brought up another menu. This time her keyboard journey took her to a screen that displayed some sort of hospital personnel duty roster for Wednesday, July 24.

"The nurse on duty was Jerry Gottlieb."

"Either of them around right now?" Dexter asked.

"Sorry, no. Jerry's on vacation, in Canada, I think, and Dr. Skadahl moved to Mankato with her husband and kids last winter. Why do you want to know this, anyway?"

"I told you, he's on a wild goose chase," Grady said.

"I'm, ah," Dexter hesitated, "I'm looking for information that may concern a recent death." His statement removed any trace of a smile from her face.

"A death? Whose?"

"Muriel Evenson."

"The girl in Higgins Point, who fell off her balcony?"

Dexter nodded.

"That was an accident, right?"

Dexter shrugged, not wanting to get into it.

"She was in the car with Vickie Lundholm the night she died. She was driving, I remember reading about it. She died last week. What night was that?"

"Thursday night."

She looked at the computer screen again. "That's kind of spooky."

"What's spooky?"

"Last Thursday was July 24th."

"So what?"

"Well, the car accident she was in was on July 24th, one year earlier to the day."

"You two crackpots deserve each other," Grady said.

As he climbed into his Cherokee, Dexter thought about the coincidence of dates and about his talk with Nick Lundholm, but he still had trouble trying to work up any real enthusiasm for him as a suspect. Grady had a lot more trouble.

"Dex, sometimes you act just like an intelligent white man, then there's times like this."

Dexter's neck muscles were starting to feel like knotted rope. He rolled his head around producing a series of grinding pops.

"I'm just following up, you know? Trying to be thorough. I'd be derelict if I didn't. Ann said so."

"You're just fixin' to give Frank Kahler something else to write about."

Trying to read the minds of the suspects in this case had Dexter imagining that everyone was guilty. He felt like a new doctor with intern's disease, imagining his patients had every symptom that he'd ever read about. Nick Lundholm—some sort of avenging demon? It didn't seem likely, but as they left the Medical Center parking lot, Dexter had to admit that stranger things happened every day all over America. Maybe this time it was just Higgins Point's turn. He decided that it was time to talk to Mrs. Lundhom.

Dexter dropped Grady at the office, where his car was, and then drove over to talk to Mrs. Lundholm. The house on Orange Street was adorned with flowerbeds, rose bushes, and ivy. The lawn was well-tended, though the house, which belonged to Mrs. Lundholm's sister, could have used a coat of paint.

A smallish woman wearing slightly faded jeans, a blue work shirt, and a wide-brimmed, straw-hat bent over a bed of peonies in the front yard. When Dexter got out and approached the house, the lady stood up, tossed a handful of weeds into a basket, and waited. He could just make out a smile under the shadow of the hat that covered her features.

"Are you Mrs. Lundholm?"

"Why, yes, I am. Is there something I can do for you?"

Her voice was soft, pleasantly musical, and seemed to resonate with an inner calm. Dexter's immediate impression was that she was one of those fortunate few who had the universe figured out and was still okay with it.

"I'm Officer Loomis with the Higgins Point Police Department. I wonder if I could have a few moments of your time this morning?"

She reached up, raised the brim of her hat, and looked at him carefully, still smiling. "Are you selling tickets?"

"Selling tickets, ma'am?"

"Tickets." She said this as though it provided some sort of explanation. When Dexter came up with a blank expression she continued, "To a police function."

"No, I'm not selling any tickets today, Mrs. Lundholm. I wanted to talk to you about your husband, Nick."

She released the brim of the hat and her face returned to shadow. "Is Nicholas all right?"

"That's what I was going to ask you."

The concern in her eyes told Dexter that she understood that they weren't talking about her husband's physical well-being.

"I haven't seen him for quite some time."

Dexter decided to start at the beginning. "Ma'am, on Thursday night a local girl named Muriel Evenson died. I suppose you've heard about it."

"Oh, I did, that was just terrible."

"I apologize for having to bring up such a painful subject, but my understanding is that Muriel Evenson was driving the car that your daughter was killed in."

There was a pause. "Yes, she was. There were three girls in the car."

Dexter had read the police report that morning and already knew that the girl in the backseat had been Cara Lynn Grovsner, the waitress at Janet's. "As I'm sure you recall, Muriel Evenson told the authorities that she swerved the car to miss a deer."

"Yes, I remember, Officer . . ." She scanned Dexter's shirt for a nameplate and found none. Dexter suddenly realized what she was looking for.

"Loomis, ma'am."

"Officer Loomis."

"Apparently, Nick didn't agree, claimed she had been drinking. He said some things at the time, about Muriel, some things which weren't too charitable."

"I never thought she did anything wrong. Heavens, a deer can pop up any time. I had a near miss myself once." Suddenly, Mrs. Lundholm understood where Dexter was headed. "But the papers said that the Evenson girl's death was an accident."

"I'm afraid that isn't the case," Dexter said.

"Oh my goodness! But that accident was a year ago, and he was just spouting off. You can't think that Nicholas would actually harm her."

"Is that what you think?"

Mrs. Lundholm's eyes were staring at nothing and her lips were moving slightly as though she were talking to someone. Finally, she found her voice. "I stayed with him for almost seven months after the accident, but then I had to leave. He made me leave."

"He kicked you out?"

"He might as well have, he wasn't the same person anymore. It got worse every day, the bitterness, and the drinking. He couldn't accept that the Evenson girl escaped blame."

"Got to be too much for you?"

"I tried drinking, I really did. But I couldn't get used to it, to the taste. I'll never understand how anyone can drink."

"I know what you mean," Dexter said, with the lack of conviction of one who enjoys his beer.

"I've been off the tranquilizers for several months now."

"That's uh, that's commendable, Mrs. Lundholm."

"Thank you. You do see that I had to leave? It was that or watch him die for his hate, because that's what he's doing, he's dying for his hate."

"I talked to him last night, and I think I know what you mean."

Suddenly her eyes were studying Dexter closely. "Yes, you said you saw him. How is he?"

"Well, frankly, Mrs. Lundholm, I think the guy could stand a little company."

"Oh, my." She looked mildly stricken.

Dexter couldn't think of anything else to ask, so he thanked her for her time and apologized for ruining such a beautiful afternoon.

Ann crossed the St. Croix River into Minnesota on I-94, squinting into the late afternoon sun. Twenty minutes later, she exited onto Payne Avenue in St. Paul and drove north for a few blocks, turning right onto York. The neighborhood was everything she'd expected: a street of neglected houses, many converted to duplexes and rental apartments, dwellings stacked above one another.

Detective Perry had finally given Ann something to work with on Monday afternoon. Eric Delisle was known to have associated with the murder victim, Casper Bottom and his current address was the lower flat on York, where Ann now stood. Its general condition didn't seem any better or worse than the other buildings around it. All the shades in both the upper and lower units were drawn closed. A dusty, rusted-out green Buick with a bent aerial sat in the driveway and gave Ann hope that Delisle was home. Ann navigated her way through castdown bicycles, discarded toys, and what appeared to be the guts of a washing machine strewn across the sidewalk. She stepped up onto the bare concrete porch and reached for the bell before noticing that there was only a pair of wires sticking out of the doorframe. She knocked, and after a minute she knocked again just as the door opened.

"Yeah?"

Ann shaded her eyes from the sunlight on the stoop, trying to see into the shadows beyond the screen door. "Mr. Delisle?" There was no response. "Eric Delisle?"

A cough came from behind the screen. "What are you sellin'?"

Ann smiled. "I'm not selling anything, Mr. Delisle. I'm Special Agent Summer with the DCI, and I'd like to ask you a few questions." Though the DCI had no jurisdiction in Minnesota, Ann doubted that Delisle knew that.

"You're a cop?"

"Yes. May I come in?"

"You need a warrant first."

"Pardon me?"

There was a slight hesitation in the voice behind the screen. "Don't you need a warrant to come in?"

Ann's eyes were slowly adjusting. She was starting to make out Delisle's basic features. He was tall and slender, and she thought she saw some facial hair.

"No, Mr. Delisle, you don't understand. I don't want to search the premises. I just want to ask you some questions."

"About what?"

Ann glanced around. "I'd rather not talk out here. Let me step inside and I promise to keep it brief, okay?"

He said nothing in reply, but after a few seconds he gave the screen door a nudge. Ann pulled it open, prepared to step inside, but Delisle remained in the doorway, so she waited, using the time to take a closer look at him. His long hair hung limp and tangled around his thin face, creased with sleep lines. The puffiness around the eyes suggested to Ann that he'd just gotten out of bed. He finally moved back just far enough to allow her to step into the front room, which smelled like stale pizza and wine.

"So what do you want to know?"

"I understand you were acquainted with a man named Casper Bottom."

Delisle's eyebrows pinched together in an expression that Ann read as genuine confusion. "I don't know anybody named Casper."

"He was shot to death about two months ago." There was still no flicker of recognition, and Ann was beginning to doubt Perry's information. "They found him in the trunk of a stolen Monte Carlo in a Rainbow Foods parking lot." That did it.

"You talkin' about C Note?"

"Let's start with what he was involved in," Ann said. "Any idea what got him killed?"

"C Note's name is Casper?"

"It was. My sources tell me he was mixed up with some meth labs. Can you confirm that?"

Delisle's small eyes, like BB's in his face, squeezed closed. "I don't know anything about any meth labs, man. Ain't you supposed to show me some kinda badge?"

Ann took her badge out of the back pocket of her jeans and held it up. "Mr. Delisle, as long as you didn't kill Casper Bottom, you have nothing to worry about."

"I didn't kill him, and I ain't got nothin' here, man. This place is clean, so I ain't worried anyway."

Ann glanced around the litter-strewn front room; it would have been charitable to call it filthy. "I don't know if *clean* is the word I'd use."

"Oh, ha ha. A funny cop." His face lost its sneer. "I don't have to talk to you."

"That's true, but a little cooperation can go a long way, Eric. I could put in a good word with the St. Paul Police." She realized how lame that sounded, but she didn't have much else to offer. "I just want your best guess. Who do you think killed Casper Bottom?"

"The cops already asked me that, and I told 'em I don't know."

"How about the circumstances? He was supposed to be dealing meth amphetamines. Was that why he was killed?"

When Delisle didn't respond immediately, Ann decided to pursue it. "Was it a bad drug deal? Did he cross somebody?"

"All I know is they were starting to deal a little in Wisconsin. But I got no idea who did it."

"They're expanding into Wisconsin with the meth labs?"

"Not anymore. Least that's what I heard, but that's it. I don't know nothin' else."

It supported what Detective Perry had told her, but nothing more. Ann put on a professional smile and said, "Thank you for your cooperation, Mr. Delisle."

It was a quarter past 11:00. Billy Deal reached for his beer, took a long pull, and stared at Cara Lynn, curled up in the Lazy-boy across the front room, watching television. Billy patted the sofa next to him, but Cara Lynn failed to notice.

"Hey, c'mon over here." His voice was thick.

Cara Lynn made a face, "I'm watching Letterman."

"He's on over here too."

"Not now, Billy." Her voice carried the whiny pleading of someone who knew it was useless.

"Don't make me get up, Cara."

Cara Lynn exhaled slowly, rose, and walked over to the

sofa and sat down heavily. As soon as she was within reach, Billy pulled her closer and started kissing her neck.

"No, Billy."

She tried to draw back, but as soon as Billy noticed her resisting, he got angry and rougher.

"I said, *no*, Billy."

"C'mon, Cara."

She got her arm between them, and her elbow accidentally connected with his chin. The room went white for Cara Lynn when, less than a second later, Billy's fist connected with her mouth.

"Why you make me do that? Why can't you be nice?" He pushed away from her and stood up. "You sure can ruin a mood, Cara."

She got unsteadily to her feet, tasting blood. It felt like her tooth was loose. She walked into the bathroom to rinse the blood out of her mouth, and when she passed Billy in the hallway, she avoided his eyes.

He walked back into the front room, sat down, and took a swig of beer. Several minutes later, after Cara Lynn had had a chance to recover a bit, she came out of the bathroom and walked to the front door. When she opened it, Billy looked up from the television.

"Where you goin' this time of night?"

"Cigarettes," she said.

He took a long swig of beer, draining the can. "Those things'll kill you," he said.

Cara Lynn did buy cigarettes at the Auto Stop, just in case Billy demanded to see them when she returned; she had learned to be careful around him. After the purchase, however, she went to a pay phone in the rear of the store and placed a call. There were several rings and then a slightly irritated voice, thick with sleep, came on the other end.

"Hello."

Cara Lynn hesitated for a moment and then plunged ahead. "I know what you did."

"What? Who is this?"

"I know what you did." She felt stupid repeating herself.

"Did what? Who is this?"

"Never mind who this is. I know you killed Muriel Evenson."

For a moment, the line became deeply quiet, and Cara Lynn could hear breathing on the other end.

"Is this a joke?"

"I figure I could call the police, or I could call you. Guess it's your lucky day."

There was another pause.

"What do you want?"

"Information should be worth something."

"So, what do you want?"

Cara Lynn suddenly realized that she hadn't even thought about how much to demand. "Ten thousand dollars."

"Where am I supposed to get—?"

"I'll call you on Thursday to tell you where to bring it." She hung up the phone and glanced over at the attendant to make sure she hadn't been overheard. When she got in her car and lit a cigarette, her hand was shaking.

Chapter Fifteen

On Wednesday morning, Dexter and Grady sat beside one another, leaning back with their feet propped up on Dexter's desk, staring at a television screen. The door opened and a young man, who Dexter judged to be in his late twenties and perhaps five feet six, walked in off the street. He had short hair that looked deliberately uncombed, a ring through his left eyebrow, and some sort of wire hanging out of his ear. Reading glasses were propped on his head, he wore a tan sport jacket over a yellow, Jimmy Buffet T-shirt, and was giving his chewing gum a good workout. It was the reading glasses that threw Dexter.

"Can I help you?" Dexter asked, suspecting he sounded like a waiter.

The young man extended his right hand. "Zack Rose, DCI. And you are?"

Dexter glanced down at his chest where his badge should have been before getting to his feet to shake hands.

"Dexter Loomis, Higgins Point Police. Sure, Zack Rose. You're Annie's partner."

"Guilty."

"This is Grady Penz, EMT out of New Richmond," Dexter said.

"Glad to meet you, Grady." When Grady stood up to

shake hands, Zack looked back and forth between them. "You guys on a basketball team? Hey, I suppose you want to see some ID."

"Nah," said Dexter.

Grady sat back down and resumed watching the television, which was positioned so that anyone on the public side of the counter couldn't see the screen. Zack produced a leather wallet and held it open in front of him.

"Security comes with a price tag," he said, "and vigilance is the price we must be willing to pay." He snapped the wallet shut and returned it to his pocket.

"I think that badge said 'CRIMEBUSTER' on it," Dexter said.

Zack looked perplexed. "No, it didn't, did it?"

"CRIMEBUSTER," Grady verified, without taking his eyes from the television.

Zack pulled out the wallet again and studied the badge while Dexter studied him.

"Son of a gun, you're right. Dexter Loomis, I am impressed. I'll bet not more than one person in ten manages to catch that detail."

"You got it in a box of Coco Puffs," Dexter said.

This time the surprise on Zack Rose's face was genuine. "Yeah, how did you—"

"Cause that's where Dex got his," Grady said.

This time Zack went to his breast pocket. "Okay, here you go." He held up a much more substantial-looking gold badge.

"Thanks, but I don't need to see it."

Zack's hand touched something on his belt. "Agent Rose."

Dexter looked up at him. "Okay, I don't need to see it, *Agent Rose.*"

"I just got here."

"Yeah, I know. You just walked in."

"I've left the mothership, and I'm mingling with the inhabitants."

Dexter wasn't sure how to respond to this. He looked at Grady, who just shrugged his shoulders.

"I've contacted the local, uh—" Zack looked at Dexter, "—law enforcement."

Dexter started to get out of his chair. "Yeah, I'm the local law enforcement. What about it?"

Zack held up one hand and tapped his earplug with the other.

"He's on the phone," Grady said.

Dexter could feel his face getting red. "Don't you think I know he's on the phone? I know he's on the phone."

"Nope, not to worry, boss, I'll talk to Ann. Right, I'll be in touch."

Zack's hand went back to his belt, and Dexter realized his phone was attached to it. Zack ended the call and then glanced at the television.

"Too early for *Jerry Springer*—must be *Sesame Street*."

"We heard that," Grady said. "We're right here."

Zack put another stick of gum into his mouth and smiled.

"Come here." Dexter gestured for Zack to step around the counter and join them.

"Check it out."

What Zack saw on the screen was a picture of a section of highway. The viewpoint was from a height of perhaps twenty feet, with the road running off into the distance. Trees were waving in a light breeze on the shoulders, and there was a running clock in the lower right corner of the screen. In the lower left corner was a larger set of numerals that was fixed at 0.0.

"So, what's this?" Zack asked.

"Dex's got a video camera mounted on a light pole outside of town," Grady replied.

A late model pickup truck popped into view and began to grow larger as it traveled toward the camera. Suddenly the numbers on the lower left of the screen jumped into action. 63.5, 64.2, 63.7.

"Got ya," Dexter said. He opened his desk drawer and pushed a small button, and then smiled over his shoulder at Zack.

"The numbers on the left are his speed?"

Dexter nodded. "The radar gun's positioned to record the car's speed as it comes into camera view." He looked at Zack's eyebrow ring. "What do you think?"

"Cool. So what's the button in the drawer do?"

Dexter got up from his chair and grabbed a ticket pad from his desktop. "That cycles the traffic signal outside, so he'll have to stop for a red light. Be back in a few minutes."

Down at the corner, Dexter explained the wisdom of obeying the local speed laws to the driver of the pickup, who was struggling to understand how someone on foot could walk up to him at a red light and ticket him for speeding. During Dexter's explanation, which ran several minutes and touched briefly on the role of relativity in time travel, he spotted Ann walking into his office. After he had discharged his official duties, and returned to the office, he extended a second, official welcome to Zack on behalf of the entire law enforcement community of Higgins Point which, Ann pointed out, currently consisted only of Dexter.

"The Lone Ranger, huh?" Zack said. "I always wanted my own town."

"I'm not the Lone Ranger anymore," Dexter said. "I got you assigned to the case, and I'll never be lonely again."

"Close, but not exactly accurate." Zack turned to Ann. "Schifsky thought that since you happened to be in town anyway, maybe you'd like to pull your weight for a change. His words, not mine."

"He wants me on the Evenson murder?"

"My impression was that he thought it would keep your mind off your father. Interested?"

Ann hesitated for just a second. "Count me in."

Dexter was pointedly not staring at Zack's eyebrow ring when Grady nudged him.

"Time we went out to the cabin, Dex. I got some scrub brushes, mops, and pails in the car."

"Yeah, let's get it over with," Dexter agreed.

Ann's expression turned serious. "Hallie and I can't thank you guys enough. This is way beyond the call of duty."

"Thanks yourself, for helping out on my case," Dexter said.

After they left, Ann provided Zack with a summary of their investigative activities on the Evenson case thus far. He had two reactions; the first was a know-it-all confirmation of his suspicion that Ann couldn't keep her hands off the local crime scene, and the second was an immediate interest in the boyfriend as a suspect. He asked for a chance to meet the guy in person, and Ann agreed, suggesting that since Dexter was going to be tied up for a while with the cabin, the two of them could drive over to the college to talk to Padgett.

Padgett was in his office in front of his computer when Ann and Zack appeared in the doorway.

"Mr. Padgett, this is Special Agent Rose," Ann said, "he's been assigned to the Muriel Evenson investigation."

"How do you do Mr, er, Agent Rose?" Padgett said, offering his hand.

"Just fine." Zack ignored his hand and flashed his CRIMEBUSTER's badge. "And yourself?"

"As well as can be expected, considering the circumstances." Ann detected a trace of yesterday's remorse creeping back into his speech.

"Yeah, it must be difficult," Zack said. "I just wanted to talk with you briefly. Kind of bring myself up to speed."

Padgett nodded.

"I understand you'd been seeing Muriel Evenson for about a year. Is that right?"

"Yes, as I told, uh . . ." Padgett glanced at Ann helplessly, and she suddenly realized that he couldn't remember her name.

"Agent Summer," she supplied, managing not to laugh.

"Agent Summer," he finished lamely.

"Seeing her how? Romantically?"

"Yes, romantically."

Zack leaned in and looked closely at Padgett's face. "Just out of curiosity, is it okay for a teacher to date his students these days?"

"I . . ."

Ann was enjoying watching Padgett struggle for a reply, so she was a little disappointed when Zack's focus took a hard left.

"Hey, what's this?" he asked, staring at Padgett's computer screen.

"That's a screenplay I'm working on." Though Padgett acted as though the distraction was an annoyance, Ann was sure she detected relief.

"A screenplay, no kidding? What, for TV, movies, what?"

"It's for a movie."

"I go to the movies. Maybe I'll watch it someday."

"Maybe."

"What's it about? Is it a cop movie?" Zack asked, around his chewing gum.

"No, it's not a cop movie."

"Good, I hate cop movies." He looked at Ann. "They never really get it right, do they?"

"About as often as we do," Ann said.

"It's a coming-of-age story set in rural Minnesota," Padgett explained, trying to both ignore Zack and answer his question at the same time.

"You lost me there, sounds like a real snoozefest. Not a chick flick is it?"

"Chick flick?" Ann rolled her eyes.

Padgett's silence conveyed his annoyance.

"You gonna try and sell it to some movie company?"

"It's already sold—optioned actually. I'm just working on some rewrites."

"You mean to tell me that you're actually a professional screenwriter?"

"I guess I am," Padgett said.

"How do you do that from out here in Minnesota?"

"It's not easy," Padgett replied, beginning to warm to the topic. "With the main writing behind me, the next phase will require a certain amount of collaboration with the studio writers, plus the inevitable meetings and so forth. I'm actually planning on moving to Los Angeles soon."

"Yeah," Zack said, "I guess they don't make movies in Hollywood anymore, do they? Ann, did you know that Hollywood isn't even a town?"

Ann, who was accustomed to this sort of information coming from Zack, made her usual reply. "Really?"

Zack turned to Padgett. "It's true, since 1910 when it was incorporated, Hollywood's been a district of Los Angeles."

Padgett just looked at Zack and said nothing.

"So tell me," Zack said, veering back on point, "was Muriel going to L.A. with you?"

Ann thought that Padgett looked a little thrown by the question.

"We were working it out when she died."

"Working it out, huh? So she might have gone with you?"

Padgett looked at Ann. "This makes twice in two days you've talked to me about Muriel. Am I a suspect? Because if I am, I can tell you that there's someone far more likely to have harmed Muriel than I."

Zack leaned forward working his gum faster. "Now we're getting somewhere. Who did you have in mind, Professor?"

"Several months ago, Muriel started to complain about her supervisor at the bank, about how he wouldn't leave her alone."

"Harassment?" Ann asked.

"It got so bad I suggested she talk to her supervisor's boss."

"Was his name Tom Manning?" Ann asked, recalling the thin, whiny loan officer with the head cold from the previous afternoon.

"That's it, that's his name. I don't suppose that it's occurred to anyone to look into that. I mean, I had an affectionate relationship with Muriel; he had to be restrained from bothering her."

Zack looked at Ann. "I love it when they solve the case for us."

"I guess there's nothing else for us to do," she said. "We might as well go home."

"Guess so. Pack up our tent and fade into the night." Then he addressed Padgett. "We'll be in touch, Professor. Oh, and don't leave town."

"I didn't know police actually said that."

"Normal police don't," Ann explained.

As they were walking across the parking lot toward Ann's Stratus, they decided to drive over to Muriel's apartment so Zack could take a first look at the crime scene. Ann knew that a fresh set of eyes would be useful, and she wanted to see the place again herself. After they got into the car, Zack said, "I hope Padgett's screenwriting is better than his acting."

"Wouldn't be hard," Ann replied.

After the two detectives left his office, Padgett sat for a moment staring at the open door. The bouncing yellow curls and flashing smile of Bridget, as she appeared suddenly in his doorway, interrupted his thoughts. She looked up and down the hallway and then stepped inside.

"Okay if I close the door?"

"Sure. Come in."

She pulled the door shut and turned toward Padgett. "Am I going to see you tonight?"

"Of course, Lady Macbeth. Rehearsal's at seven."

She pouted with a smile, stepping closer to him, lowering her voice. "No, I mean later."

Sitting in his office chair, Padgett smiled and opened his arms and Bridget stepped into his embrace. With Padgett's head gently pressed against her breasts, Bridget spoke into his hair.

"I want to talk about L.A. tonight, Geoffrey. I want us to be together."

Too cautious to suggest anything serious in his office, Padgett allowed his hand to drift up the inside of her thigh.

"Sure," he purred, "we'll talk tonight."

Chapter Sixteen

The yellow police barricade tape strung across the driveway of Muriel's apartment told Ann that Sheriff Hicks had followed through on getting the crime lab out there. They entered the front hall and climbed the carpeted stairs. The same stairs, Ann thought, that Muriel's killer had climbed. At the top of the stairs, they encountered a second length of tape across the door.

They walked through the rooms while Ann pieced together her version of Thursday evening's events for Zack. His comments remained noncommittal, offering little in the way of agreement. During one last swing through the apartment, Ann happened to notice a tiny trace of white powder on the floor in the hallway. Looking up, she saw the trapdoor to the attic, which was a plywood hatch approximately two feet square. It was supposed to drop into place, but it hadn't seated completely the last time it had been used and was slightly ajar. Zack came over and stood next to Ann, looking up.

"Got something?"

"The attic door wasn't like that when I was here yesterday morning."

"Maybe the lab techs were up there and left it open."

"Could be," Ann said. "Or maybe someone stopped by last night after they were finished here."

Zack got Mrs. Tophler to open the garage so they could borrow a ladder, and Ann grabbed a flashlight from her car. A few minutes later, Ann was standing on the ladder with her head and shoulders in the attic, shining the flashlight at something.

"See anything?" Zack asked.

Ann descended the ladder and handed him the flashlight. "Take a look for yourself."

The heat in the attic was oppressive, and the dust that Ann had stirred up, roiled in the beam of Zack's flashlight as he guided it slowly around the large, dark space. The attic wasn't used for storage, and the light revealed only the interior construction of the roof and a thick layer of pink insulation. When Zack brought his gaze from the far reaches of the attic down to the vicinity of the hatch, he saw what Ann was talking about.

"I see it," he said. What he saw was a small amount of white powder spilled across one of the rafters near the opening and a torn remnant of plastic hanging on an exposed nail. The plastic also had traces of powder on it. He climbed down, taking care not to step on the powder on the floor.

"That plastic was probably part of a bag," he said.

"Let's get the lab back out here," Ann said.

They went back down to Mrs. Tophler's apartment and asked her if anybody had been up to Muriel's apartment lately.

"Those people from the Sheriff's office came out yesterday afternoon." She waited a moment and then added, "The only person other than Muriel that has a key is Cara Lynn."

"Who?" Zack asked.

"A friend of Muriel Evenson's," Ann explained.

"If you talk to her, could you please ask her to return it to me?" Mrs. Tophler asked.

"We'll be happy to," Zack said.

Ann explained that Cara Lynn worked at Janet's Café in town anzd filled him in on her previous interview.

"I may be wrong," she said, "but I think I established a rapport with her. When we get there, let me ask the questions."

The lunch rush was just beginning when they walked in and sat down. Ann caught Cara Lynn's attention and waved her over, and when she got to their table, Ann just had time to identify a fresh bruise on her cheek before Cara Lynn's smile disappeared and she looked down at her ordering pad.

"This is Agent Rose form the DCI," Ann said. "Do you have a few minutes to talk?"

"I s'pose so," she replied, sitting quickly on a nearby chair. Her eyes still avoided Ann's.

"Were you in Muriel's apartment last night?" Ann asked.

She looked at both of them in turn with large eyes. "God, no!"

"You do have a key to her apartment, don't you?"

"Yes," she said after some hesitation.

Zack leaned forward. "Could we see it?"

"I don't have it right now."

"Where is it?" Ann asked, trying to send a psychic message to Zack to let her ask the questions.

"I gave it to Billy."

"Billy?" Zack asked, looking at Ann.

"Billy Deal, her boyfriend," Ann said.

"Why'd you do that?"

Cara Lynn looked at Ann and answered Zack's question. "Because he told me to," she said softly.

"Did he tell you why he wanted to get into the apartment?" Ann asked.

"Uh uh," The way Cara Lynn shook her head gave Ann

the impression that maybe she did know. "Do you know if he used the key to get in last night?" This brought only another shake of her head.

Zack picked up a menu. "How's the pecan pie?"

Cara Lynn didn't say anything, just wiggled her hand and made a face, and then glanced back at the kitchen.

"We just have a couple more things we want to ask you," Ann said. "Did you know Muriel was pregnant?"

Cara Lynn looked down, "Yeah." She said it softly, and then, as an afterthought, added, "but Geoff wanted her to get an abortion."

Ann placed a restraining hand on Zack's arm. "Wasn't he okay with her pregnancy?" she asked.

"Did he tell you that? God! No way! They were having huge arguments."

"About whether or not she would have his child?"

She nodded, "Muriel was a mess. She was, like, crying all the time."

"Was Padgett trying to talk Muriel into an abortion?" Zack asked.

Cara Lynn tore off an unused check from her pad, scribbled something on the back, and slid it across the table to Ann. "This is the abortion clinic he took her to in Minneapolis."

As Ann accepted the paper she took care to look into the girl's eyes and not at her bruised face.

"Did Muriel ever say anything to you about moving to L.A. with Padgett?"

"He told her he was taking her with him, but I don't think he was going to if she was pregnant. She wanted to have the baby. Like I said, she was a mess."

Ann changed directions. "Cara Lynn, I understand you were involved in the car accident where Vickie Lundholm was killed."

Cara Lynn looked momentarily confused by the shift in

topics and took a moment to answer. "Yeah, I was in the car."

Ann proceeded carefully, not wanting to put words into Cara Lynn's mouth. "You were taken to the emergency room?"

"Uh huh."

"Tell me what happened."

Cara Lynn took a deep breath. "Well, I was asleep in the backseat, but I guess Muriel saw a deer and ran off the road. I woke up flying around the backseat, and the next thing I know, there's this huge jolt, and I slammed into the back of the front seat. Turned out we hit a tree. Took me a couple of minutes before I could even climb out of the car. Then I saw Vickie lying on the hood of the car. I guess she went through the window and hit the same tree that the car hit. They said later that she was dead when she got to the hospital. They took Muriel and me in a different ambulance. We were just beat up a little."

"Did Mr. Lundholm come to the emergency room?"

She nodded. "Vickie's dad showed up, and when he found out about Vickie, he went off his nut."

"Did he get violent?"

"Violent? I thought he was going to kill me, and I wasn't even driving."

"What did he do?"

"Started knocking things around, you know, some of the medical equipment, and yelling stuff."

"What did he yell?"

"Mostly he wanted the cops to check how much we'd had to drink." She looked at Ann. "There were some people drinking at the party, but not us. I swear."

"Did he threaten Muriel?"

Cara Lynn paused, and Ann could see a light go on in her eyes. She slowly moved her head from side to side. "I don't think he killed Muriel."

Zack leaned forward. "She didn't say he did. Answer the question."

"That was a year ago." She shook her head. "He's Vickie's dad. I knew him. He's not like that." She glanced at the kitchen, "Look, I gotta go."

Ann looked at Zack to see if he had anything else to ask.

"Does anyone else know you gave the key to Billy Deal?" he asked.

Cara Lynn shook her head.

Zack smiled. "Why don't you tell us how to find this boyfriend of yours."

"We rent a house about a mile south of Higgins Point, off Highway 35," Cara Lynn said. She scribbled down the address for them. As she handed the paper to Zack, she added, "Do me a favor. Don't tell him I gave you this."

"Don't worry," Ann said, and then added, "and take care," hoping Cara Lynn knew that she was referring to Billy Deal.

Zack snapped his gum. "Probably should check in on Speed Trap Loomis, see what kind of trouble he's in."

Ann rose from her seat. "I'll meet you back there, but I've got something to take care of first."

"This is a new way to stick me with the check?" Zack shouted, as Ann disappeared through the door.

Dexter and Grady sat at an outdoor table next to a sandwich board that stood propped up on the sidewalk. The sign heralded the entrance to the *Daily Grind Espresso Café*, featuring *'Seattle's Best Coffee'* in decorative script. The cleanup at the cabin had gone fairly quickly. Dexter's memories of Paul Summer were sufficiently faded by time, so that any real sense of personal grief was kept at arm's length. But remembering what he could about Paul took Dexter back many years. Sitting in front of the café, he looked up and down the length of Higgins Point's Main Street and thought about the evolution of the town over the years. There were definitely less basic service type establishments and more antique shops and art galleries than there used to be. Dexter was surprised to realize that he felt a mild resentment toward the changes taking place in his hometown. He wondered if he was becoming one of those old farts who sat around on park benches all day, complaining.

"Sheriff Hicks is comin'."

Grady's remark brought Dexter back from his thoughts. The sheriff was just getting out of his car, which was parked in front of a fire hydrant a few yards down the sidewalk. He stood beside his car for a moment, wearing a pair of reflective sunglasses, and took a slow look up and down the street. Then he ambled up the sidewalk to where Dexter and Grady sat and pulled a chair over from another table. When he sat down, he left his sunglasses on. Dexter realized the sheriff had a folded up newspaper with him and got a sinking feeling in his stomach.

"Afternoon, Moses," Dexter said.

"Dex, Grady. You fellas enjoyin' yourselves?"

Dexter didn't want to go into explaining what they had just spent the last few hours doing, so he simply said, "Taking a little break."

"That's good, we all need a little break now and again." Hicks tossed the paper on the table. "Had a chance to see this morning's Pioneer Press yet?"

Grady looked at Dexter, but said nothing.

"Moses, I saw the article. It was the most slanted piece of—" Dexter stopped suddenly. "Did you say *this morning's* paper?"

"Yeah, Dex, this morning's paper."

"I, ah, read the article in *Tuesday's* paper."

The sheriff smiled. "So did I. Made you look like an idiot. No offense, Dex."

"None taken, Moses."

"I'm talkin' about this morning's paper, where Kahler makes *me* look like an idiot. Seen it yet?"

"I guess I haven't."

"Did I mention he interviewed me yesterday, *after* he talked to the D.A.?"

"He did?"

"Yes indeed, he surely did. So when I told him that I was movin' forward with the Evenson investigation, he was able to inform me that the D.A. had asked the DCI to come on board."

"I was going to—"

"Tell me? That'd have been real considerate, Dex. Then maybe we could of saved Kahler from havin' to write' stuff like . . ." Hicks opened the paper and read from it. "*When asked about the investigation on Tuesday, Sheriff Moses Hicks apparently wasn't aware that the Madison office of the DCI had been asked to assist on the case. This reporter has to wonder, is there a reason why the sheriff is being kept out of the loop?*"

"Moses, I really was going to tell you."

The sheriff refolded the newspaper and tossed it into a nearby trash container. Nobody spoke for a minute. Finally, Hicks removed his sunglasses and said, "I used to have Frank Kahler in a box."

"Moses, I—"

"In a box, Dex. He didn't say anything about Curran County business 'less I told him to. After a couple of interviews with you, he thinks he's Bob Woodward."

"It's my fault, I'm sorry. Things have been happening pretty fast the last couple of days. I've been busy."

Hicks glanced around at the café tables in the immediate vicinity. "Yeah, you look busy as hell."

"Grady and I have been—" Dexter stopped, and started again. "Here's what's been going on so far. After we saw you at the autopsy on Tuesday, Ann and I talked to some of the people who knew Muriel. Ann was just sort of helping out unofficially. I asked the D.A. to request help from the DCI on Ann's suggestion. Then, this morning, a DCI agent named Zack Rose arrived in town and told me he was assigned to the case. He also said that Ann Summer was officially assigned to it too. Today, Ann and Zack talked to some more people, and I'm pretty sure Ann took Zack over to see the crime scene. That's everything."

"You forgot somethin', Dex," Grady said. "You went and had a talk with Nick Lundholm."

"That's right," Dexter said, wishing Grady had kept his mouth closed. "I talked to both Mr. and Mrs. Lundholm."

"What do the Lundholms have to do with Muriel Evenson?"

"Probably nothing," Dexter explained, "it's just something I did for Dick Evenson."

Sheriff Hicks clearly didn't follow but seemed willing to let it go. He put his sunglasses back on and stood up. "We all got to work together, Dex. That's how professionals do it. Keep me informed from now on, okay?"

"I'll do that, Moses. And I'm sorry about Kahler's article."

Sheriff Hicks walked away, speaking over his shoulder. "Yeah, me too, seein' how I'm runnin' for reelection in a couple of months."

Chapter Seventeen

After Ann's talk with Eric Delisle produced no new information about the Casper Bottom murder, Ann made a decision about the gun. She didn't want to turn it into the Curran County Sheriff's Department until she knew why her father hadn't done that himself. But Detective Perry's office was handling the Bottom case, and he seemed okay to her, so she decided to give it to him.

It was close to noon when Ann returned to Perry's St. Paul office. When the desk officer called Perry up to the front, Ann immediately informed him of the gun she was carrying in her bag. He accepted it from her and led her back to his office. The first thing Ann noticed was the open pizza box covering the Detective's desk; she'd managed to interrupt his lunch for the second time.

"Sorry about my timing," she said.

"Don't worry about it. Half the time I'm eating while I'm driving. Want a piece?"

Ann smiled. "No thanks."

He handled the plastic bag carefully while he examined the evidence tag attached to the Luger. "How long have you had this?"

"I found it Sunday night. I want it run for ballistics and prints."

"Oh, don't worry about that," he assured her. "In the meantime, why don't we see if we can trace the registration?"

He picked up his phone, read the serial number off the gun to somebody at the other end, and asked them to run a check. Then he turned his attention back to Ann.

"That shouldn't take too long, if the computers don't crash. Where did you find it?"

"In my father's freezer."

"His freezer? Your father worked for the Sheriff's Department, any idea why he didn't turn it in to them?"

Ann shrugged. "No idea. That's why I hesitated to turn it in myself."

"You said you found the gun last Sunday?"

"Uh huh."

"Then you knew about it when you came to see me on Monday."

"Yeah," Ann admitted.

"You playing me, Miss Summer? You know some people would call what you did, withholding evidence."

"I suppose some people would. But it's yours now."

"Ah, what the hell, I guess it is." Perry picked up a slice of pizza. "Sure you don't want some?" Ann shook her head. He took a bite just as his phone rang. He picked up the receiver, grabbed a pencil, said "Shoot," and wrote some notes on a pad of paper. When he was done, he thanked whoever was on the other end and hung up.

"Apparently, the computers didn't crash. We have some interesting information. The Luger was used in an armed robbery six months ago in Roberts, Wisconsin. The perp was some guy named," he glanced at his pad, "Thomas Puggart, currently serving eighteen months at Waupun State Prison."

"One of our state's more charming institutions. When was Bottom killed?"

"Two weeks ago."

"That doesn't make sense," Ann said. "If Puggart's serving eighteen months, he couldn't have killed Bottom."

"Right. A Wisconsin correctional facility has supplied him with the best alibi he could hope for."

"So how could the gun he used in the robbery be used in Bottom's murder?"

Perry smiled. "Ah, that's the interesting information I mentioned. It seems that this Luger," he indicated the gun, lying on the desk between them, "is currently in the evidence locker of the Curran County Sheriff's Department."

"It is?"

Perry shrugged his shoulders. "It was supposed to be. Unless I'm mistaken, we have just discovered that it's missing." He picked up a pizza slice and took a bite.

Ann leaned forward. "If we assume, for the moment, that my father didn't steal the gun himself and murder Casper Bottom, then he must have somehow acquired it after it was used by the real killer."

"Agreed." Perry took another bite of pizza.

"Then I guess we're waiting to see if there are any usable prints on the gun."

"And if it was really used in the Bottom murder," Perry added.

"You'll let me know?"

Perry set down the pizza, picked up the Luger, and gazed at it, smiling. "It's the least I can do."

Dexter looked up from the phone records in front of him and stared at Zack's eyebrow ring. They were seated across from one another at Dexter's desk, going through Muriel Evenson's calls with a reverse directory and making a list of people she'd talked to in the days before she died.

"Okay, that makes three calls to her boss, Tom Manning," Zack said, looking up suddenly. Dexter didn't bother trying to hide the fact that he was staring.

"Does that thing hurt?"

Zack looked confused for a second. "The earplug?"

"The ring, through your eyebrow. Does it hurt?"

Zack grinned. "The truth? Constant excruciating pain." He leaned forward. "Takes a hell of a man to stand it."

Dexter tossed his pen on the desk and leaned back. "Okay, it was a stupid question."

"No, not at all. There are no stupid questions, Dexter, only stupid—hey, Ann!"

Ann stood in the doorway. "Are you two playing nice together?" She closed the door, walked over to the desk and glanced over Dexter's shoulder. "Anything interesting?"

"We're making a list of Muriel's calls," Dexter said, handing it to her.

She looked it over while she set her purse on the desk. "Some calls to Padgett, no surprise there."

Zack tossed a stick of gum into his mouth. "One call to Billy Deal," he said.

"That would be to Cara Lynn Grovsner, she lives at the same address," Ann said.

"Still could be a tie-in with the drugs."

"What drugs?" Dexter asked. "What are you talking about?"

Zack put on an innocent face for Ann. "I forgot to tell him."

Dexter looked from Zack to Ann. "Tell me what?"

"We stopped at Evenson's apartment earlier," Ann said, "Someone's been by, and they left a mess behind."

"Traces of white powder and a torn piece of plastic bag," Zack added. "Found it in the attic."

Dexter looked disturbed. "You found that in Muriel's apartment, and you're sure it's drugs?"

"We had the lab come by to collect it," Ann said. "We'll get the results in a day or two, but we're pretty sure it's cocaine."

"And," Zack added, "it turns out that Miss Cara Lynn Grovsner had a key to Evenson's apartment and gave it to Mr. Deal, no doubt in response to his persuasive charm, judging from the marks on her face."

"Drugs in her apartment?" Dexter leaned forward, placed his elbows on the desk, and put his face in his hands, as more of Muriel's innocent façade crumbled away in his mind.

"Look," Ann said, "the drugs were in her place, but they probably belonged to Deal. He may have been paying her to keep them there. We'll look into it. In the meantime, why don't we sort out what we have so far? We can start with Padgett."

Dexter welcomed the chance to think about anything else.

"He didn't have an alibi for Thursday night past ten-thirty," he said. "And what about Lady Macbeth? Maybe murder is how Padgett breaks up with old girlfriends."

"Lady Macbeth?" It was Zack's turn to look confused.

"One of his students," Ann explained. "Muriel's understudy for the play *Macbeth*."

Zack looked from Ann to Dexter. "Maybe there's a tie-in with the abortion business."

"Abortion?" Dexter looked confused.

"Padgett claims he was fine with Muriel having his kid," Ann explained, "but Cara Lynn says otherwise."

"And she gave us the name of the abortion clinic they went to in Minneapolis," Zack added. "Let's get a subpoena so we can access the record of that visit. If he's lying about his attitude on this abortion thing, we may have our motive."

Ann was skeptical. "Padgett's single, so there's no wife for him to worry about finding out, and he's getting ready to quit at the college and move to L.A. so he's not worried about them finding out. I don't see any angle where an unwanted pregnancy's a motive for murder."

"Hey, a guy's headin' for L.A., doesn't need any extra baggage. She won't get an abortion, and he doesn't want to bother with child support. I'm not saying it's pretty, but it's been done."

"Who do I talk to about a subpoena?" Dexter asked.

"The clinic's in Minneapolis, so talk to a Hennepin County district judge," Ann said. "What's the consensus on Billy Deal?"

Zack shrugged. "If he killed her for the drugs, why didn't he just take them Thursday night?"

"Because," Dexter said, "when he threw her off the balcony, the dog probably went crazy and wouldn't let him back inside. He would have had to wait until the dog was removed to go back for the drugs."

"The traces we found in the attic suggest that somebody was in the apartment after the lab techs," Zack said. "But since Deal was known to go up there on occasion, wouldn't he have known about the dog already?"

"Maybe he's not very bright," Dexter said.

Ann shook her head. "I'm starting to wonder how bright you two are. The disposition of the dog has nothing to do with it. It looks like those were Billy Deal's drugs, and the Evenson girl was letting him stash them there—maybe as a favor, maybe for a price, I don't know. But it doesn't make sense that he'd kill her for the drugs if she was letting him hide them in her apartment."

Zack and Dexter looked at one another. "Ann always had a tendency to give felons too much credit," Zack said.

"And Zack has a habit of talking about people in the third person when they're standing right there," Ann said.

Zack grinned and then returned to the list. "She called Tom Manning three times in the last month."

"Muriel was working for him," Dexter said. "He even mentioned that she used to take work home. The calls were probably business."

"Probably," Ann said, "but Padgett claimed Manning

was harassing her at work. It's easy enough to check out." She glanced down at the phone record again. "Her last call to Manning was placed at seven-thirty on the evening of the murder. I'll have another talk with Mr. Manning."

"I can go over to Minneapolis to see about those clinic records," Dexter said.

"By the way," Ann said. "I asked Cara Lynn Grovsner about Nick Lundholm."

Dexter was a little surprised that Ann was humoring him. "How'd that go?"

"It was a little weird. She said he almost had to be restrained at the hospital and then insisted that there was no way he could have done it."

"Think that's weird?" Dexter said. "I checked with the hospital records. Muriel Evenson's murder occurred on July 24, exactly one year to the day after the accident that killed Nick Lundholm's daughter."

Ann and Zack looked at one another. "And?" Zack said.

"And Muriel was driving the car. Maybe Lundholm's some kind of psycho."

"Revenge," Zack said, "is the enemy of logic."

"I thought you said rash action was the enemy of logic," Dexter pointed out. "And who says a killer has to be logical?"

"Revenge *is* a rash action and therefore an enemy of logic. Try and pay attention please."

Dexter ignored him. "The Grovsner girl was in the car too. If Lundholm was involved in Muriel's death, isn't it possible that he'd want to shut her up?"

"But that means we'd have another year to get ready for him." Zack was grinning.

"Very funny, lawboy."

"Meanwhile, back on planet Earth." Zack pushed himself up out of his chair and walked to the door. "Ace gumshoe, Zack Rose, acting on a hunch, ripped the case wide open."

"Where are you going?" Ann asked.

"Confucius say, 'Follow the drugs'. I'm going to have a talk with Mr. Deal."

After Zack was gone, Ann said she'd like to stretch her legs and get some air. She asked Dexter if he would like to take a walk, and he said he would indeed. They left his office and strolled through the neighborhood, enjoying the late afternoon breeze that had taken the edge off the day's heat.

"My biology teacher used to live there," Ann said, pointing at a two-story stucco with a porch that spanned the front of the house. "She was always out working in her garden. She used to wave at me. Her name was Mrs. Iverson."

"Short woman, kind of heavy," Dexter said. "Wore floral dresses."

"Yes! That's her. How's she doing?"

"She taught me biology too." Dexter cleared his throat. "She passed away about three years ago. Sorry."

Ann looked at the house again. "I wonder who lives there now?"

"Her son lives in St. Paul and rents the place out. I gather it's mostly to a younger crowd. Last summer Chief Coffers busted the residents for growing marijuana in the back yard."

"You're kidding."

"I swear. They had a patch of it surrounded by corn. Problem was, the marijuana grew faster than the corn and one of their neighbors spotted it and called Lewis." Dexter grinned. "During the trial, it came out that they used Miracle-Grow on the marijuana but not on the corn. A documented case of nature weeding out the stupid."

Although he'd only seen Ann a few times since she'd gotten to town, Dexter was beginning to tune in to the subtle nuances in her manner. At the moment, he had the impression that there was something on her mind besides the peculiar behavior of the residents of Higgins Point. He wasn't sure when she intended to let it out, or if, but it was a nice afternoon, and he was enjoying her company, so he was willing to wait. He didn't have to wait long.

"After Zack and I were done today, I drove into St. Paul."

"What's in St. Paul?"

"A detective who's working on a murder case."

Ann told Dexter about discovering the Luger in her father's house, and then establishing that it had been stolen from the Curran County Sheriff's Department.

"I'm almost certain my father was investigating a homicide that it was used in."

"Wouldn't that be a matter of record?"

"It wasn't a case he was assigned to—it was unofficial."

"My God, Annie, this is huge!"

"I know. It means my father didn't kill himself."

"And now you can get the full investigation you wanted."

"Not quite yet," Ann said. "Not until we tie the gun to a murder. Then there'll be a motive to bring to the D.A."

"Who's 'we'? The detective in St. Paul?"

Ann nodded. "His name's Perry. I'm basically treading water until he gets back to me with the ballistics and fingerprint work-up."

"Did you tell Moses yet? I mean about the gun being stolen from his office?"

Ann shook her head. "No, and for the time being, I'd like to keep it quiet."

"Why?"

"I'm not really sure. I knew my father pretty well, and he must have had a good reason for not turning the Luger in to Sheriff Hicks. I guess I just want to wait and see."

"Well, anyway, this is great news." Dexter tempered the jubilant tone in his voice. "I'm sorry, Annie, I didn't mean 'great', I meant . . . I don't know what I meant."

"That's okay, Dexter." Ann reached up and touched his shoulder. "I know what you meant."

Eventually, they arrived back at Dexter's office, and he excused himself to wrap up some office work. Ann continued walking south toward the First National Bank. She passed in and out of the afternoon shade that was provided by the ash and basswood trees along Delphi Street. She tried to enjoy the sunshine and the breeze that carried the scent of the nearby river, but her thoughts were all over the map. While the breeze had her thinking about sailing with Dexter on Sunday, the sunshine reminded her of her father's funeral.

Ten minutes later, Ann entered the bank and found that Tom Manning was still there, busy with a loan customer. She got herself a cup of coffee and a cookie from a courtesy tray set up near the entrance, and took a seat. The small town touch, she thought. After a few minutes, Manning's customer, a man in his sixties, rose and passed Ann on his way out of the bank. She got up and approached Manning, who was obviously surprised to see her.

"Mr. Manning, hello. I'm Agent Summer. I spoke with you yesterday. I'm sorry to bother you again, but this should only take a few minutes."

He smiled and sniffed. "Please, have a seat." He indicated a chair in his cubicle and then produced a tissue from his desk drawer. Turning away, he blew into the tissue, took a quick peek and deposited it into his wastebasket.

"Excuse me," he said.

"I have just one or two follow-up questions I would like to run by you." Glancing at his desk, Ann noted a large amount of paperwork. "Business must be good."

"We're pretty busy right now. I guess you never really appreciate how much help someone is to you until they're gone." He shifted in his chair, apparently sobered for a moment by the thought of what he'd just said, and then brightened. "So, what sort of loan were you interested in?"

Ann laughed, "On my salary, I'm afraid all I can afford is the loan of your time."

He crinkled his eyes in a smile, blinking several times. "What can I do for you?"

"Mr. Manning, exactly how well did you know Muriel Evenson?"

He looked at her for a moment, and the crinkled eyes vanished. "I know what this is about."

Ann waited until he sniffed twice and then continued.

"Several months ago I went through a period—" he paused and started again. "I had a problem."

"You were pursuing Muriel Evenson, and she wasn't returning your affections."

"Sounds like you've already heard someone's version of it."

"Now I'd like yours."

Manning looked around anxiously. "Look, I admit I had a silly infatuation for a while. It was a lapse of judgment on my part, okay, a bad lapse. But I dealt with it."

"Why didn't you mention any of this yesterday?"

"Because it was over, and I knew what you would assume."

"She filed a formal complaint, Mr. Manning. You understand how that appears."

He looked like a runner trying to catch his breath. "My wife found out about my—interest—in Muriel. One night, I came home from work and she had her suitcases out. She never looked back, never gave me a chance. All I had left was my work. I begged Mr. Meadows to let me stay at the bank, and he agreed, if I attended counseling. I managed to keep some part of my life from falling apart. Muriel and I worked through it; we worked together ever since it happened."

Ann listened to the pleading in his voice and judged his

apprehension to be sincere, but as to whether it was from a fear of being falsely accused or a fear of being discovered a murderer, she couldn't tell. Manning pulled out another tissue and blew his nose. Ann waited for him to take a peek and throw it away before continuing.

"When was the last time you spoke to Muriel?"

Manning thought for a moment, "Here at the office on Thursday."

"Not later that night?"

"No."

"Mr. Manning, phone records show a call from her house to you at," Ann glanced at her notepad, "seven-thirty on Thursday evening."

Tom Manning looked blankly at Ann for a second. "I'm sorry. I thought you meant spoke with her in person."

"So you did speak with her Thursday night?"

"As I recall, she did phone me." Manning picked up a paper clip and was rolling it over and over in his fingers. "I didn't make a note of the exact time, but I'm sure your records are accurate."

"Could you tell me what the call was about?"

"She had a question about some loan papers, something she was trying to finish up. Like I said, she used to take work home."

"What was it she wanted to know?"

"I don't remember exactly."

"Approximately will do." Ann watched him closely.

"I'm afraid I have to apologize, but I don't recall what it was she asked me. If it's that important to you, given a little time, I'm sure I could come up with it."

"I'm sure you could too. Mr. Manning, the phone records also show two other calls from the victim to you over the last two weeks. I suppose they were also business?"

Manning blinked his red eyes, sniffed, and nodded. "Of course."

"Could you tell me, please, where you were on Thursday night around eleven-thirty?"

"I was at home."

"In bed?"

"No, I sat up and watched a movie."

"What movie?"

"A classic, *Dial M for Murder.*"

"Were you alone?"

"Yes, I was." Manning smiled weakly at Ann. "In your line of work, I guess you would say that I have no alibi."

Manning was watching Ann leave the bank when his supervisor, Larry Meadows, the bank's president, materialized at his desk, his pungent cologne foreshadowing his presence. Meadows was carrying a computer printout and holding it like a hymnal. He looked at it as he spoke to Manning.

"Say, Tom, strangest thing. Can't seem to locate a loan file."

"What's that?" Manning asked.

"Dersval, Robert Dersval, lives in Baldwin." He looked at Manning over his glasses. "File's not in the cabinet."

Manning rubbed his forehead for a moment. "Dersval. It's got to be one of the files that Muriel Evenson was working on at home when she was—when she was murdered. Why, what's up anyway?"

"Came up past due this morning, and a flag went up on my computer. The loan's for less than fifteen thousand, so normally I wouldn't ever see it, but like I said, it came up past due."

"Well, I've been trying to retrieve the files," Manning said, "but the police seem a little touchy about letting us remove anything from their crime scene."

"I'm sorry about the Evenson girl and all, but what do our files have to do with her death?"

"I'll keep on them about it, don't worry. In the meantime, why don't you let me handle Mr. Dersval?"

"With pleasure," Meadows said, as he wandered away studying his printout.

While Tom Manning watched Meadows walk away, he reached for another tissue.

Chapter Eighteen

By Thursday morning, Ann still hadn't heard a word from Detective Perry. Although her mind was on the Luger, she forced herself to return to the First National Bank again, where a young brunette receptionist with her smile on automatic asked her if she could help her. Ann asked to see the branch president. The receptionist picked up her phone and, after a moment, directed Ann to an office in the back corner of the bank.

Larry Meadows' office had dark wood paneling and windows looking out onto the main area of the bank. As president of the branch, Meadows was the one to whom Tom Manning reported. Ann introduced herself and showed him her identification. Meadows was a medium-sized man slowly going to fat in his office chair. He was fair-skinned and had thinning hair with the washed out look of a former redhead. He smiled and waved Ann into a seat.

"I'm sorry to bother you, Mr. Meadows," Ann began, "I'm investigating the death of Muriel Evenson, one of your employees."

Meadows looked down for a moment and when he looked back up, the smile was gone. "That was a terrible business, just terrible. Of course, I'll help in any way I can."

"At the moment I'm following up some information that we received about Tom Manning, one of your loan officers. Apparently there was some sort of trouble between him and Muriel Evenson."

"Well, for God's sakes, Tom told me that you'd brought it up, but I thought he'd explained it all to you."

"As his supervisor, I'm interested in your take on the incident."

"The sheriff came around yesterday and talked to me about it. Once he understood the situation, he didn't think there was any reason to suspect Tom."

"Sheriff Hicks talked to you?"

"Sat right where you're sitting now. Said he didn't see any merit to that idea at all. 'That dog won't hunt,' is how he put it, I think."

"Why don't you fill me in," Ann said, "so I can feel good about Tom Manning too."

Meadows let out a sigh intended to let Ann know what a pain in the ass she was being.

"There was some trouble. A while back, Tom made some advances toward Muriel Evenson, which weren't very well received. It got to the point where she came to me and said he was harassing her." His monotone speech came to a halt, as he apparently waited for a cue from Ann.

"Was he harassing her?"

Meadows rubbed his forehead. "Yeah, I think he was. I mean it's a gray area, but when I talked to him, he seemed to realize how unwelcome his advances were. He basically ended up admitting it."

"What happened then?"

"After we had our talk, he asked for another chance. He promised to clean up his act and stop bothering Muriel Evenson. Apparently his wife walked out on him, and I didn't want to see him fall completely apart, so I said okay."

"That was the end of the harassment?"

"It's the perfect example of the system working. Tom attended counseling sessions and he and Muriel continued working together. There hasn't been a hint of unpleasantness since."

"Muriel Evenson is dead. That's unpleasant," Ann said evenly.

Meadows's scowl made it clear that he didn't appreciate her sarcasm.

"You mentioned that they continued working together after her complaint. Is that normal?"

"I really don't have a great deal of experience with this sort of thing, but it was Miss Evenson who asked that they continue working together."

"Why would she do that?"

"I have no idea, but it certainly speaks well of Tom's sincerity."

Ann looked at Meadows and tried to marry his version of Manning's behavior with the nervous, sniffling man she'd questioned. Her suspicion that Manning had not been totally forthcoming was at odds with Meadows's glowing version of his good intentions.

"What was Muriel Evenson's level of responsibility here at the bank? Did she cover for Tom Manning when he went on vacation?"

"Well, actually, she'd only been with the bank for about a year, and I didn't think Tom's been on vacation since she started. But in any case, she didn't deal directly with customers. She assisted with the paperwork, that's all."

"Why didn't Mr. Manning take a vacation this year?"

Meadows seemed surprised at the question. "Why? As I recall, two days before he was supposed to leave, he came in with a bandage on his wrist—a bad sprain, or something. Said he didn't want to waste the cost of a trip to Cozumel when he couldn't enjoy it. It made sense to me."

Ann was wondering what else she could ask when Meadows beat her to it.

"If it's my opinion you came here for," he said, "what happened between Muriel and Tom is old history. I can't believe it could be the basis for murder, any more than I could believe that Tom would commit such an act."

The statement was Meadows's signal that he had nothing left to say, and he would like to get back to work. Ann thanked him, and as she made her way through the bank to the front door, she happened to notice that Manning was standing at someone's desk, watching her. As she pushed the door open, she smiled at him and nodded.

Dexter and Grady sat beside one another behind Dexter's desk, staring in silence at the television screen and passing a bag of Fritos back and forth. After a couple of minutes, Grady said, "Dodge Minivan." They both glanced at the corner of the screen. "Thirty-three miles an hour."

"No, Chrysler," Dexter said.

"Chrysler?"

"That's Mrs. Lightner; she drives a Chrysler. Doesn't know where the gas pedal is."

They studied the screen in silence for another minute.

"I thought about getting a minivan," Grady said, "but, you know, the gas mileage and all."

"Nice cargo room, though," Dexter said, "if you do a lot of hauling."

"Yeah, nice cargo room."

Dexter threw some Fritos into his mouth. "You don't do a lot of hauling."

"I do some hauling, plenty of hauling."

"But not enough to need a minivan."

Grady looked at Dexter. "Oh, and I suppose you do."

"I do more hauling than you do. Who borrowed my Cherokee last fall to take their leaves down to the compost?"

"That's exactly what I'm trying to say. I need to haul things from time to time, same as you."

"Well, if that was true, you'd always be—"

"Good morning, gentlemen." Sheriff Hicks stood in the doorway, holding a large manila envelope. He walked around the counter and tossed it into Dexter's lap.

"Morning, Moses." Dexter started ripping the envelope open. "What's this?"

Sheriff Hicks didn't say anything, just walked over to the coffeepot while Dexter pulled out the papers and began reading. After the sheriff finished pouring a cup of coffee, he supplied a summary. "Chemical analysis confirmed the white powder in Muriel Evenson's attic was cocaine all right. The level of purity indicated that it was cut down and was ready for sale on the street."

Dexter slowly placed the report back inside the envelope. He kept picturing the young, laughing girl on his sailboat and couldn't understand how that sunny little kid could evolve into the corpse lying in the driveway. Even if the drugs in her apartment belonged to Billy Deal, how did she come to be involved with people like that in the first place? He shook his head and tossed the lab report on his desk. "No way this was Muriel's stuff. Dick doesn't need to hear about this."

Sheriff Hicks took a sip of coffee and then studied his cup. "If the drugs don't figure into the murder case, I don't see any reason to bring it up."

Dexter felt a small relief.

"Speaking of Dick Evenson," the Sheriff said, "He collared me this morning and started goin' on about Nick Lundholm; some nonsense about how Muriel Evenson drove the car his daughter was killed in? Says you were investigating it for him."

"I mentioned yesterday that I talked to the Lundholms as a favor to Dick." Reading the expression on the sheriff's face, he made the decision not to bring up the issue of the coincidental dates.

"Guess you're free to waste your time any way you want, Dex."

What went through Dexter's mind was *you also thought it was a waste of time to do an autopsy on Muriel Evenson*, but what came out of his mouth was "It's mine to waste, Moses."

"Talk about wastin' time." Sheriff Hicks moved around behind Dexter and Grady. "You fella's watchin' television?"

"We're fishin'," Grady said.

Dexter looked at Grady. "We're operating a synchronized, radar-enforced, video-enhanced, speed violation traffic station."

"We're fishin'," Grady said again.

Dexter took Sheriff Hicks briefly through the setup and was unable to suppress a surge of pride when the sheriff expressed admiration. But when he was leaving, Hicks turned in the door and said, "It'd never work down in Kentucky, where I come from."

"Why is that?"

"Them old boys would just shoot out the camera."

Ann arrived a few minutes after Sheriff Hicks left. While Dexter poured a cup of coffee for her, she surprised him with an invitation to dinner that night.

"The four of us; Hallie and Ted, you and I. And you don't have to worry about the food. Hallie's doing the cooking. She's already taken charge of the kitchen."

"Sounds very nice. Plus they'll be perfect chaperones for our third date," Dexter pointed out.

"So you *are* counting the autopsy as a date. Isn't that a little tacky?"

"Maybe a little, but not inconsistent with my general character. What time should I show up?"

"Hallie said 'eightish'."

"Thanks, I'll look forward to it. Plus it'll be fun to see

Hallie again after all these years. I can be judgmental about this Ted character she married; it'll be like a high school reunion."

Grady, who had been sitting there watching the exchange, said "Ann, Dex needs to know something." He looked at Dexter. "He needs to know should he bring anything to dinner with him? Like maybe a bottle of wine?"

"Oh, yeah, Grady's right. Is there anything I can bring?" Dexter smiled at Ann, while he silently settled a curse upon Grady and all his descendants.

"Hallie didn't mention anything, so I guess it's up to you."

"What's your sister cookin'?" Grady asked.

Ann thought for a second. "I think she said something about a pot roast. I get the impression that Ted's your basic meat and potatoes kind of guy."

"Then Dex'll bring a red wine. Won't you, Dex?"

"Of course." Dexter looked at Grady. "What kind will Dex bring?"

"A nice, expensive Merlot should do."

Dexter looked at Ann again. "I should explain that I only keep him around to remind me how inaccurate the stereotypes of the black man in America are."

Grady grinned. "That and to plow his back forty."

After everybody settled back down, Dexter remembered to mention that he'd gotten a subpoena for the abortion clinic records of the counseling session, and turned it over to Zack late yesterday. Ann said they were way overdue to check into the car that Muriel's landlady had reported hearing on Thursday night. They decided to canvas Muriel Evenson's neighborhood, and Grady offered to pitch in. Dexter would cover Vine Street, where Muriel's apartment was, and the other two would take a street on either side.

Ardella had used the phrase "in the distance" when describing the sound of the car, and Dexter wasn't sure how far from Muriel's house they should check. Higgins Point was a small town with an abundance of undeveloped lots, so the houses didn't tend to crowd one another. An eighth of a mile probably encompassed no more than five houses. They finally decided to start with five houses in each direction, on each side of the street. That meant twenty houses on each street—sixty in all. Dexter turned off the television, or the RadarVid Station, as he had decided to call it, and the three of them drove over to Ardella's house to go to work.

When the people were home, they tried to be helpful, but Dexter found that they usually had more questions than answers. He found some people who were up at eleven-thirty on Thursday night, but none remembered seeing or hearing a strange car. Ninety minutes later, when Dexter finished the last of his houses, he walked over and found Ann with a few more houses still to check, so he joined her. They were just finishing up when Grady found them.

"Could have somethin'," he said, glancing at his notepad. "Mr. Brian Chadwell, at 341 Maple, was letting his cat in around eleven-thirty, and remembers seeing a white sports car on the street near his house. Never saw the car before."

"Don't suppose he saw the driver," Dexter asked.

"No driver in sight, probably too dark to make out a face anyway."

"How about a license plate?" Ann asked.

Grady shook his head. They covered the few remaining houses, and on their way back to Dexter's office, Ann explained how they could get the state police to initiate a computer search for white sports cars registered locally.

When they walked in the office, Zack was sitting in Dexter's chair, chewing gum with his feet up on the desk. "So, fellow crime fighters," he said, "what's up?"

Ann explained what they had been doing, and Zack asked if they'd had any luck.

"Possibly," Ann said, "A strange car was seen down the

street and one block over from Evenson's apartment on Thursday night, a white sports car."

Zack cocked his head. "A white sports car?"

"Muriel's landlady thought she heard a car starting around the time of the murder," Dexter explained. "We're gonna do a computer search, see what pops up."

"Were you able to talk to Billy Deal?" Ann asked.

"Wasn't home last night when I stopped by, but I did put the subpoena to work."

"The clinic records?" Dexter asked.

Zack nodded. "Seems Mr. Padgett wasn't completely forthcoming with us. The record of the counseling session showed a definite pro-choice attitude on his part, an attitude that was apparently not shared by Miss Muriel Evenson."

"He was pressuring her to abort?" Ann asked.

Zack nodded. "Looks like Padgett was lying about wanting Muriel to have his baby."

"It's still seems thin, Zack," Ann said. "So he lied about wanting his girlfriend to abort their kid. It's still not—"

"A motive for murder?" Zack said, finishing the sentence for her. "What if she felt like a weight around his neck? What if he was interested in traveling fast and loose when he got to the coast?"

"Cara Lynn told us that Muriel was expecting to go to Los Angeles with Padgett," Dexter said, "and Padgett said the same thing. What makes you think he wasn't willing to take her with him pregnant or not?" Even as he asked the question, Dexter found himself doubting Padgett's good intentions.

"Made one other stop yesterday," Zack said, "Metro Airport." He paused for effect.

"And . . ." Ann finally prompted.

"And, it turns out one Mr. Geoffrey Padgett has purchased an airline ticket to L.A. One ticket, one way."

"You don't expect him to buy a ticket for a girl who's been murdered, do you?" Dexter suddenly realized the stupidity of his statement, and asked, "When did he buy the ticket?"

Zack, who was grinning while he worked his gum over, had apparently been waiting for that question. "Week ago Tuesday, two days *before* Evenson died. Guess he had a hunch she wouldn't be needing a ticket, huh?"

"When's the flight? Ann asked.

"Who cares? Week from next Saturday." Zack seemed annoyed that his news didn't elicit more response.

Ann raised her eyebrows. "Not exactly what I'd call a quick getaway."

"These guys never think they're going to be found out," Zack said, and then added, "By the way, I think I can help out with the search for the white sports cars. Padgett owns a white Mazda Miata."

Chapter Nineteen

Dexter and Grady sat at a window table in the Riverview Tavern across the street from Janet's Café. Grady was examining a newspaper that was spread out on the table.

"This is the third article in three days, Dex. Ain't three times supposed to be enemy action?"

Dexter sat with his shoulders hunched, one hand wrapped around a half-drank bottle of Miller Lite. "I don't get it, what'd I ever do to this guy?"

"You wouldn't let him into the backyard last Thursday to see Muriel Evenson's body. I wouldn't have either."

"If he'd stop writing these articles, I'd give him a guided tour." Dexter took a swig of beer. "Did you read the part about my training?"

"Yeah." Grady focused in on the paper. "*Apparently sixteen years as county engineer and three months of criminology courses is what passes for adequate law enforcement training in Higgins Point.* That's a cheap shot, Dex. Everybody's got to learn things for a first time."

"It doesn't help that he points out that the city council never had a chance to weigh in on my appointment."

"They don't need to. You're supposed to be temporary."

"Yeah, but still, considering how much I've contributed

to the case so far, it's hard to argue with him." He took another swig of beer.

"Dex, you're lettin' this pencil pusher get to you. Knock it off."

"Oh yeah?" Dexter turned the paper around and read, "*With the second death in as many weeks, and no clues to point to, Higgins Point is quickly becoming the murder capital of western Wisconsin.*"

Grady folded the paper up and threw it on a chair. "You ain't got nothin' to do with Paul Summer's death. Besides, that was supposed to be a suicide."

Dexter looked at Grady. "Just between you and me, Annie doesn't think so."

Grady just nodded his head slowly in understanding. Both men stared at their beers, while Dexter resolved that as long as he was wearing the badge of police chief, he was going to try and make more of a difference. Even if he couldn't contribute know-how, he could sure contribute hard work. He touched his shirt pocket where his badge was supposed to be and realized that he'd left it at home on the dresser.

At ten after six, Cara Lynn stepped out of Janet's Café and squinted at the sun, beginning its slow descent over the St. Croix River. She walked around the corner of the building, into the parking lot, and didn't really notice the tan Ford station wagon that had pulled up next to her on her left. After it moved along side of her for several feet, keeping pace, she glanced over and recognized it as the car that Vickie Lundholm's mom had used to chauffeur her and Vickie to soccer matches and swim meets. She bent over and looked in the open passenger side window at Vickie's father.

"Guess you were surprised to hear from me."

Cara Lynn didn't say anything.

"Okay with you if we talk?"

"I guess."

"Why don't you get in? I'll drive, we'll talk."

"Why don't we talk right here?"

"There's something I want to show you."

Cara Lynn looked around. The parking lot and street were almost deserted late on Thursday afternoon, and only the distant squeal of the gulls down by the river broke the stillness. She looked at Vickie's father again and shrugged.

"Sure, okay." When she opened the door, the hinges squeaked in protest.

Grady was still staring at the beer in front of him, and Dexter had switched and was now staring at a mural that had recently been painted on one of the walls of the bar. It featured a tuna fish singing into a microphone. The tuna fish bore a striking resemblance to Tina Turner.

"Does that fish look like anyone you know?"

Grady studied it for a minute and shook his head. "Nope."

"Doesn't look like anyone you know. You're sure?"

Grady took another look. "Yup."

"Suddenly, I'm having dinner with John Wayne." Dexter took a sip of beer and turned toward Grady. "That doesn't look like Tina Turner to you? Tina Turner, Tina Tuna—get it?"

Grady looked at the mural again. "Yeah, I know it's supposed to be Tina Turner."

"You just said you didn't know who it was."

"No, I didn't. I said it's not anyone I know, which is what you asked me. I never met the woman in my life." He took a sip of beer.

"You try to have a civil conversation with *some* people."

At that moment, Dexter happened to glance across the street and see Cara Lynn Grovsner getting into an old Ford station wagon. When the driver turned back to face the road, Dexter recognized Nick Lundholm, and for one of the few times in his life, his gut instinct took charge. He threw some money on the table and hustled Grady, protesting loudly all the way, out of his seat and out the door. They jumped in Dexter's Jeep just in time to follow Lunholm's station wagon north out of town, on Highway 35.

Lundholm drove north for a few miles and then east for another five. During the time they spent in the car together, neither he nor Cara Lynn spoke. Eventually, they turned onto a gravel road, which led through some woods to a smaller dirt road that ended at the door of a cabin. It stood in a small clearing with pine trees close enough on three sides for the branches to brush the roof. Cara Lynn thought it could have used a little upkeep.

When Lundholm got out of the car and began walking, Cara Lynn just sat where she was. Lundholm turned around, and when he saw that she hadn't followed, said, "What I want to show you is in here," and disappeared through the front door.

Cara Lynn got out of the car and stood for a moment, her faded pink waitress uniform contrasting with the collage of evergreens around her. She finally walked to the cabin door, hesitated for a second, and then passed from the light to the darkness within.

Once he was behind the wheel of his Cherokee following the station wagon, Dexter had a chance to calm down and think. Why would Cara Lynn willingly get in Lundholm's car? Maybe he'd somehow talked her into getting in, or forced her. He could have even been flashing a gun, out of Dexter's view. Eventually they turned east, away from the river. The further they got from town, the crazier this whole thing seemed in Dexter's mind, and Grady wasn't exactly providing positive reinforcement.

"You outta your mind, boy?" pretty much summed up Grady's take on the situation.

Half a dozen times Dexter almost turned around, but each time he did, one thought made him keep going; what if there was just the slimmest chance that Lundholm was the killer? What if they turned back and then Cara Lynn's body was discovered later? Dexter didn't think he could live with that.

When the station wagon left the main road and began snaking through the pines, Dexter hung far enough back so they wouldn't be noticed. Eventually, they came to a small dirt turn-off where dust still hung in the air announcing the station wagon's passing. Before venturing further he pulled to a stop and reaching across Grady, took his .38 out of the glove box. Then he opened the console and took out several bullets.

"What's that thing for?"

"It's okay. It's just insurance."

"That ain't insurance, and it sure as hell ain't okay."

"Grady, I'm a professional. Relax." Dexter started putting the bullets into the gun and dropped several onto the floor of the Jeep.

"Professional, huh? Dexter, you're my worst nightmare—a civil engineer with a gun."

Cara Lynn stopped just inside the door. The cabin's dark interior still held the heat of the day, and the musty odor told her that the cabin hadn't been used at all this summer. Lundholm was lighting a lantern.

"Electricity's been turned off. No need for it, haven't been up here all year." He motioned for Cara Lynn to come in. She stepped closer and he began to speak to the lantern.

"Been a year since Vickie was taken from us. Hasn't been a good year. The Missus left me, an' I'm drinkin' more than I ought to."

He moved to a cupboard next to the sink and opened the

cupboard door. Cara Lynn crossed her arms and cocked her head to one side, watching him.

"Three girls in the car that night. Now two's gone, just you left."

He pulled a silver urn from one of the shelves and set it on the table between them.

"I guess Evenson's finding out for himself what I been going through the past year."

He towered over Cara Lynn, and the lantern light was erratic as it moved over his face, bringing out the deep relief of the veins in his forehead.

"Police was by my house couple of days ago, asking if I killed Muriel Evenson. Got me thinkin'. Things have gone on long enough. Maybe it's time to put an end to 'em."

They abandoned Dexter's Cherokee and proceeded on foot, the fallen pinecones and dead wood alongside the road crackling under their shoes. There was little breeze in among the thick trees, and the sweat rolled down the side of their faces as they crept forward.

When they finally spotted the cabin, Dexter saw that the clearing it sat in was very small, allowing them to stay under the cover of the trees until they were right on top of it. They crept up and Dexter pressed himself against the rough logs, urging Grady to do the same. Grady rolled his eyes but did as he was asked. Inching up to one of the side windows, Dexter peered in. The cabin was empty, and he was suddenly aware of a sound coming from out back, a soft, repetitive scraping. As they made their way to the rear of the cabin, Dexter was able to identify the sound—somebody was digging.

Standing in the tiny clearing behind his cabin, surrounded by blue spruce and red pines, Lundholm threw on the last shovelful of dirt. He stepped back, inspecting the fresh earth in silence. The empty urn lay on the ground beside him, and Cara Lynn stood a few feet away watching.

"I'm a builder, I work with lumber, roofing, some cement work." Lundholm stared at the ground before him as he spoke. "My hands are rough. First time I ever held Vickie was when we brought her home from the hospital. I wouldn't touch her in the hospital, too afraid. But when the Missus got home, she just laughed at me and put Vickie in my arms. Most amazing thing that I could hold something as soft and delicate as that child in these hands and not hurt her. I was looking down on her little tiny face, wondering how I would ever be able to protect her from the world when, just like that, she starts crying. She was crying so hard I thought my heart was gonna stop, thought it was something I'd done. The Missus takes her, and checks her, and finds a safety pin that let loose. Pretty soon she's quiet and happy again. Tells me not to worry, kids are tougher than ya think. After that, I couldn't hold her enough. I'd find myself thinking about holding her when I was at work."

Lundholm looked over at Cara Lynn. "A lot's happened in twenty years, but to this day I can remember like it was this morning what I felt when I thought I'd hurt her. Funny, the things that stick with you."

Cara Lynn picked up the urn. "Mr. Lundholm, why don't you take me back to town, and get your wife, and bring her out here?"

Lundholm was staring at the ground again. "I believe I'll do that." He leaned the shovel against the cabin and they began walking around to the front.

Dexter stood frozen in place. Rather than witnessing the scene of homicidal carnage that he had feared, he had just watched Nick Lundholm bury his daughter's ashes. He felt more like Inspector Clouseau than Inspector Poirot and suddenly realized that he would rather be almost anywhere else in the world than where he was at the moment. He was turning around to try and sneak away quietly, when Lundholm and Cara Lynn came around the corner of the cabin.

Cara Lynn looked stunned to find them there, but Lundholm's expression told Dexter that he picked up on what was going on right away.

"I, ah . . ." No words came, only the sound of the crickets and birds, and Dexter wished he could just blend into the trees. He suddenly realized he was holding his .38 in his right hand and quickly hid it behind his back. "If, ah, if everything's okay here, we'll just, ah, we'll head back to town." He turned around, and as they hurried away, he could hear Grady next to him, laughing quietly.

When they got back to town, Dexter dropped Grady at his car and then went and sat on a bench in front of the Riverview Tavern. It was still a little more than an hour before he was due at Ann's house for dinner. He was trying to decide whether to go inside and have a beer or just go home and was starting to make progress on a decision when he spotted Zack Rose coming out of Terry's Tattoo Parlor on the other side of the street. When Zack saw Dexter, he waved and then walked across the street to join him.

"Did you just get a tattoo?" Dexter asked.

Zack sat down on the bench. "No, I was just checking out the local talent."

"You have any tattoos?"

Zack stopped chewing his gun for a minute and looked at Dexter. "That's pretty personal. I don't think another lawman's ever asked me that before."

Dexter shrugged. "Just curious."

"You're not hitting on me, are you?"

"What?"

"I'm as liberated as the next guy, Dexter, but I'm afraid I'm not interested."

"What are you talking about?"

"No offense, okay? I'm just not *that way*."

"What way? I don't care what *way* you are."

"Yeah, I know. Denial's part of the whole latent thing, but you're just going to have to accept it."

"There's no *latent thing*. I'm—"

"You're what, forty years old? Still single?"

Dexter stopped blabbering for a minute and looked at Zack. "You're psychotic."

"By the way, Dexter." Zack glanced up and down the street. "You could be a little more discrete."

Dexter fought to keep his voice under control. "I was just curious about the tattoos. Ever heard of small talk?"

Zack held up his hands. "Whoa boy—settle down. This is obviously a bigger issue for you than it is for me."

While Dexter was trying to conjure up a reply to this insanity, Zack's hand went to the phone on his belt.

"Rose here."

While he waited, Dexter reflected on how miraculous the recent advances in cell phone technology were, making it now possible to interrupt people virtually anywhere. After a moment, he noticed that Zack's ever present grin had vanished, and he was doing more listening than talking. And, more significantly, his gum was at rest. Zack reached down and ended the call, and sat staring at the sidewalk.

"I take it that wasn't good news?"

Zack seemed to suddenly remember that Dexter was sitting beside him. "That was the Madison office."

"Okay."

"An undercover cop in Milwaukee was murdered a few weeks ago. We got a tip that the murder weapon was in this gangbanger's apartment, but the judge wouldn't give us a search warrant."

"Why not?"

"Conflicting information on the application."

"So you didn't get to search for the gun?"

"No."

"And the guy's still walking around?"

"No. This call was to tell me he's in custody for murder; a drive-by shooting."

"Sounds like good news to me."

Zack slowly removed the foil from another piece of gum. "It would be, but one of his rounds went through a window and killed a twelve-year old girl in her front room. She was watching TV." He shook his head. "Goddamn it! I told Ann to leave that other crap off the application!"

"You're blaming Ann?"

Zack seemed surprised by the idea. "For the murder? No, of course not. But she's so constipated with procedures that she ought to be working for the ACLU. The judge even gave us a chance to rewrite the application. He did everything but wink at us."

"Ann wouldn't go for it?"

"Ann *couldn't* go for it," Zack clarified. "She's not wired that way."

"If I know her at all, she's going to take this kind of hard."

"She'll probably find out about it eventually, but we're not going to tell her. What's the point of letting her beat herself up over something that was inevitable?"

"How could an accidental shooting be inevitable?"

"The shooting wasn't—the warrant denial was. Ann wouldn't hedge on the application because she didn't recognize it as an option. It wasn't in her nature."

They sat beside one another for a few minutes while Zack folded the foil gum wrapper and Dexter imagined himself being shot while watching television. Finally, Zack said, "Yesterday you mentioned Padgett was putting on *Macbeth* at his college, right?"

Dexter nodded.

"Are they rehearsing tonight?"

"Thursday night? Yeah, I think so."

"Why don't we go over there and see what kind of adlibs

Padgett comes up with to explain that trip to the abortion clinic?"

Dexter looked at his watch. "I'm due at Annie's house at eight for dinner, but I guess I have time. Sure, I'll drive."

"Ann's cooking for you?"

"Actually, I think she said Hallie was making a pot roast."

"But she asked you to dinner?"

"You sound shocked."

"Not shocked so much as impressed."

While they were walking back to the office, a question occurred to Dexter.

"So you're telling me a judge can reject a search warrant application because it has too *much* information on it?"

"Basically, yeah. Why?"

"Seems ironic, that's all."

"Not really, but you want to know what *is* ironic?"

"What?"

"The gangbanger never even hit the guy he was actually shooting at."

Chapter Twenty

At 7:00 PM, the parking lot in front of the Lakeview College theater building held less than twenty cars. Dexter and Zack entered the front door and walked through the lobby to the back of the dark auditorium. Only the stage area was lit, and there were perhaps a dozen students standing around. Dexter could see more people at the back of the stage painting the "flats," the large canvas-covered wooden frames that would comprise the scenery for the production. The smell of fresh paint filled the auditorium. There didn't seem to be a scene underway at the moment, and the actors on stage were standing around, talking among themselves. Off to the side, Geoffrey Padgett was using exaggerated gestures to explain something to one of the students. Dexter and Zack walked down the center aisle toward the stage. When Padgett saw them approaching, he dismissed the student he was talking to and stood waiting for them with his arms folded.

"Mr. Padgett," Zack said, "we have a couple more questions for you."

"This isn't exactly the best time. Couldn't it wait until tomorrow morning in my office?"

"It could, but it isn't going to."

Padgett gave an audible sigh and cocked his head slightly. "What is it—I'm sorry, I've forgotten your name."

"Agent Rose, and this is Chief Loomis."

Dexter had an insane urge to raise his hand and say, "How."

"What would you like to know?"

"The last time we talked to you, you claimed you didn't have a problem with the fact that Muriel Evenson was pregnant with your kid." Zack smiled. "So we'd like you to explain something."

When Zack didn't go on to say what he wanted explained, Padgett finally spread his hands. "I'm listening."

"I got a look at the records of the abortion clinic in Minneapolis, where you took Muriel Evenson. Seems like their version of the conversation doesn't agree with your pro-life stance."

It was several seconds before Padgett found his voice.

"I am *not* guilty of homicide."

"Calm down, Professor, no one's accusing you of homicide." Zack smiled. "That what you thought?"

"Well, your questions seem so—"

"Homicide's a broad term; it includes things like self-defense, state executions, justifiable killing. No, we're leaning more in the direction of cold-blooded murder. So, why don't you humor us and explain why you lied about the baby?"

Padgett's shoulders seemed to slump in resignation, and he pulled out a linen handkerchief and wiped his forehead. "Maybe I lied about wanting her to have the baby because—I've got my own priorities. But that doesn't make me a murderer."

A white sports car was seen in the vicinity of the victim's apartment around the time of the murder. You drive a white Mazda Miata, don't you?"

Padgett nodded.

"And there's also the issue of the airline ticket you purchased several days before the murder. A single ticket. How did you know, two days before Evenson was murdered, that she wasn't going to be needing a ticket?"

Padgett almost exploded. "Do you have any idea what kind of odds I'm up against? How hard it is to get your foot in the door of any studio? I do not need a family following me around in L.A."

Dexter stepped back slightly to avoid the spray of spittle.

"I'll need room to move out there. I'll have to keep my options open, but that doesn't mean I would ever harm Muriel. I loved her."

"If you loved Muriel," Dexter asked, "why are you coming on to the other coeds?"

"I . . . I"

"C'mon, Professor," Zack said, "give us the truth, and it'll set you free."

Padgett's expression suddenly adopted the wide-eyed honesty of a zealot.

"You want the truth?" His voice dropped. "The truth is . . . I nail 'em all, okay? I can't stop myself. Is that what you want to hear? In fact, let me introduce you to the flavor of the month: the young lady I was with on Thursday night when you say Muriel was being murdered." He turned to several actors on stage and called out. "Bridget, could you please come over here for a minute?"

The blond girl that Dexter recognized from his visit to Padgett's office, broke away from the others and walked over to them. When she got there, Padgett placed his arm gently around her shoulder and spoke softly.

"Bridget, this is very important. I want you to explain to these men that you were with me at my house last Thursday night."

"Slow down a minute." Zack turned to the girl. "Bridget. That your name?"

"Uh huh."

"That's a very pretty name. So Bridget, is it true that you were with him last Thursday night?"

Bridget hesitated, looking in turn at each of the three men confronting her.

"It's okay, Bridget," Padgett said. "It's okay to say you spent the night."

"Hey, Professor, you want to shut up any time soon?" Zack addressed the girl. "So, how about it, Bridget?"

"Yeah, I was there."

"And what'd you two do?"

"What do you mean?"

"It's not appropriate to ask her that," Padgett said. "What do you think we did?"

"A guy who acts like you do is going to lecture me on what's appropriate?" Zack turned to Bridget. "Okay, what'd you two have for dinner? Two people spend the night together, they have to eat something." Before Padgett could open his mouth, Zack stuck his finger in his face. "And don't say one word, not one—"

"We cooked spaghetti with meat sauce." Everyone looked at Bridget. "And there was salad and key lime pie for dessert."

Padgett and Zack looked at one another, and then Zack asked, "What else did you do? Watch any videos, go anywhere?"

"No," Bridget said, noticeably more assertive. "After dinner, we just did the dishes and then turned on some music."

"What music?"

"Classical," Padgett said, causing Zack's head to swivel back in his direction.

"Light classical," Bridgett added.

"Forget it." Zack turned away for a second and then swung around to confront Padgett again. "You better watch your script, professor. Fictional alibis have a habit of coming apart."

Padgett scowled. "I assure you, Agent Rose, the script is strictly non-fiction."

"Fiction or non-fiction, it's still gonna tumble, and when it does, I'll be waiting in the wings with a hook."

As they walked out of the auditorium, Dexter said, "Hey, Zack. 'Waiting in the wings with a hook?' Don't you think maybe you were a little heavy on the metaphors back there?"

"It was an extended metaphor," Zack explained.

"Extended? I think you broke it."

Ann moved the blade of the knife rhythmically up and down through the celery, trying not to cut off her own fingers. Next to her, Hallie was bent over, peering into the oven, checking the pot roast and humming softly. Ted was in the front room watching the news on television. It was obvious to Ann that 'Mr. Sensitivity' was accustomed to letting Hallie do all the work in the kitchen. Back in Seattle, Ann doubted if Ted knew where the kitchen was.

In the week since they'd been there, Hallie had cleaned their father's house from top to bottom so that Ann barely recognized it. The kitchen was cozy and warm with the aroma of the roast. The front room had been straightened, and all of their father's old magazines and papers were gone. Hallie had even put a blanket on their father's old brown chair, where Ted was currently entrenched, hiding its imperfections, and, Ann thought, removing its character.

Ann reminded herself that her sister meant well and that each little change she made, taken individually, made perfect sense. Why not toss out his old magazines? This wasn't a shrine. Why not improve the look of the furniture? It would make the house show better when they tried to sell it. They hadn't actually discussed selling the house yet, but Ted had mentioned getting a real estate agent. Ann knew that she couldn't live in this house. Her job was three hundred miles away in Madison, and she hadn't seriously considered becoming a landlord. With everything else that was on her mind, Ann was inclined to just let Ted and Hallie plan things. She was actually grateful that they were willing to take the lead.

Hallie straightened up and closed the oven door. "Ted has this idea." She hesitated. "He thinks that since your friends went up to the cabin and cleaned it up the other day . . ."

"Since they cleaned it up, what?"

"Well, he thinks it would be a good idea for us to spend the weekend there."

"At the cabin where he died?" Ann almost nicked her finger. "Don't tell me. For closure, right?"

Hallie nodded. "That's what he says. He wants all three of us to go up there for Friday and Saturday night. He says we can talk about dad and tell stories, and it would help us to accept things."

"You mean it would help me to accept things."

Her sister didn't respond; instead, she opened the refrigerator and poked around inside.

"Hallie, that gun I pulled out of the freezer the other night was probably tied to a homicide, just like our father thought. That gun means I don't have to accept anything. It's like a ticket to be skeptical." She sighed. "Well, it's a weird idea, but then your husband's a weird guy. And I guess I can appreciate the fact that he does have good intentions, if a bit misguided. Okay. I'll join you, but I can't go up until Saturday. That okay?"

"Thanks, Ann. And you never know; it might actually do some good."

"Probably can't hurt."

"Say, what time did you tell Dexter?"

"Just what you told me, 'eightish'."

Hallie smiled. "I only saw Dexter for a minute at the funeral. I didn't really get a good look at him. How does he look? Is he still thin as a rail?"

"He's still tall. I don't know, I guess I haven't really thought much about his looks. He's not really thin, but he's certainly not overweight. I guess he's slender."

"You haven't thought much about his looks, huh?"

Ann pushed the small pile of sliced celery aside, and reached for a tomato. "Not really."

"You're not getting off that easy, little sister; you're a cop. You're trained to be observant. What if you had to describe him for your job?"

"My job?" Ann thought about it. "Okay. Male Caucasian, slender, six-feet-three-inches tall, tan complexion, large ears and medium length black hair—should use a comb more often."

They both laughed, and then Hallie said, "That's not bad, maybe a little sinister."

Ann shrugged. "If I had to describe him for my job, he'd probably be a felon."

"What about his eyes?"

"Grey, with little dark flecks in them," Ann said, surprising herself.

Hallie smiled. "I see."

"By the way," Ann said, to change the topic, "have you told Ted about Dexter being your old boyfriend?"

"Of course I did—this afternoon, after you told me he'd accepted the invitation."

"You never mentioned Dexter to him before now?"

"Nope," was Hallie's simple reply.

"I guess there's no reason why you should have to tell your husband about your high school boyfriends."

"Nope," Hallie agreed. "That and he never asked."

Hallie began slicing a loaf of French bread. "Seriously, Ann, you could sure do worse than Dexter. He's a great guy, or at least he was when I knew him."

"You're shameless, big sister. And if he's such a catch, why did you let him get away?"

Hallie paused with her bread knife. "You know, I don't

remember why we broke up." She resumed cutting the bread and casually asked, "Why haven't you gotten married?"

Ann considered throwing a tomato at her sister. "That's a pretty rude thing to ask, isn't it?"

"Not for a sister, and I noticed you didn't answer me."

"Darn right, I didn't answer you," Ann said.

"Do you let criminals off that easy when you're questioning them?"

"Is that what you're doing, questioning me?"

Nobody said anything for a minute, while they both worked in silence. Finally Ann said, "I was engaged once."

Hallie's mouth dropped open. "I don't believe it. Seriously?"

Ann nodded.

"You were engaged and you never told your own sister? Who was he?"

Ann shrugged and grabbed another tomato. "A guy named Don Huftel."

"When did this all happen?"

"A few years ago."

"Well, tell me about it."

"Not much to tell. I would have mentioned it at the time, but I guess I had my doubts as to whether it was actually going to work out. Don always had a tough time dealing with my occupation, and when I transferred into homicide, he just took a hike. End of story."

"Think you're getting off that easy? Ha!"

The doorbell rang, and Ann smiled and set her knife down. "Saved by the bell. I'll get it." She paused on her way out of the kitchen and added, "Not a word about this to Dexter, or I'll kill you."

When Ann opened the door, Dexter was standing on the porch wearing tan slacks, a maroon, open-necked shirt, and a sports jacket. Ann was pleased to see that he'd taken her invitation seriously enough not to wear cutoffs and a Packers T-shirt. He was holding a brown paper bag that obviously contained a bottle of wine, and Ann would have bet serious money that it was Merlot. He handed the wine to Ann as he entered and thanked her for the invitation. She, in turn, thanked him again for the sailboat ride on Sunday. Dexter said hello to Hallie and Ted and offered to open the bottle of wine which, Ann noted, was indeed Merlot.

"That would be nice," Ann said, leading him into the kitchen, where she handed him a bottle opener. "Thanks."

A half an hour later, when they were all in the dining room at the dinner table, Dexter tried to explain his feelings. "It feels odd," he said. "I mean, I dated you in high school, Hallie, and we knew each other pretty well. But I haven't seen you for twenty years. And I know next to nothing about you, Annie, but I've been seeing so much of you this past week, it seems like I know you better than Hallie. It feels odd."

"Why Dexter," Hallie said, smiling, "I'd be more than happy to tell you all about my little sister."

"Hallie." Ann's voice carried a warning clear to all.

Dexter smiled. "I'd like that. Maybe we could have lunch some time and you could sort of bring me up to speed. Let me know what makes the old girl tick."

"Oh my God!" Ann said. "I'm in hell."

The phone rang. "I'll get it," Ann announced, "and no talking about me while I'm out of the room."

In the front room, Ann picked up the receiver and it was Detective Joe Perry from St. Paul. He told her that the ballistics results were in.

"The bullet we dug out of Casper Bottom definitely came from the Luger you brought in. Looks like your old man had it right."

"Anything on the fingerprints yet?" she asked.

"Not so far, but I'll let you know."

Ann thanked him and returned to the table. After she sat down, Hallie asked her who had called.

"You know the victim's name we found attached to the gun in dad's freezer? That was the St. Paul detective who's running the case." Ann explained. "He was just letting me know that ballistics confirms that the gun did kill Casper Bottom. So Dad got the name of the victim right."

"Then he was investigating a murder when he died," Dexter said.

"It looks like he was getting close to something."

Chapter Twenty-one

"Why are you calling me?"

"I told you why already." Cara Lynn felt less nervous this time, more sure of herself.

"And I told you, whatever game you're playing, I'm not playing along."

"We're already past that part. You know Braden Flats, out by the reservoir?"

"No. This is crazy, and you're crazy, and I'm not doing this!"

"Then my next call is to the police."

Cara Lynn waited through the long pause and was beginning to suspect that he'd hung up.

"Okay, Braden Flats," he said. "What about it?"

"Be there tonight, eleven o'clock, and bring the ten thousand."

Cara Lynn had plans for the money—plans that included Florida, but didn't include Billy. She hung up the pay phone in the back of the Auto Stop and glanced around to be sure no one had listened, and then went up to the counter for a pack of cigarettes.

When she got back to the house, Billy's black Trans Am was parked in front, but he didn't seem to be home. She decided he must be out with one of his buddies, and that this would be as good a time as ever.

She went into Billy's room and pulled out the bottom drawer of his dresser and kept pulling until it fell out onto the floor with a muffled thud. On the floor, in the space below the drawer, there was something wrapped in a towel. She picked it up; it was heavier than she'd expected. She set it on the bed. She put the drawer back in place, sat on the bed, and opened the towel, holding the shiny, chrome gun in her hand. Billy had told her it was a .38 revolver. She opened the cylinder and saw that it had six bullets in it, but she was careful not to point it at herself; she wasn't stupid. The bullets looked peacefully nestled in their chambers. Cara Lynn had decided to bring Billy's gun with her just in case the guy had other ideas besides paying her the money. As she closed the cylinder, she heard a noise only a few feet away and almost jumped out of her skin. But she didn't start to actually shake until she looked up and saw Billy standing in the doorway.

Seven miles north of Higgins Point, County Road J curved to the east and ran along the north edge of the county reservoir. There was a dirt road cutoff that ran south through the woods, eventually leading into a large open area known locally as Braden Flats, an expanse of packed dirt and crabgrass atop an old landfill bordered by dense trees. It was fairly secluded and a favorite spot of high school kids on the weekends, but at 11:00 on Thursday night, it was deserted and silent. Billy Deal's Trans Am gave a throaty growl as he downshifted to make the turn onto the dirt road. Billy always kept his hand on the floor shift when he drove; the vibrations felt satisfying, and he liked to feel the power.

Earlier that evening, when he'd caught Cara Lynn with his gun, there had been an anxious moment. Luckily, he'd managed to hold off on his first impulse, which was to beat the hell out of her until he learned everything. It blew his mind when Cara Lynn told him the guy's name, and it turned out to be one of his coke clients. This was going to be a lot sweeter than selling him a little coke. This blackmail gig could go on and on. He couldn't understand why everyone made such a big deal out of it. Hell, it was a snap! She'd made a couple of calls; now all he had to do was swing by and collect ten thousand.

He emerged from the woods, and in the moonlight, Billy saw the sports car that Cara had said to look for, parked on the far side of the clearing. *He's early*, he thought. *He's so freaked he can't wait to hand over the money.* He parked about fifty feet behind the other car and pulled his revolver out from under the seat. He checked to make sure it was loaded, but then decided he probably didn't need it. He was putting it back when he realized that the guy had gotten out of his car. He rolled his window down and changed his mind about stashing the gun, instead laying it on the passenger seat.

Billy was wondering why the guy was waiting by his car when he realized that someone was standing right next to his car. He glanced up in time to see the dark cylinder peek over his door. A split second later, there was an explosion, and a searing heat tore through his shoulder. He threw himself to the right, landing roughly against the passenger door. His shock from the attack was replaced by rising terror as he groped around for the gun, only realizing then that he was lying on it. A second deafening explosion, and this time he could feel the shock of the bullet's mass as it struck him in his left hip. Acid smoke stung his throat as his hand finally closed over the handle of his own gun. Enraged, his own pain forgotten for the moment, he twisted his body around and brought his gun up. *Just get one in him to stop him*, he thought, *then I can do him right.*

His ears were ringing so furiously that as he pulled the trigger, he could barely hear the sound of his own gun.

Whoever it was had jumped to the side, and Billy realized that all he'd done was shoot into his own door. He screamed in frustration, adjusting his aim up a little and firing three quick shots, which passed harmlessly out the open window. The car was now full of smoke, and then the gun appeared again. Everything was happening in slow motion. He couldn't seem to move quite fast enough.

There was a flash of fire, and a blinding pain erupted in his chest. He could taste blood in his mouth, as a veil seemed to wash over his senses. He became dimly aware that the air that he was trying to force in and out of his lungs had a thick, frothy quality. When the fourth bullet hit him in the neck, the gun slipped from his hand. He slumped against the passenger door, his senses shutting down, his body stiffening in shock. A final bullet hit him just in front of his left ear and came out the other side of his head, shattering the passenger window.

Cara Lynn lay on her bed in the dark, nursing her bruised cheekbone and thinking about the kind of day she'd just had. That morning, in the restaurant, Mr. Kerlach had bumped her from behind when he was trying to help his wife out of her seat and into her walker. The impact had sent the hot coffee she was pouring at the time into an unhappy customer's lap. Cara Lynn, of course, assumed the blame and apologized, hoping that Mr. Kerlach would turn around and say something. But Mr. Kerlach staggered off with his ancient wife and had no idea what had happened. There'd been no tip.

And what was that business after work with Vickie's dad? Bringing her out to his cabin to bury Vickie's ashes bordered on eerie. She sincerely hoped that he got some help, because she could tell he needed it. Then, when the cop suddenly appeared out of nowhere! It had taken a minute, but it finally dawned on her that he thought he was protecting her from Mr. Lundholm. She never thought she was in any danger; why would he think that? The whole thing was really weird. Then, just when she was finally going to get the money from Muriel's killer, Billy walks in. Lying on the bed, Cara Lynn's only cheerful thought at the moment was the possibility that the guy would show up without the money and piss Billy off, and maybe Billy would shoot him. Then, at least, Muriel's murder would be avenged.

Cara Lynn was thinking about maybe taking another Tylenol for her headache, which was the result of Billy's version of 'talking' things over, when she heard the unmistakable sound of someone walking across their wooden front porch. She was sure it wasn't Billy, because she hadn't heard his Trans Am, which could be heard all the way down the street. *Too bad*, she thought; *I don't feel like company tonight*. The footsteps left the porch and things quieted down again. After about a minute, it occurred to Cara Lynn that whoever had come to the door had left without knocking or ringing the bell. Just as she was deciding that this was a little odd, there was a creaking groan from somewhere in the back, followed by a violent cracking sound that resonated through the framework of the house.

Cara Lynn rolled off the bed and stood frozen in the center of the bedroom, completely alert. She knew what was happening; some drug dealer thought the house was empty and was coming in to help himself to Billy's stash. She'd met some of these types from time to time, and she knew what they were capable off. She also knew that whoever he was, she didn't want to get in his way.

There was no weapon in the bedroom because Billy had taken the gun with him, and the windows were painted shut. The only way out of the house was past the intruder. She took three quick steps to the closet and slid the door open as quietly as she could manage. Out in the dining room, she heard the sound of drawers being pulled out of the old buffet, and their contents landing on the floor. She slipped into the closet, pushing aside blouses and coats, and buried herself far back in the darkness, fighting a rising panic, and trying to will herself to be invisible. Her mind was going a thousand miles an hour, trying to think of any weapon that might be at hand. She could hear muffled thuds in the front room and the sound of a knife ripping through fabric.

It was when he started in on the bathroom, working his way toward the two bedrooms in the back of the house, that Cara Lynn realized how thorough he was being. If he was taking the time to look under the bathroom sink, there was no chance that he wouldn't find her in the closet. She emerged from the shelter of the closet nauseous and a little light-headed, and stood behind the bedroom door wondering where to go. The man was only one doorway away, literally six feet down the hallway, on the other side of the wall. And then he wasn't.

Footsteps were approaching the bedroom. When he got to the two doors leading to the bedrooms, the footsteps stopped, and only when Cara Lynn heard the violent crash of the sliding closet door being slammed open did she realize he had chosen the other bedroom. For unbearable seconds she stood frozen in place, listening to things being thrown around in the next room. Finally, she peeked around her door, and then edged out into the hallway. Her plan was to try and get to the front door and then run like hell. After only two steps, a sound behind her told her that he was coming back out, so she ducked sideways into the bathroom.

She stepped into the bathtub and as silently as possible pulled the opaque shower curtain closed in front of her, thinking that it made sense to hide where he'd already looked. He tore up the second bedroom, while she endured a wait that seemed to last forever, and fought to keep her heart from beating so loud it would give her away.

The sound in the bedroom stopped, and she thought,

when he goes to the basement I'll make a try for the front door. She was beginning to believe that she might get away, when a white hand appeared around the edge of the shower curtain, only inches from her face. She let out a small gasp. His fingers were splayed across the tile wall for support, while he bent down, apparently searching behind the toilet, and she realized that he was wearing white rubber gloves. He must have come back because he'd forgotten to look behind the toilet tank.

The man was breathing heavily from his exertion, which was probably the only thing that had prevented him from hearing her gasp. Cara Lynn focused her eyes on the image of a tattoo, buried amid his curled black wrist hairs, and partially obscured behind the material of the thin, white glove. She wondered for a terrifying instant whether or not he would remember that he had left the shower curtain open.

And then the hand was gone, and he was walking down the hall toward the basement, and Cara Lynn almost threw up. She crept to the front door when she heard his heavy tread on the basement steps, hoping his sounds would mask hers. She opened the front door silently and slipped out, closing it behind her, and as she ran down the street, savoring the impossibly sweet night air, she didn't look back.

Chapter Twenty-two

On Friday morning, Ann strolled down Delphi Street toward Dexter's office. She nodded to a lady who was setting plants outside of her flower shop and smiled at an old gentleman with bushy eyebrows, slumped like a boot on a shaded wooden bench in front of Keilor's Drugs. As she walked by the First National Bank, she noticed an English sports car, a pale yellow Triumph, parked in the bank lot. It was located in one of the far corners, where an employee would park in order to leave the closer spots for customers. A thought occurred to her; at night, under the washed-out light of a street lamp, a pale yellow car could be mistaken for a white one. On an impulse, Ann walked into the bank.

She asked the receptionist if she knew who owned the Triumph parked outside and was told that it belonged to Tom Manning. She walked over to his cubicle, and when he looked up, she smiled and apologized for bothering him again. The smile he supplied in return was strained, and he asked her to have a seat in a tone that suggested she keep it brief.

"Mr. Manning," Ann said. "There's been a new development."

His eyebrows went up. "A break in your case? What is it?"

"In a manner of speaking, your car's the break."

Manning's face was completely expressionless. "I'm afraid I don't understand."

"It was seen in the vicinity of Muriel Evenson's apartment the night of the murder."

Ann added nothing else, just watched Manning's face. The statement, of course, was untrue, or rather if it was true, she wasn't aware of it, but there was no law that prohibited a cop from lying to a suspect. Manning finally blinked, and the expression on his face gave Ann the same feeling that she used to get when she was fishing with her father and she would feel that familiar tug on her line.

"I—stopped by Muriel's apartment on Thursday night," he said simply, and then swallowed with a bit of difficulty. Ann just looked at him for a moment as she realized what he was telling her.

"This is the third time we've talked, and you haven't mentioned this before now? And please," Ann held up her hand, "don't say it's because I didn't ask."

"Well, technically you didn't." He hurried to explain himself. "What I mean is that you asked if I'd seen her on Thursday. Actually, I didn't *see* her."

"But you just said that you stopped by her apartment."

"I did stop by, I rang her bell and knocked, but there was no one home." Manning paused, apparently remembering that Muriel was found dead there. "I mean no one came to the door."

"When did you stop by? What time?" Ann had her pad and pen out.

"Around eleven o'clock, perhaps a few minutes before. So you see, the last time I talked to her was on the phone on Thursday evening, and the last time I saw her was at work earlier that day, as I stated before."

"And you felt like keeping this a secret, why?"

Manning reached over for a tissue, blew his nose, took a quick peek, and threw it in his wastebasket. "Because I was concerned that you would jump to the exact conclusion that you're jumping to now, that I was still pursuing Muriel."

"But you weren't?"

"No."

"Then what were you doing at her apartment so late at night?"

"Larry told me that you talked to him yesterday."

"That's right."

"And that he assured you that I've maintained a professional relationship with Muriel."

"Mr. Manning," Ann said, unable to keep the edge out of her voice, "answer the question."

"I stopped by to get those loan files that I mentioned to you when we first talked, the ones you won't let us have."

"But why so late? What's wrong with Friday?"

"Muriel had asked for Friday off, and I realized I was going to need the files. I know her play rehearsals usually run until around ten-thirty, so she would probably still be up."

"Is there any record of her request?"

"We're not that formal around here."

Ann sighed and glanced at her pad. "Okay, so you stopped by the apartment around eleven, rang the bell and knocked, and then left without seeing Muriel Evenson."

"That's right."

"Did you see or hear anything out of the ordinary, anything that could help us?"

Manning lowered his head for a moment, apparently in thought. "I don't recall anything that stands out; the house was dark and quiet."

Manning's story, his latest version, didn't exactly inspire Ann's confidence. The way his explanations seemed to curve back on themselves was setting off a soft alarm. His former harassment of the victim made him a suspect, so he withheld that information because of how it would make him look.

Ann couldn't think of anything else to ask him for the moment, so she left him at his desk, cluttered with work. As she walked to Dexter's office, she was preoccupied with the absence of a motive for Muriel's murder. Manning's former harassment of Muriel seemed like a dead end, and in spite of her instincts, Ann was at a loss to think of another motive that Manning might have had. Zack's belief that Padgett killed her because she was a millstone around his neck likewise felt weak. Could there have been any importance attached to the loan papers that Manning kept referring to? The bank file folder in Muriel's wastebasket had been empty. If she had taken files home with her, where were they? And how could they tie in as a motive for murder?

When she entered Dexter's office, he was sitting at his desk next to Grady. They were both eating ice cream bars. She told them about her conversation with Tom Manning's boss, Mr. Meadows, the previous afternoon.

"Apparently, your sheriff has been by to talk to him," Ann said. "He tossed out the whole notion that Manning's sexual harassment is a possible motive. 'That dog won't hunt', is how he put it. Pretty colorful for Wisconsin, don't you think?"

"He's a transplant from Kentucky, Annie. Never lost the accent, and he doesn't even like cheese, as far as I know." Dexter dropped his feet to the floor and stood up. "Hey, Friday's ice cream day around here. You want a bar?" He started across the office to the small refrigerator in the corner.

"No thanks," Ann said, "I'm driving. By the way, any new developments on your Nick Lundholm angle?"

Dexter glanced over at Grady with a suspicious look on his face. "Why? Did Grady talk to you?"

"No, I was just curious."

"There's nothing there, dead end."

Ann thought that Dexter seemed curiously anxious to move on. "But I thought you had this big revenge theory about Lundholm."

"I'd believe him if I were you," Grady said and took a bite of his ice cream bar.

Dexter changed the topic. "Me and Zack went and had a talk with Padgett last night, at his play rehearsal."

Ann watched Dexter eat his ice cream bar. She noticed that he always took two bites at a time, never one or three, always two. "Did Zack haul him off in cuffs?"

"No, actually he came up with an alibi—named Bridget."

"Our Bridget? You mean Muriel's understudy?"

"Yeah. It took a little prompting from the wings, but she says she spent the night with him."

"Do you buy it?"

"Not really."

"Did Zack?"

"He didn't arrest him on the spot, but I don't think it was because of Bridget's performance. I think he realizes that even without the alibi, we don't have much of a case against him."

"I dropped in on Manning a few minutes ago," Ann said.

Dexter took two quick bites, and leaned back in his chair. "Oh?"

"On a hunch, I told him that his car had been seen near Muriel's apartment on Thursday night."

"He doesn't drive a white sports car, does he?"

"He admitted it," Ann said simply.

"He admitted what?" Dexter's chair squeaked loudly as he rocked forward. "You mean you placed Tom Manning at Muriel's house on Thursday night?"

"We were wrong about the white sports car?" Grady asked.

"His car's pale yellow; it's close enough. He claims he

stopped by around eleven o'clock, but no one was home. Says he never saw her."

"She should have been back from rehearsal by then." Dexter rocked back again. "But I suppose she could have gotten in later."

"Says he rang the bell and knocked," Ann said, "but didn't hear anything from inside. Could she have been dead already? Maybe our time of death is off?"

"Ardella said she looked at her clock, and the dog went ballistic at eleven-thirty. I trust that fact. And it makes sense that the dog went off when she was attacked." Dexter looked at Ann with a quizzical expression. "Did you say he rang the bell and there was no sound from inside?"

"That's what he told me."

He thought for a minute. "There's something Ardella said on the night of the murder. She said when Muriel wasn't home, Brando would only bark if someone came to the door. But Ardella didn't hear any barking at eleven o'clock when Manning says he was there, so either Muriel was home but chose not to answer—"

"Or she answered the door and let him in," Ann said.

"And Manning's lying," Grady concluded.

At that moment, the door opened and a young blond girl walked in with a stricken look on her face. Right on her heels was a man in a business suit and a woman with heavy eye makeup and lacquered hair. They appeared to be her parents and seemed to be more than a little upset. The three of them shuffled up to front of Dexter's desk and stood there for several seconds waiting for someone to say something.

"Uh," Dexter began.

"Go on," said the woman.

The girl lurched forward, pushed from behind, and Dexter suddenly recognized her.

"You're Bridget, right?"

Bridget was torturing the hem of her sleeveless blouse

in her twisting fingers. She looked back at her parents, glanced at Ann, and then finally looked at Dexter.

"Tell him," commanded the father, and then cleared his throat and folded his arms.

"I, uh, what I told you last night, I was . . . lying."

"You mean about being with Geoffrey Padgett last Thursday?" Dexter asked.

"Yeah." Her voice was barely audible.

"You weren't with him after the rehearsal?"

"No."

"Then you didn't," Dexter glanced at the father, "spend the night with him?"

"Oh God." Bridget buried her face in her hands.

Whack! A slap on her arm from her mother. "Tell him, tell him what you told us."

"I only went along with it, because I wanted him to like me."

"Just to be clear, you can't account for his whereabouts after the rehearsal on Thursday night?"

"No."

"Bridget, do you think it's wise to be dating someone that much older than you, not to mention the fact that he's your teacher?"

Bridget started to say something, then stopped.

"Don't be too hard on her, Dexter" Ann said, and then addressed Bridget's parents. "Geoffrey Padgett's a charming predator, and we're finding out that he doesn't place a lot of moral restrictions on himself."

The father nodded and after the three of them had made their disorganized way out of the office, Dexter turned to Ann.

"This news is going to make your partner's day."

"He wants to pin this thing on Padgett, all right," she agreed.

"You still don't seem convinced."

"I'm not."

"If he's innocent," Grady pointed out, "why would he have to invent an alibi?"

Ann shook her head. "I don't know."

The phone rang, and Dexter picked it up. "Higgins Point Police, Loomis speaking."

Ann watched Dexter's face, but his expression hardened to the point where she was unable to read his reaction to what he was being told. After a couple of minutes of listening, he simply said, "Thanks," and hung up.

"That was Zack," he said. "Some kids hiking out by the reservoir found a body."

"Any ID?"

"He didn't know. The reservoir's a few miles north of town. It's county jurisdiction, but let's have a look anyway." Dexter grabbed his keys from the desk. "I'll drive."

Chapter Twenty-three

Fifteen minutes later, Ann, Grady, and Dexter emerged from under the canopy of tree onto the flat expanse of the county reservoir, and for a moment, Dexter thought he was at a law enforcement convention. Parked outside of the police barricade were a number of county sheriff's vehicles, state police cars, and the crime lab van, several with their flashers going. Uniformed men were everywhere, walking around with some unknown purpose, or just standing around, talking, and drinking coffee from Styrofoam cups. The crackle of several radio conversations floated over the scene.

The center of attention was a black Trans Am at the edge of the clearing, about two-hundred-feet away from where Dexter parked his Jeep. A small group of lawmen surrounded the car, and included in the group were Sheriff Hicks and Zack Rose. Ann, Dexter, and Grady ducked under the barricade tape, and as they approached on foot, Sheriff Hicks turned around and spotted them.

"Dexter, Grady, Miss Summer." Hicks's soft, deep voice sounded like a Johnny Cash song when he spoke.

"Moses," Dexter said, staring at the Trans Am.

"Who's in the car?" Ann asked.

"Excuse me just a minute." Hicks turned back toward the general group of men and raised his voice to a considerable volume.

"Hey, you fellas want to kill them lights? This ain't no damn highway!" He turned back around, muttering. "I swear, any excuse these fellas can find to run them flashers and sirens." Then he refocused on Ann's question. "Male Caucasian, multiple gunshot wounds—looks like maybe a drug-related shootin'."

"What kind of drugs?" Dexter asked.

Hicks looked at Ann for a moment and then at Dexter. "We're way outside of your town jurisdiction, Dex."

"Absolutely, Moses. You're welcome to this murder, we already have one of our own."

"Found traces of a white powder in the trunk," Hicks said, apparently satisfied. "Looks like cocaine."

They approached the driver's side of the car, and Zack stepped back so they could look inside. When Dexter saw the shattered, plaster white face of the victim, he swallowed quickly and squeezed his eyes shut for a moment. When he opened them again, he was still barely prepared for the scene before him. The car's interior looked as if it had been spattered with red paint. The wide-eyed corpse was chalk white, with blackened bullet holes visible in his neck and left temple. Thick blood had dried in midflow from both wounds, and his shirt was soaked in blood.

Ann touched Dexter on the shoulder, "Are you all right?" She said this very quietly, and he nodded in response.

Zack stepped in closer and mimicked Ann's quiet tone. "How come you never ask how I am?"

"The other side's the pretty view," Hicks said. "When the bullet exited, it took out the window and deposited the right side of his head all over my reservoir."

"Got an ID?" Ann asked.

"Yeah, we found his driver's license laying on the ground."

"You're gonna love this," Zack said.

Hicks placed his glasses on his face and held up the plastic bag containing the license. "William Lawrence Deal," he recited, and removed his glasses again. "Resident of your town, I believe, Dexter."

Dexter was concentrating on taking deep breaths, and it took a moment for him to accept that this gruesome object in the car was the same man he'd watched through Janet's Café's window a few days earlier.

"No wonder he stood me up last night," Zack said.

"You know this guy?" Hicks sent a wad of chewing tobacco a respectable distance.

"Just by reputation," Zack said and spit his wad of chewing gum almost as far.

Hicks stared at Zack's eyebrow ring for a minute and then said, "He was shot a total of five times." He flipped back through his notepad. "Shoulder, hip, chest, neck and head. Course, that's preliminary until the medical examiner takes a look. No positive ID on the weapon used yet. There was a .38 found in the car that apparently belonged to Deal, had two bullets left in the cylinder. Looks like he might have got four shots off, put one bullet through his own door."

"Did he hit what he was shooting at?" Ann asked.

"No blood on the ground." Hicks grinned, "Guess it wasn't his night."

Suddenly Frank Kahler appeared out of nowhere. "Hey, if it isn't Barney Fife, master of ceremonies for the biggest crime wave in western Wisconsin."

"I'm not saying anything to you," Dexter declared.

"That's the smartest thing you've said yet," Grady observed.

"How'd you get past the tape?" Dexter demanded.

Kahler smiled. "Sheriff Hicks."

"Calm down, Dex," Hicks said. "You got to know when to hold 'em, and when to fold 'em."

"There's a trade-off for good press, Chief," Kahler explained. "A little access and we're all friends. Right, Sheriff?"

"Don't push your luck, Frank, just get your story."

Hicks led them around to the back of the car. The trunk lid was smeared with fingerprint powder and sitting open. He pointed at a small spill of white powder.

"When we got here, the trunk was shut and the keys were in it," he said. "Somebody went through it."

Dexter turned to Ann. "Can the lab compare this stuff with the cocaine you found in Muriel's apartment?"

"They should be able to tell how close it is in purity."

"If this stuff's a match, these homicides could be related," Hicks said.

Something seemed to occur to Ann. "The license was lying on the ground?"

"That's right."

"If the shooter took the trouble to dig it out of Deal's pocket, he must have been after his address. Anyone been over to Deal's house yet?"

"Way ahead of you. Soon as we ID'd him, I sent Tilsen over," Hicks said. "He called, said the place was trashed. Someone even took a knife to the mattress and couch cushions, real thorough job, probably looking for the rest of the drugs. Makes sense."

It didn't make sense to Dexter. Why would a drug dealer sew his product up inside a couch, where it would be hard to get? But having no experience in these matters, he decided to keep the thought to himself.

Ann looked at the Sheriff. "What about Cara Lynn Grovsner? She lives with Deal. Any sign of her?"

"No." The Sheriff slowly shook his head. He seemed to take his time thinking this over.

"I think someone should look into the Grovsner girl's whereabouts," Ann said, "make sure she's okay."

Hicks shook himself away from whatever he was thinking about. "We can do that." He pulled out his cell phone and was dialing as he walked away.

Kahler scurried off to interview somebody, and Ann, Dexter, Zack, and Grady all walked back toward their cars. Ann noticed Dexter shaking his head. "What?" she asked.

"I don't think whoever searched Deal's house was looking for drugs," he said. "I think they were looking for something else. I mean, a major stash inside couch cushions? It doesn't make sense."

Ann smiled at him.

Dexter saw the smile and stopped walking. "What?"

"I was thinking the same thing. See, Zack, I told you," she said, punching Zack's shoulder, "he's a natural cop."

Zack groaned and then Dexter remembered Bridget's confession.

"Hey, Zack, you'll never guess who stopped by the office not more than an hour ago."

"You're right," Zack agreed, "I'll never guess, because I won't try."

"None other than the lovely and semi-talented Bridget."

"Lady Macbeth, yeah?"

"The very same. In a fit of honesty, inspired by her parents, she took it all back. Says she wasn't with Padgett the night Muriel was murdered."

"No kidding." Zack said smiling. "So the Professor's improvisational theatre closed out of town, huh? I'm genuinely glad to hear that."

Ann glanced at her watch. "I'm going for a bite to eat. Anyone else interested?"

A vision of Billy Deal lying in the front seat of his car flashed in front of Dexter. "I'll pass," he said.

"Me too," Grady said.

"Atta' boy, Dexter," Zack said, grinning. "I'm in, Ann.

I don't like to arrest people on an empty stomach. You buying?"

"I'll buy, but you're not arresting anybody yet."

Dexter dropped Grady off at the office, and ten minutes later, stood on the sidewalk in front of Ardella Tophler's house, gazing up at the triple windows of what had been Muriel Evenson's front room. Mrs. Tophler had lowered the shades, no doubt to keep the summer heat out of the unoccupied apartment. Rather than walking up to the front door, Dexter went around the side, following the driveway to the back of the house until he reached the faded bloodstain on the pavement. He stood looking out over the neighboring yards and felt like a visitor at a shrine.

A sports car had been seen in the area. The jury was still out as to whether it belonged to Manning or Padgett. But no matter who was driving, if he was innocent, he would have left by the front steps, but if he was guilty, then he would have been out on the deck and left by way of the driveway where Dexter now stood.

Dexter knocked on the door and when he asked Ardella Tophler if she could let him into the upper apartment, she told him that the door was still unlocked. She was insistent that he have a cup of coffee, but Dexter was just as insistent in his refusal. When Ardella started up the stairs behind him, he asked her if she would wait downstairs. "I'd probably be lousy company anyway," was the way he put it.

He entered the apartment and walked through the rooms, thinking about Muriel Evenson, and remembering the young girl he'd known. After her funeral, she would exist only in memories and mementos. Her belongings would eventually be removed from the apartment, and there would remain no indication of her ever having been there. Dexter thought of footprints on a beach.

Muriel had always been popular, and as far as he could remember, had always had aspirations to sing and act, but apparently, she'd wanted her dreams so desperately that she allowed them to cloud her judgement. She'd become involved with an obvious manipulator like Geoffrey Padgett, probably because he told her things that she wanted to hear. And her friendship with Cara Lynn Grovsner had caused her to veer into the path of Billy Deal and his drugs.

Dexter passed through the living room and kitchen and finally walked into the bedroom. Standing there, surveying the array of personal effects that cluttered her dresser, he imagined Muriel getting out of bed and going downstairs to let her killer in, wearing only her robe. It was obviously someone she knew well enough to trust. Dexter knew this wasn't a drug homicide—this had been personal.

He spotted the discarded manila bank folder lying in the wastebasket. He picked it out and was looking at it when the glint of something white sticking out from under the dresser caught his eye. He bent down and pulled out a photograph of Muriel and Padgett, standing together at what appeared to be a cast party. He studied Padgett's longish hair and self-assured smile, but his face offered up no clues as to his guilt or innocence. Finally, he laid the photo on the dresser and left the room.

Back out in the front room, Dexter sat on the green sofa and slouched down with his head back. He gazed at the old chandelier in the center of the room, and tried to put himself into Muriel's life. Gazing deep into the dusty glass shards, he tried to imagine what aspect of her life had finally steered her into the path of a killer. She had been saddled with an unexpected pregnancy, but in spite of her ambitions, and to her credit, was apparently determined to have the baby. She'd allowed a creep like Billy Deal to use her apartment to stash his drugs, but there was nothing to suggest that she'd ever used drugs. She'd successfully navigated her way through sexual harassment at work, somehow managing to salvage things and stay on working terms with her harasser.

He absentmindedly examined the folder he still held in his hands, noticing that it seemed stretched out a bit, as though it once held a reasonably thick packet of paper. What had been in this folder—the loans that Tom Manning seemed so desperate to retrieve? If it was loans, did Muriel remove them from the folder, and what had she done with them? And if it wasn't her, then did the killer take them? And for what possible reason?

On a hunch, Dexter went back into Muriel's bedroom and took a closer look at her bookshelf. Sandwiched among a hodgepodge of textbooks was a section of scripts. He pulled the entire section out and began leafing through them. There were a couple of dozen scripts ranging from Greek drama to English comedy, but no bank files. When he started looking past the title pages, however, and examined the contents of Sheridan's *The School for Scandal*, in place of Sheridan's wit, he instead found the missing bank files. *Appropriate choice of plays*, he thought.

Chapter Twenty-four

Dexter placed a call to Janet's Café, interrupting Ann and Zack's dinner, and ten minutes later, they met him outside of the First National Bank. The three of them entered the bank, showed their identification, and Dexter asked the receptionist if they could speak with Meadows, the branch president. The receptionist spoke briefly on the phone, and then directed them to his office. On the way across the lobby, Ann glanced at Tom Manning's cubicle and noticed that it was empty. They entered Meadows's office, and when they were all seated, Dexter produced the sheaf of loan papers.

Tom Manning was away from his desk, buried among the file cabinets in the corner when he happened to see the three law enforcement officers enter the bank. He paused in his work and watched as they walked back to Larry Meadows's office. He was certain he knew why they were there. After they entered Meadows's office and closed the door, Manning set down the files that he was working on and quietly returned to his desk. He opened his briefcase, emptied it, and began refilling it with personal items. The photograph of his parents, a pair of carved wooden figures—a memento from his trip to Jamaica—and his employee-of-the-month plaque all went inside. He was dying for some cocaine, but it would have to wait until he got out of the bank. He took a bottle of Maalox out of his desk drawer and contented himself with a long pull. He rose from his chair, put on his sport jacket, and walked across the bank towards the vault.

In Meadows's office, with the door closed, it only took a few minutes to establish that the files were current loans issued through their branch. Meadows specifically recognized the name 'Dersval' as one of the missing files that Manning had been trying to get released from the crime scene.

"What can you tell us about these loans?" Ann asked.

"Well, let's see." Meadows began thumbing back and forth through them, reading quickly. "They all appear to be garden variety, small loans, nothing that would raise any eyebrows."

"Nothing unusual?" Zack asked.

"Nothing that leaps out at me." Meadows's voice trailed off as he concentrated on the pages that passed more slowly under his hands. After a minute he looked up.

"They all appear to have been issued by Tom Manning."

"Did Muriel Evenson assist any other loan officers?" Ann asked.

"Yes, she occasionally worked with all three of them."

Then Dexter joined the conversation. "How many loans do we have here?"

"Let's see, looks like nine, yes, nine loans."

"What's the largest amount?" he asked.

"The largest is for—fourteen thousand dollars."

"Ever see any of these loans before, ever review them for the bank?" Dexter asked.

Meadows looked up. "No," he said simply.

"None of them? Is that normal?"

"Completely," Meadows assured Dexter. "Tom's lending

limit is fifteen-thousand, so any loan for less than that amount wouldn't require a review by our committee."

"Which is another thing they all have in common," Ann pointed out, leaning forward. "Just a thought, Mr. Meadows, why don't we check to make sure that these loan recipients actually exist."

Before stepping out of the bank's vault, Manning adjusted his sport coat to camouflage the several packets of large bills with which he had carefully lined the waistband of his trousers. He felt amazingly calm, though he suspected it was due to the fact that thus far he was refusing to think about the big picture. He knew from experience that as soon as he was away from the bank and able to access his cocaine, he was going to feel totally in control, but he wasn't kidding himself; he was going to need help. He was going to have to make a call. Back at his desk, he grabbed his briefcase, and as he walked past the receptionist and into the late afternoon sunshine, he nodded and smiled; just another office drone knocking off a little early on Friday.

They divided the loans up and all four of them went to work with their cell phones. After fifteen minutes of calls, the results were in: nine loans and nine fictitious recipients—they simply didn't exist. Calls to work numbers given on the loan applications yielded only confused employers who had never heard of the people, and calls to home numbers found only wrong, or non-existent, numbers. Larry Meadows, who had started looking pale after the first couple of calls, now sat staring at the pile of papers on the desk before him, the forefinger of his right hand convulsively strumming his lower lip.

"It's a classic pattern," he said softly.

For a moment, the other three were willing to wait for

Meadows to gather his thoughts and continue. Zack finally broke the silence.

"Yeah, right, a real golden oldie."

Meadows ignored the remark. "Tom hasn't had a vacation in two years."

"Is that important?" Dexter asked.

"Embezzlers don't take vacations, right, Mr. Meadows?" said Ann, who had spent several years in the white-collar crime division. Meadows looked at them, fighting back the embarrassment he clearly felt for a trusted employee.

"No, they find reasons not to. There's the danger that they would be discovered if someone was reviewing their work while they were away."

"How did he expect to get away with this?" Zack asked.

"I think when we look into it," Ann said, "we'll discover a series of stock market investments or maybe a gambling habit, or some similar scheme to multiply the money. Embezzlers often start out intending to just 'borrow' it."

"But what blinded him to the logic that says eventually the facts would probably come out?" Zack said.

"Arrogance," Ann suggested.

"Arrogance is the enemy of logic," Dexter said. "Sorry, Zack."

"Muriel obviously knew about this," Zack said. "The fact that she didn't take this to the authorities means only one thing—blackmail. When she approached Manning, he must have decided it was cheaper to murder her than pay her. Looks like we finally found our motive."

Ann stood up. "Let's take him into custody. We can start with embezzling, and that'll give us some time to work up a murder charge."

She glanced over at his cubicle and still couldn't see him. "He's in the bank right now, isn't he?"

"I spoke with him sometime after lunch," Meadows said glancing at his watch. "He should be around for a little while yet."

Two minutes later, they stood at the front desk while the receptionist informed them that Tom Manning had left a little while ago.

"He had his briefcase with him. I think he's probably gone for the day," she added, trying to be helpful.

They walked over to Manning's desk and when Meadows noted that his pictures were gone along with his employee-of-the-month award, they knew that their bird had flown the coop. They called the state police and had them issue an APB, and arranged to have a car swing by and look for him at his home.

After they left the bank, Dexter and Zack dropped Ann off at her car. She got in and had just turned on the ignition when the passenger door suddenly opened, and then Cara Lynn Grovsner was sitting next to her. Her eyes were red, and she looked exhausted. Ann wasn't sure what to say to her, what to ask her first. She wondered whether or not Cara Lynn had heard about Billy Deal. As it turned out, she didn't have to ask anything; Cara Lynn had come to talk. Ann grabbed a pad of paper and a pen and listened as Cara Lynn began with a confusing series of seemingly unrelated statements. Finally, Ann asked her to start at the beginning.

"Muriel didn't tell me anything about what she was doing until about a week before she died. The whole thing was an accident."

"What was an accident?" Ann asked.

"Finding out what her boss, Tom Manning, was doing. She was just trying to be thorough, you know, and she ended up finding out that one of his loan guys didn't exist. Then she looked closer and found out a bunch of them didn't exist. He was giving loans to fake people and keeping the money."

"Any idea why she didn't bring this to the attention of the bank manager?"

Cara Lynn's laugh was quick and nervous. "Want the short answer? Money. Muriel was pregnant, but she wanted to go to Hollywood as bad as Padgett. She figured he was a lot more likely to let her come along if she could pay her own way."

Ann nodded. "So she decided to blackmail her boss. We found a stack of fraudulent loans issued by Tom Manning in Muriel's apartment, so we knew she was involved somehow."

"Then you guys know it was Manning who killed her."

Ann nodded.

"Did you arrest him?"

"We'd love to. Don't suppose you know where he is?"

"He's gone?"

"For the moment. As soon as he sticks his head up, we'll grab him. Tell me something, if you suspected that Tom Manning murdered Muriel, why didn't you come to the police with the information?"

Cara Lynn looked out her window and mumbled something. When Ann asked what she'd said, she fixed her eyes on Ann and spoke clearly. "I said, I was going to blackmail him for murdering her."

"Are you serious?"

Cara Lynn hesitated for an instant and then nodded. "I made some calls to him and you should have heard him. He was so innocent; he was like 'who is this? what do you want from me?' "

"What happened?"

"I had a meeting set up for last night, then Billy found out. He got me to tell him about Manning."

"He beat you up?"

She looked away, and Ann waited. "He was really angry."

"He didn't know anything about this?"

Cara Lynn shook her head.

"That thing out at the reservoir, that was supposed to be the meeting?"

"Yeah."

"That could have been you. I take it you've heard what happened."

"That Billy's dead? Yeah, that's why I decided to come back and tell what I know."

"You think Manning shot him?"

"Who else? That's who he was going out there to see." She paused while something seemed to build up inside her. "I don't care about Billy, but there's no way Manning's getting away with killing Muriel."

Ann stared at her notes for a few minutes and tried to picture the runny-nosed bank officer pumping five bullets into Deal's body. Then a question occurred to her.

"Why did you leave Higgins Point?"

"When the house was searched last night, I freaked."

Ann tried to make sense of this, and then the realization came. "Are you telling me that you were in Billy's house while someone was searching it?"

"It's my house too. Yeah, I was there. I was waiting for Billy to come back from the reservoir, when some guy broke in the back door. I had to hide in the closet. God, it was straight out of a horror movie. He would, like, walk into a room and start tearing it apart, and I would creep down the hall to another room. I figured it was some drug dude ripping off Billy. I know what they can do, and I definitely didn't want him finding me there."

Ann thought about this for a minute. "You thought it was a drug rip-off?"

"Yeah."

"Did you get a look at this person? Could you ID him?"

Cara Lynn shook her head. "I never saw his face. I was hiding, you know. He almost caught me. I thought he was leaving, but he came back into the bathroom where I was hiding behind the shower curtain. He had these creepy gloves on."

"You saw his hands but you didn't see his face?"

"Right."

"What sort of gloves, rubber?"

"Yeah, thin white rubber, or something, like he was a doctor. He was so close I could see the tattoo on his wrist."

Ann reached into the backseat of her car for a pad of paper, which she handed to Cara Lynn along with a pen. "Think you can sketch the tattoo for me?"

Cara Lynn accepted the paper and pen. "It was six inches from my face. I don't think I'll ever forget it."

"Then what happened?"

"When he went down to the basement, I ducked out the front door. Came back later for my car and drove to St. Paul."

"And that's where you were last night?"

"Uh huh. I slept in my car, only I didn't sleep much."

No one said anything for a few minutes while Cara Lynn sketched the tattoo. When she was finished, she handed the paper and pen back to Ann. "That guy in my house wasn't really looking for drugs, was he?"

Ann shook her head. "I believe he was looking for the loan files. The person in your house," Ann said, "killed Billy."

"But I know the guy in my house wasn't Tom Manning," Cara Lynn said. "I know the hand I saw wasn't his."

Ann glanced down at the sketch of the tattoo. It was a crude picture of a bulldog's head with the words 'BRAVO COMPANY' above and 'VIETNAM' below.

Chapter Twenty-five

It was 10:00 on Saturday morning, and the light from the table lamp gave the motel room an artificial yellow cast, which jarred with the shaft of natural sunlight slipping through the crack in the closed curtains. Tom Manning was standing next to the bed, thinking again about Muriel Evenson's last moments on earth.

When he'd stood over her still form on that dark driveway ten days earlier, there'd been a moment when he was absolutely certain that he couldn't go through with it. But the dog making all the noise upstairs had shaken him into the realization that he *had* to act. He'd bent over her, pinched her nose and covered her mouth, and waited. There was a weak jerk at the end, and that was all. She was gone.

He never intended for it to happen. He went to her apartment thinking he could talk to her, reason with her. When he brought up the idea of the two of them going away together, she laughed in his face, but it wasn't until she told him that she was pregnant with Padgett's child that he snapped. Almost before he realized he'd done it, he forced her out onto the deck, grabbing the Statue of David off the table on the way by. The dog was barking non-stop, and he was on the verge of panicking; he wasn't himself. He closed the door against the dog and when she struggled, he hit her.

When she slumped down, he dragged her to the edge of the deck and threw her over. Then he broke the railing out to make it look like an accident. In hindsight, it was a stupid idea, but he deserved a little slack; he wasn't thinking clearly at the time. Every second that passed, he thought the dog's barking would bring someone. At least he had the presence of mind to take the statue with him and throw it into the St. Croix River later. When he lowered himself down to the ground, he didn't even realize that Muriel was still alive, that he would have to do more.

Now he needed help, he had to make a call. He sat down on the edge of the bed and dialed the phone, trying to compose himself. When the voice he was expecting came on the other end, he started speaking in mid-thought.

"You didn't tell me you were going to kill him."

Manning sat motionless, listening, and then spoke into the receiver.

"I don't know what I thought you were going to do. You told me to wait by my car and you would take care of it. But I didn't think—"

Manning ground his teeth together and listened for a moment before trying again. "But I had to call to you. How else—"

Frustration finally forced his words out. "Well, to tell you the truth, right now I care very little about what you think is smart and what isn't. I listened to you once, and now I'm actually running from the law!"

He bowed his head and ran his hand over his forehead. "You've got to help me get out of here. I managed to take a little of the bank's money with me when I left. There's ways for people to disappear, right?"

He rose from the bed, holding the phone, and began pacing back and forth like an animal on a leash.

"I *am* calm. I'm very calm for someone in my situation. When I saw that damn investigator dragging everybody down to the deposit box area, I knew they were on to us. She just wouldn't let go.

"Yes I said 'us'. Listen to me carefully. No, you listen to me. You don't want them catching me."

He stopped moving and sank to the bed once more. "No, no, I'm not threatening you, I'm only trying to clarify the situation.

"That's better. That's all I'm asking for, a little help. I'm at the Billick's Motel on Sheridan Road, room 18."

The line went dead at the other end, which struck Tom Manning as very rude. He placed the phone back on the table. *There's just no excuse for treating people like that,* he thought.

The sparse shrubs across the front office of the Billick's Motel were brown and dying, and the cracked asphalt of the parking lot radiated heat up into Dexter's face. In the window, a small, red neon sign, feeble in the Saturday afternoon sunlight, announced 'VACANCY'. They were six miles from Higgins Point, and the whole gang was there; it was a repeat of the circus at the reservoir. Ann and Dexter were standing next to Manning's yellow Triumph while a lab tech was busily tagging and bagging several suspicious looking packages of white powder in the car's trunk. Dexter noticed that a piece of tape covered a small tear in one of the bags.

"This didn't have to happen," Ann said, quietly. "This wasn't necessary."

A stretcher emerged from the open door of room 18. Ann walked over and stopped the two attendants who were wheeling it away. She reached down and pulled back the white sheet, brilliant in the sunlight, far enough to view the chest wounds; two closely grouped black holes in the center of Manning's blood-soaked shirt. His face was the washed-out color of paper, and no one had closed his eyes. Dexter looked at him from a distance and tried to think of Muriel Evenson.

Ann placed the sheet back over his face, and Dexter followed her into room 18. As they passed from sun into shadow, Dexter momentarily lost some of his sight, but his hearing was fine.

". . . thought sure he was gonna come in quiet."

Sheriff Moses Hicks was speaking to a state police investigator, who was taking notes.

"Didn't leave me no choice, yanked out that pistol and was gonna open up on me. Hell, if I was a little slower, you'd be talkin' to him right now,'stead of me."

Bob Tilsen was talking quietly to Zack in the corner of the room. When they saw Ann, they came over and Ann introduced Tilsen to Dexter. Dexter recognized the name as the man who had led the investigation into Ann's father's death.

"What happened?" Dexter asked.

"Apparently the sheriff got an anonymous phone tip that Tom Manning was at this motel," Tilsen said. "He used a pass key to unlock the door, and when he got inside, Manning pulled a gun on him, so the sheriff shot him."

"Twice," Ann said. "Did Manning get off any rounds?"

"Apparently not."

Ann glanced over at Hicks. "Pretty lucky."

"Guess it wasn't Manning's day." Tilsen didn't seem too concerned.

Dexter tried to savor some sense of justice, to find some worth to this ending, but he just felt empty. He looked at Ann. "Is it always this much fun when you wrap up a case?"

Ann was watching Hicks, and answered without taking her eyes off of him. "Is this case wrapped up?" She brought her gaze to Tilsen. "No stray shots, no near-misses, and the grouping's a textbook 'double tap.'

Dexter read clear concern in Tilsen's expression.

"Why don't we let these people work," Tilsen said, as he gently ushered everyone toward the door.

When they were back outside, breathing in the hot air off the asphalt, Ann asked Tilsen if there were any witnesses.

Tilsen shook his head. "Not to the actual shooting, no."

"How is that possible?" Ann asked.

Tilsen was watching the traffic move past the motel. "Apparently, he came to the motel alone." Ann looked at Dexter and Zack, and then back at Tilsen.

"He didn't bring any back-up with him?"

"Apparently, he thought it was going to be routine, thought he could bring him in peacefully." Tilsen shrugged. "It went bad. He called it in after it was over."

Zack leaned in closer to speak. "Isn't a county sheriff a little senior for that kind of Rambo stuff?"

Tilsen leveled his gaze at Zack and spoke slowly. "He made an error in judgement, he admits it, end of story." He started to turn away and then sighed heavily and turned back. "I guess he knows the Evenson family. He had a personal reason for wanting to arrest Manning himself. But as for witnesses, the only people who know what happened in that room are Sheriff Hicks and Tom Manning, and Tom Manning won't be making any statements."

"History is written by the survivors," Zack said. "It gets better, tell her the best part."

"Manning's gun is a 38, the same caliber that killed Billy Deal," Tilsen said. "They're gonna run it through ballistics."

Ann looked around the group of men. "Well, that puts a bow on it."

"And," Tilsen continued, "they found several bags of cocaine in Manning's trunk. If they're a match for the traces they found in Deal's car, it would tie Manning to his murder.

Ann looked around. "Am I the only one here having trouble believing the bank clerk's a mad dog gunman?"

Dexter slowly raised his hand.

Zack leaned in toward Dexter. "I think that was a rhetorical question."

Sheriff Hicks stepped out of the motel room, filling the doorway, and headed out into the parking lot. As he was walking past the line of cars, he happened to glance down into Ann's Dodge Stratus and came to a sudden stop. He was staring at a pad of paper lying on the backseat with a sketch drawn on it, a crude rendering of a bulldog with the words 'BRAVO COMPANY' and 'VIETNAM' around it. It matched the tattoo that he had on his wrist. He glanced back at the motel and continued walking.

Ann stepped back into room 18 and approached a member of the lab team who was collecting fingerprints. He was a slightly-built, serious-looking man with wire rim glasses and receding hair.

"Did you get any prints from the gun?" she asked.

"Sure did, nice clean set." His hands continued to work as he spoke.

"How about the bullets?"

The man paused, looking over his glasses. "Excuse me?"

"Get any prints off the bullets?"

The man's mouth hung open for just an instant while he considered the question. "Well, no."

"Could you?"

"You want me to print the bullets?" He hesitated and then let out a sigh. "Why the hell not."

The .38 was lying on the bed. He pulled it out of the bag and carefully emptied the bullets from the cylinder onto a piece of white paper. When he'd dusted the first bullet, he sat back and looked at Ann.

"Nothing."

He dusted the rest of them while Ann watched and found no prints on any bullets.

"Thanks," Ann said and stepped outside to rejoin the group in the parking lot.

Tilsen took one look at her and said, "Something on your mind?"

"I was just wondering why there aren't any fingerprints on the bullets."

"Why there aren't any what?"

"Fingerprints on the bullets in Manning's gun. There aren't any. Just wondering why."

Tilsen grinned at the rest of them and then looked back at Ann. "Beats the hell out of me."

"Seems odd, doesn't it? Why would Manning think to wipe the bullets clean when he was loading the gun? Assuming he even knew how to load the gun."

Tilsen didn't try to hide his irritation with the question. "I can't account for the habits of that fastidious little jerk any more than you can. Who the hell knows why he'd do something like that?" He walked away, ending any chance for a reply.

Suddenly, like a bad penny, Frank Kahler was back. He had his notepad ready and was already talking as he walked up to Ann and Dexter.

"Holy God. I'm not coming back here without a bulletproof vest, Chief."

"Very funny, Kahler."

"Call me Frank. Let's see now, this is the fourth stiff in two weeks. You folks better do something about this quick, or there isn't going to be anybody left in town to vote for the sheriff."

"The sheriff's the one who shot Manning," Dexter said.

"Moses did this?" Kahler scribbled on his pad.

"Self-defense," Dexter explained.

Kahler spotted Hicks across the parking lot, excused himself, and was gone as quickly as he had arrived.

With Manning's body on the way to the medical examiner's office, and the lab team finishing up, there was no reason to stay. Ann asked Dexter to walk her to her car. When they got there, she fished around in her purse for her keys while she spoke.

"Hallie, Ted and I are driving up to my father's cabin tonight. We're planning to spend the night."

"At the cabin, where he died? Does that strike you as a good idea?"

"It's something Ted dreamed up. I'm just trying to go with the flow. The point is I want you to arrange a meeting for Monday. You, me, and Zack, okay?"

Dexter took out his notepad and pen. "Manning was just killed in a shootout with the sheriff. I thought that's what you called 'case closed'.

Ann shook her head. "It's not about Manning. It's about your sheriff."

This brought Dexter's writing to a halt. "Suddenly he's *my* sheriff? What about him?"

Ann started her car. When she put it in gear, Dexter placed a restraining hand on the door. "Annie, why are you going up to the cabin?"

"I have to retrieve my father's Winchester for a lab analysis."

"Are you going to tell me what's going on?"

Ann sat looking forward with her hands on the wheel for a minute and then put the car back in park. She explained how the tattoo on Hicks's wrist matched the tattoo that Cara Lynn had seen on the man who had searched her house on Thursday night.

"We figured that whoever searched the house also shot Billy Deal," Ann reminded Dexter.

"Why would the sheriff want to shoot Billy Deal?" Dexter asked.

"It's not exactly clear yet. Deal was at the reservoir to

blackmail Manning, and now Hicks has apparently killed both Manning and Deal.

"I thought we figured out that Muriel was blackmailing Tom Manning?"

"She was, but Muriel told Cara Lynn about it before she was murdered."

"And if Cara Lynn knew, then Billy Deal probably knew."

Ann nodded. "He beat it out of her."

"And the sheriff's mixed up in it all?"

"I think he may be behind it all," Ann said. "I also suspect that he murdered my father."

"What?"

"You know that gun I found in my father's freezer? The guy it was used to murder, the guy named Casper Bottom, was apparently killed because he was trying to establish methamphetamine labs in western Wisconsin. I think Hicks controls the meth labs locally and murdered Bottom to protect his turf. I believe my father was going to bring that gun in to the DCI just before he died. That's why he told me he wanted to drive down to Madison personally and see me about something. I asked myself why he didn't turn the gun in to the sheriff's department, and the only reason I can come up with is that he'd figured out that it was the sheriff he was after. Coming to the DCI makes good sense if you're trying to take down a sheriff.

Dexter looked over at the door to the motel room where Hicks was talking to Frank Kahler. "Then this wasn't self-defense?"

Ann shook her head. "I'm betting my badge it wasn't, but I don't want to say anything until I've got my ducks lined up. I want to see you and Zack in your office on Monday morning for a meeting. Will you arrange it with Zack?"

"Annie, you can't go up to the cabin; it's too dangerous.

It sounds to me like Hicks has gone completely round the bend."

"I'll be fine. There'll be three of us up there, and besides, Hicks is no threat to me if he doesn't know I'm on to him."

Dexter grudgingly allowed her to drive away, too stunned by what she'd told him to think up a good argument. He went back into the motel to talk to Zack but was told he had left, so he called him on his cell phone.

"Agent Rose."

"It's Dexter."

"Yeah, Chief?"

"I was just talking to Annie; she asked me to arrange a meeting with the three of us on Monday morning."

There was a pause. "I was expecting to go back to Madison this afternoon. If Ann wants some kind of postmortem powwow, why wait until Monday? Can't we do it now?"

There was no way Dexter was going to discuss what Ann had told him over a cell phone. "She's already gone. She's spending the night at her father's cabin."

"Great, she goes fishing, so I have to sit around here all weekend."

"You work with her, you tell me. Would she ask for a meeting for no reason?"

Zack sigh. "I suppose not. We'll meet at your office?"

"Yeah, say nine AM."

"I'll see you then."

After Zack ended the call, he turned to Sheriff Hicks, who had asked him for a lift back to his office. "Looks like I'll be enjoying the hospitality of Higgins Point this weekend."

"Thought you said you were headin' back?"

"Dexter says Ann wants some kind of meeting on Monday."

"What about?"

"Didn't say."

"What was that about going fishin'?"

"I guess Ann's going up to her father's cabin tonight."

"Alone?"

"I don't know, I suppose."

"Well, maybe she's finally decided to accept Paul's suicide and stop buttin' her head against a brick wall. Maybe she's goin' up there to make her peace with her old man."

"That and fish," Zack said.

"Paul's cabin's on Eden Lake as I recall," the sheriff said. "They stopped stocking bass out there years ago. If she wants any fish out of that lake, she better bring dynamite."

At 4:00 that afternoon, when the fax came across Dexter's machine, there was nobody in the office to receive it. It was only by chance that Dexter stopped by a little later and happened to spot the paper lying in the fax machine's basket. It was a copy of the phone records for calls made from the Billicks Motel earlier that day. A friend had pulled some strings to obtain the record quickly as a favor for Dexter, who had requested it at Ann's direction.

The calls were broken out and charged to individual rooms. The record showed a single call from Manning's room, placed at 10:00 that morning. Dexter tried to identify the number that had been called, using his reverse directory, but it was unlisted, so he dialed the number himself. When no one picked up at the other end, he had to settle for an answering machine, and suddenly he was listening to the voice of Sheriff Moses Hicks, the person Manning had called just before he died. Dexter hung up without leaving a message. I guess the tip Hicks got wasn't so anonymous after all, he thought.

The Bluffs Restaurant in Higgins Point was slightly misnamed since Higgins Point wasn't far enough above the river level to have any bluffs. The place was fairly empty early Saturday evening when Dexter arrived, thinking of fried catfish. He walked in and said hello to Lyle Krellhearn's oldest daughter, Alice, who was doubling as hostess and waitress tonight. As she was leading him to his table, Dexter spotted Zack sitting near a window, so he veered over and asked if he could join him. Zack took a few seconds to chew and swallow his food and run his napkin across his mouth.

"Sure," he said, nodding at the table.

Dexter sat down and ordered a draft beer and tried not to look at Zack's eyebrow ring.

"Dexter, you seem to be on good terms with Ann, maybe you can answer a question for me."

"I can try."

"A textbook double tap? Why was she going after the sheriff like that?"

Dexter knew that Ann intended to explain things on Monday, and he wasn't so sure she would want him to say anything. "I think it was just an observation."

"And what was that bit about no fingerprints on Manning's bullets?"

What the hell, Dexter thought, *Zack's a DCI investigator; he ought to be in the loop*. "I have some bad news for you, Zack."

"Bad news, what bad news?"

"This case may not be quite as wrapped up as we thought, Ann thinks maybe there's more to it."

"She said that?"

"She thinks someone else is involved. But there's good news. She thinks she knows who."

Zack didn't say anything for a minute, and then finally, in a quiet voice, he said, "Okay, let's have the good news."

"That was the good news, now I'm afraid we're back to the bad news. Have you noticed that Sheriff Hicks has a tattoo on his wrist?"

"This is about the sheriff?"

"That's the bad news that I mentioned."

Zack stared at Dexter for a moment. "Yeah," he said finally, "I spotted something on his wrist about his unit in Vietnam when he held up Deal's driver's license out at the reservoir."

The waitress appeared next to the table, set Dexter's beer down in front of him, and asked if he was ready to order. Dexter said he needed a few minutes, and when she was gone, he turned to Zack.

"Cara Lynn Grovsner identified that tattoo," Dexter said. "She saw it on the wrist of the man who searched Billy Deal's house right after Deal was murdered. Apparently, she drew a sketch of it for Ann."

"We figured whoever searched the house—"

"Right, also murdered Deal."

Zack took a long slow breath. "Also murdered Deal."

"A little while ago, a fax came in," Dexter said. "Phone records for the Billicks Motel. You'll never guess who Manning called at 10:00 this morning."

"Sheriff Hicks," Zack said, almost to himself.

"Bingo. Now, why would a man on the run from the law call the county sheriff?"

"Hicks said he received an anonymous tip," Zack said. "Maybe Manning wanted to give himself up."

"Simpler to just walk into a police station. But if he was looking for help from his partner, it begins to make sense."

"This is why Ann called the meeting on Monday, to go after the Sheriff?"

"Uh huh. When she finds out I spilled the beans, she's not gonna be happy."

Zack tried to smile, but it wasn't too convincing. "I may have some bad news for you too. This afternoon, when you called me on my cell phone and told me about the meeting, I was giving the sheriff a lift back to his office."

Dexter shrugged. "So, he knows about the meeting, no

harm done. Hell, I hope he shows up—but if he does, I'm putting the bullets in my gun."

"He also knows that Ann went up to her father's cabin tonight, alone."

Zack's expression conveyed a little more concern than Dexter felt comfortable with, but the embarrassment of the Lundholm incident was still fresh in his mind. "Probably no big deal," he said. "She's not alone, Hallie and Ted are with her. Besides, there's no reason for him to suspect what Ann's got in mind."

"You really believe that?" Both men stared at each other for a minute, and then Dexter said, "I can call his house."

Hicks's wife, Marjorie, answered. She explained that Moses wasn't in and wouldn't be back until tomorrow. She wasn't exactly sure where he had gone, because although he'd left her a note, which she'd found when she got home from work, it wasn't very clear. She only knew that it was some business that would take him away for the night. Dexter tried the sheriff's cell phone next.

Chapter Twenty-six

One hundred feet from the access road, on a small gravel turn off, the Black Hummer was placed beneath low hanging boughs that provided shade from the rapidly rising moon. The engine had ceased making tinging sounds and was silent, leaving only the sound of the crickets, as the darkness deepened around Sheriff Moses Hicks, who sat motionless behind the wheel. No breeze could reach him close in among the trees, and the open window was little help against the humidity. A quarter of a mile to the north, through dense evergreens, was Paul Summer's cabin.

He removed a small bottle of chloroform from his glove box and put it in his shirt pocket, then glanced at his watch for the tenth time in an hour, and for the tenth time, tried to figure out how things had managed to get fouled up so fast. Only a week ago, life was good; they were unloading all the product that his meth labs could put out, payoffs from that whiny embezzler, Manning, were sweetening the pot, and everybody was keeping their mouths shut. Hell, when Paul Summer got too close to the meth operation, and Hicks had to take him out, he'd even forced him to write the note and managed to get the suicide ruling to stick. He was starting to believe he could do anything. Then, Dick Evenson's daughter had to get greedy and try to blackmail Manning. Apparently, Manning had been to one too many movies; after he panicked and killed the girl, he actually thought he was going to 'disappear.' What an idiot. When Manning called him and told him he'd killed Muriel Evenson, Hicks had had no choice but to help cover his tracks; he had a vested interest in keeping Manning out of jail. But even back then, he'd known what Manning finally realized only seconds before he died—that Hicks could never afford to leave him in any condition to talk, in jail or out.

Now, Manning was out of the way, and Hicks had even managed to blame Deal's murder on him. But that still left one thing to take care of. Manning had told him that the blackmail calls had definitely been from a woman, so when he'd walked up to the Trans Am at the reservoir, he'd been expecting to find a female behind the wheel, not some local coke dealer with a gun. That meant that there was still one person walking around who knew something, and it hadn't been a giant leap to finger Deal's live-in girlfriend. One last loose end, but one that he had to deal with quickly. His only regret was that he'd had to kill Manning before he could pin her murder on him too. Now that would have been artful.

But now there was a new problem: Ann Summer. If she hadn't stuck her nose in things, he wouldn't be out here now feeding the mosquitoes, and her prospects to collect a pension would be a hell of a lot better. Finding the sketch of his tattoo, in her car, had jolted Hicks. He wasn't sure exactly how much she knew, but she obviously had him in her sights.

Hicks jumped when his cell phone went off and hesitated for a moment but then turned it off. He waited another fifteen minutes and then looked at his watch one more time. It was 10:00, and the moon was rising and growing brighter by the minute. He decided it was time.

The trek to Summer's cabin was difficult because Hicks

had to fight through the undergrowth in order to avoid the road; he didn't want a set of headlights fixing him in anybody's memory. Progress was slow, but after twenty minutes, he stopped, concealed in the last stand of trees before the clearing that surrounded the cottage. The cabin was a one-story, wood-framed dump, typical of local retirees on a limited budget. Ann Summer's Dodge Stratus was parked on the near side, but there was a second car there too, one he wasn't familiar with. That obnoxious DCI agent, Zack Rose, had told him Ann would be alone at the cabin; those guys couldn't get anything straight.

The front door of the cabin was out of his view, but from his position, approximately sixty feet away, he was able to look into two brightly-lit windows. He could just make out the faint sound of voices coming from the cabin. While he watched the windows for movement, his hand went to his shirt pocket, absentmindedly assuring him that the chloroform bottle was still there. The plan was for Ann Summer to disappear quietly, no trace. He saw her walk past one of the windows and, a moment later, emerge through the front door carrying a flashlight and what appeared to be a rifle case. She walked to her Stratus and opened the rear door, leaned into the back seat, and then returned to the cabin without the rifle.

All his life Hicks had been the sort of person who took care of problems quickly, before they became complicated. His style was to go straight through, not around, obstacles. He pulled a pair of rubber kitchen gloves from his back pocket and tugged them over his large hands, then checked the chloroform bottle one last time. He began walking toward the cabin, intending to go straight through this obstacle.

He had only moved a couple of feet when the slam of the screen door told him that she had come out again. This time, however, the bounce of her flashlight beam led away from him and toward the trees approximately forty feet from the cabin. He liked things simple, but he was also a pragmatic man who was capable of adapting when necessary. He knew that the lake was in that direction, and that water wreaked havoc with forensic evidence. Maybe she wouldn't have to disappear. He moved quickly to follow her, examining the possibilities.

When Ann had arrived at the cabin early Saturday evening, Hallie and Ted were more than ready for her. Since they'd arrived on Friday, Ted had been busy dreaming up a regime of grief therapies. Mostly, they seemed to involve the three of them sitting around the table while Ann and Hallie took turns telling stories about their father. Initially, it had been almost as painful as Ann feared it would be. Then, gradually, Ann and Hallie's stories began to meld together into a kind of family history monologue that included their mother. After a couple of hours, they all decided that they were tired of looking at Paul's Winchester, and Ann took it out to her car. When she returned, she announced that what would do the most good for her right now would be a moonlight swim. She changed quickly, grabbed the flashlight, and excused herself.

The warm, evening air folded itself around Ann as she stepped from the cabin. Wearing a dark blue swimsuit, with a towel draped over her shoulder, she trotted toward the trees, trying, in vain, to stay ahead of the mosquitoes. The day's light was gone, but the moon had almost risen to its full brilliance; her figure cast a moon shadow across the grass. She crossed the lawn and stepped onto the path, inhaling the deep scent of the trees around her, braving the twigs and stones.

She had gone perhaps fifty yards down the trail, when she thought she heard a crunch on the path behind her. She swung her light back in that direction but saw only the empty trail winding away under the dark branches. She decided it was nothing and continued walking until she reached the beach. She twisted her feet down into the cool sand as she walked, finally stepping up onto the dock. Ann thought of all the afternoons that she had spent sitting on these familiar, worn planks with a line in the water, many of them with her father.

At the end of the dock, the moon's reflection on the water's surface looked like a silver highway dancing away from her toward the opposite shore. She set the flashlight down and, with no hesitation, dove hard and flat out onto the silver flecks and began swimming strongly toward the middle of the lake. The cool water running along her skin provided a delicious chill, washing away her thoughts. After several minutes, she became unconsciously aware of the distant whine of an outboard motor, but it didn't register with her because the sound was completely natural given the surroundings. She slowed her swimming, and then finally turned over and floated on her back, looking up into the night sky.

With her ears underwater, Ann again picked up the straining pitch of an outboard motor that seemed to be increasing in volume. It grew louder until Ann finally became aware of what she was actually hearing. She sat up in the water and turned toward shore to see the dark outline of a boat hull racing straight toward her. If she had paused for even an instant to process this information, the boat would have hit her, but pure instinct took hold, and she dove to the side and down. The scream of the motor closed over her and a burst of pain erupted in her left foot, and for an instant she thought her foot had been shredded by the propeller.

The sound of the motor grew fainter and Ann swam upward, aware now that her foot had actually glanced off the metal hull of the boat. She broke the surface prepared to give the unobservant boater a piece of her mind. It was just plain stupid to race a boat at that speed in the dark.

The boat, which had been traveling straight from shore

initially, had circled around and was returning, traveling parallel to the shore. Ann waved her arm and yelled "swimmer!" To her amazement, the boat adjusted its course, veering straight toward her, the rising pitch of the motor signaling its increasing speed.

This time, with adequate warning, Ann was able to dive to avoid the boat, but it occurred to her that if this was some sort of homicidal maniac, he could make it very difficult for her to reach the shore. Her foot was sore, but didn't seem to be broken. A third pass, unsuccessful from the boater's point of view, clearly qualified as enemy action, and Ann suddenly felt extremely exposed treading water so far from shore.

Then, something was different. Ann realized that the motor's pitch had dropped during its last turn, and the boat was now closing on her slowly. She turned and began swimming for the beach, which was about three hundred feet away, using her fastest crawl stroke. When a backward glance confirmed that the boat was almost on top of her, she dove and continued swimming underwater. She swam for a while until she needed air and had to come up. When she broke the surface, a hand grabbed her hair, twisting her head sharply, and she was lifted partly out of the water.

She had only a split second to glance upward in the moonlight, recognize the face of Sheriff Moses Hicks, and take in a breath of air, before she was thrust underwater again.

That he was going to drown her if he could, was something that Ann understood without having to think about it. She instinctively tried to pull downward but only dangled helplessly in the water, unable to fight the buoyancy of the boat. She thrashed back and forth like a landed fish, but the fingers clenched in her hair were unyielding, and she only succeeded in using up precious oxygen.

After a minute, Ann could feel the beginning of the familiar burn in her lungs, and knew she was running out of air. Though she could hold her breath for a respectable length of time, she had only managed a quick gasp before going under, and there was a certain amount of mental stress affecting her. Fear was becoming more of a player with every passing second. On an impulse, she raised her legs up over her head, not exactly sure what might happen, only to have them slapped down by the Sheriff's free hand. Then her hands found the aluminum hull and pushed against it for leverage, but the water offered no resistance, and Hicks' grasp remained determined.

Ann hadn't had a breath for almost two minutes by this time, and though her brain knew this, her body did not. Her blood continued to deliver carbon dioxide to her straining lungs and take away any oxygen it could find to replenish her cells. As the carbon dioxide built up, the burn became more intense, its severity entering territory she had seldom explored. Encased in the black water, blind and helpless, her thoughts were becoming more erratic. On an impulse she reached up with both hands and dug her nails into the Sheriff's arm. If he drowns me, she thought grimly, I want his DNA under my fingernails. But her attack had no discernable effect; Hicks merely reached down with his free hand and peeled her hands away, apparently content to worry about scratches after she was dead.

Ann was rapidly reaching the point where she would lose control of her reflexes, and try to inhale water, and then the drowning would begin. Panic now had a firm anchor within her. Her thoughts were becoming jerky to match the twitching of her body. Her legs flailed out, striking the hull of the boat, and she felt it quiver, and roll slightly. With the last vestige of reasoning left to her, Ann realized that in order to hold her under, Hicks must be on his knees, leaning out over the side of the small boat. She reached her hands up out of the water, found the gunwale of the boat, and jerked down sharply with all the strength left in her.

The boat rolled instantly and Ann felt the grip on her

hair release, and then she was treading water and gulping in the night air. Her head was slowly beginning to clear when Hicks thrashed to the surface only a few feet away. He lunged for the overturned boat but then he saw Ann and changed direction. With his arms closing over her, she fought every instinct in her body and forced herself to duck down into the dark water once again. She slipped sideways out of his grasp and pushed away from him. Her left hand brushed over the holstered gun at his hip, and then she surfaced, swimming toward shore with what strength she could find. Hicks started swimming in pursuit. Normally, the sheriff would have been no match for Ann in the water, but she was exhausted. When she finally dared to look back, the sheriff, though losing ground, was still within thirty feet of her.

Dexter and Zack almost missed Sheriff Hicks' vehicle. They were trying to figure out where the cutoff to Paul Summer's cabin was from the directions they'd gotten from Bob Tilsen. Zack was throwing his flashlight beam around, when he spotted the sheriff's black Hummer partially hidden under some trees. Its presence took everything they had been speculating on beyond any possibility of coincidence. Dexter's foot hit the accelerator and he barely kept the Cherokee on the road while he covered the remaining distance to Paul Summer's cabin. When they got out of the Jeep, Dexter took his .38 with him.

They could hear voices coming from inside the cabin as they stepped up onto the porch, but Dexter couldn't make out what was being said. The interior seemed well-lit, and all things considered, the scene certainly didn't seem too threatening. Dexter knocked on the door, and when Hallie answered, she looked surprised.

"Dexter?" She looked past him at Zack.

"This is Zack Rose, he's a DCI Agent. Zack, this is Annie's sister, Hallie. Could we come in?"

"Of course."

Hallie moved aside, and Ted stood up as they stepped inside. Dexter introduced Zack to Ted.

"Is everything okay?" Dexter asked.

"Of course," Ted offered. "Why wouldn't it be?"

Dexter looked at Zack and raised his eyebrows, wondering how much, if anything, he should reveal about Sheriff Hicks. Zack took it as a signal to make the decision.

"We've got reason to believe that Sheriff Moses Hicks may be complicit in several murders."

"Murders?" Hallie looked at Dexter. "Is he your boss, Dexter?"

Dexter smiled. "No, he's County, I work for the town of Higgins Point."

"The thing is," continued Zack, "Ann's apparently been gathering evidence against him, and we're pretty certain that he followed her up here."

"We spotted his Hummer parked down the road," Dexter added.

Ann swam until her hand touched the sandy bottom; then, she was up and running. She ignored her burning lungs and pumped her legs high to get them out of the water, while she thought about the gun that she'd felt on Hicks' hip. The water was ankle deep when she veered to the left, toward the entrance to the path that led back to the cabin. She heard the hollow report of a gun behind her, and there was a splintering snap among the dark trees somewhere in front. When she finally stopped to look back, he was almost out of the water and moving surprisingly fast for someone so large. He paused on the beach, and for an instant, the two of them were looking directly at one another in the moonlight. A distance of perhaps ninety feet separated them. His arm came up, and Ann saw a flash. There was a sharp buzzing as the bullet passed within inches of her head, and a crack as it impacted somewhere in a tree behind her.

Then she was running again, her bare feet flying over the dark path through the trees, littered with stones, leaves, and small branches. As she was trying to negotiate the turns on the trail, Ann thought about Ted and Hallie in the cabin and the Winchester in the backseat of her car. It was unloaded, but Hicks didn't know that. Whatever happened, she knew she couldn't lead the rampaging sheriff into the cabin.

The intense exertion of the past few minutes had Ann's adrenaline pumping furiously and had actually helped clear her head. Her mind bounced back and forth between the impulse to flee or fight. Then, a sharp pain in her shin was accompanied by an unscheduled headlong dive onto the path. The impact of her face on the ground stunned her momentarily. She spit dirt from her mouth and could hear Hicks grunting somewhere in the darkness behind her. He was on the path, but unable to move as quickly as Ann, not being as familiar with the trail as she was.

Ann got to her knees and threw herself sideways, rolling into the thick foliage that lined the trail. She was bruised, cut, still wet from the lake, and covered with dirt. Mosquitoes swarmed around her while she froze, hidden in the undergrowth, listening. From the sounds, she judged Hicks to be about thirty seconds behind her. It occurred to her that she could hide where she was until he passed, and then head back toward the lake and perhaps disappear onto the neighboring property. If Hicks didn't catch her, was he likely to bother Ted or Hallie? Probably not, they didn't even know he was here. But then Ann remembered the sheriff's voice in his office, lamenting how tragic Paul Summer's suicide was, and she made up her mind.

Above Ann's head, about five feet from the ground and illuminated in a shaft of moonlight that seemed to be sent just for that purpose, Ann saw a thick, dead branch, perhaps three inches across, and four feet long. It was sticking out almost horizontally from an old, dead elm. She got to her feet, grabbed the branch with both hands and pulled down sharply. A loud crack broke the stillness. Hicks had obviously heard the noise; the quiet on the path told Ann that he had slowed down and was advancing more cautiously. As quietly as she could, Ann went to one knee, still hidden by the undergrowth, and drew the branch back into batting position. From the path, if Hicks were able to see it in the patterns of light and shadow, the branch should look like any other tree limb. She waited, fighting to silence her breathing.

What's my target? she wondered, *His head, his gun hand? Maybe his leg. If I manage to hobble him, I can sprint for my car. But if that's all I want, I could let him go by and disappear toward the lake*. She gripped the branch harder and fought the instinct to wave it back and forth like a batter. She didn't have long to wait. Moving in and out of the patches of moonlight, seeming to appear and disappear randomly, Hicks came into view. Ann managed to catch a glimpse of his right hand holding the gun out in front.

She was holding the branch in a position to swing across her body, but when she spotted his gun at the last second, she decided that was her target. To be able to bring the branch down across his hand, she had to telegraph her attack by first raising the branch up slightly. It was a tiny movement, but Hicks must have seen something, because at the last second, he flinched and began to draw his gun hand back, although not quite quickly enough. The branch came down in a wicked arc, and slammed into his hand with a satisfyingly solid feel. Hicks let out a pained bellow, the gun discharged and fell to the ground, and the branch broke cleanly in half. Ann didn't hesitate. She stepped forward with her remaining two-foot length of branch, drew a bead on his face, and swung with all the strength left in her. When she made contact, the branch broke in half again and his bellow was silenced abruptly, as he dropped to the dark path, disappearing from sight.

Ann stood there for an instant wondering what her odds would be of finding the fallen gun before he did. He was a powerful man, and Ann wasn't sure how much damage she'd done. The problem was that he easily outweighed her by more than a hundred pounds, and if she joined him down in the dirt, and he got to her before she got to the gun, she could be dead fast. But then, Hicks's hand emerged from the shadows, and a metallic gleam told her that he already had the gun. She leaped over him like a deer and was thirty feet away before he could stagger to his feet.

She covered the remaining distance to the cabin, veered around to the cars parked in the front, and threw open the rear door of her car. She could hear his feet on the lawn behind her. She grabbed the rifle case, unzipped it, and threw it aside. Clutching her father's Winchester, Ann whirled around to face the Sheriff. She made a show of cocking the empty rifle as loudly as she could. When he skittered to a panting stop thirty feet away, she was pointing it directly at his face. His gun, which was pointed right back at her, was now held in his undamaged left hand. She looked down the barrel at him, eye to eye. Ann was wet, covered with dirt, and still exhausted from her ordeal in the water, but she fought to keep both the rifle and her voice steady.

"You don't look so good, Sheriff."

"I think you broke my nose."

In the bright moonlight, Ann could make out a generous smear of blood across his face and drew a measure of gratification from the thickness in his speech.

"Drop your weapon."

Hicks didn't fire, but he didn't drop his gun either.

"Gonna shoot the sheriff?"

"Right in the eye, if I have to. I said, drop your weapon."

They were only a few feet from the front door of the cabin. Apparently, Ted and Hallie hadn't heard the gunshots down by the lake, or if they had, they hadn't thought anything of it. Ann stepped carefully to her right and forward one step, hoping to divert his attention from the cabin. Hicks didn't move, only his gun hand followed her. His tongue ran over his lips as he seemed to consider his options. *After trying to kill me*, Ann thought, *what could he possibly say to me*?

"Let's not do nothin' hasty here, Summer. Maybe we can work something out."

Unbelievable. "You are some piece of work, Hicks."

"You manage to get some bullets into that rifle, did ya?"

Ann had no illusions. She understood that she had brought a club to a gunfight, and if she was going to live through this, she was going to have to get close enough to use it. As much as she hated to move further into his 'kill zone', she took another step toward him.

"You killed Manning and planted the gun on him."

The sheriff's eyes narrowed. "I don't believe that gun's loaded, Miss Summer." He slowly lowered his own pistol, keeping his eyes on her.

"That's why there weren't any prints on the bullets, because you wiped them clean when you loaded it." Ann took another step closer.

"Little idiot thought I was gonna help him get away." Hicks laughed. "When I shot him, he was the most surprised guy in the room."

"And it was you who killed Billy Deal."

Hicks shrugged. "A temporary fix, just to keep Manning out of trouble until I could figure out what to do with him."

"Then you put Deal's cocaine in Manning's trunk to frame him for Deal's murder."

"Nobody's useful forever—including you."

"You control the meth lab in this part of Wisconsin, don't you?"

This brought a fleeting look of genuine surprise to the sheriff's face. "How you know about that, huh? How?"

"Because it was you who murdered Casper Bottom."

"That was just a little dust-up over turf. I taught the runts a little lesson and sent 'em back to Minnesota with their tails between their legs."

"My father found out about the drugs and was closing in on you when you murdered him." Ann could feel the oily remnants of the fingerprint powder on her father's rifle. "This rifle look familiar to you?"

Hicks focused on the Winchester, his face distorted by the smeared blood. "Well, I'll be damned! You know something? Your father had the same problem you got—he didn't know when to quit either. And I got the same solution for you."

Hicks raised his gun again.

"Where's Ann?" Dexter asked, glancing around the room.

"She decided to take a moonlight swim," Hallie said. She left maybe twenty minutes ago."

"The way she swims," Dexter said, "it's probably the safest place for her. But maybe I'll take a walk out to the dock, just make sure she's okay. In the meantime, why don't you folks pack up and get ready to head back to town."

Dexter walked over to the front door, and as he opened it, he was surprised to hear the voice of Sheriff Hicks say, "And I got the same solution for you."

He stepped through the doorway and stopped. The sheriff was standing perhaps twenty feet away, facing Ann, who was pointing a rifle at him. When the sheriff saw Dexter, his hand swung toward him, and Dexter realized too late that it held a gun.

The discharge was sharp and blunt. The dense pines around the cabin ate up any chance of an echo. It felt like someone thrust a burning poker into Dexter's side, and his legs dissolved under him. As he fell, he saw Ann step forward and swing the rifle, bringing its butt flat across the side of the sheriff's head. The solid wood stock held, and the sheriff's head absorbed the force of the impact. Hicks collapsed like a steer in a slaughterhouse. Dexter felt Zack's arms trying to hold him up as he sat down in the doorway and slid sideways in slow motion, unable to catch his breath. *She's using the wrong end of the gun*, he thought to himself, as the floor rose up to welcome him.

Chapter Twenty-seven

The report of the rifle fire that echoed across the St. Croix River valley had the synchronized feeling of shots fired not in anger, but in honor. The seven riflemen lowered their weapons, snapped the bolts back and forward in unison, and raised them to their shoulders again. Another volley, and then a third. With no casket to look at during the salute, Ann's gaze lingered on the anonymous white gloves that held the rifles. She squeezed her sister Hallie's hand on her left and then glanced at Dexter to her right. Ted stood beside Hallie, and behind them stood Zack and Grady. Zack's gum was getting a good workout, and Ann wouldn't have had it any other way.

At the conclusion of the memorial service, Dexter had insisted on accompanying her on the walk from the church to the gravesite, but they had been standing for twenty minutes now, and she could tell that he was beginning to feel the strain. In the week since he had been shot, Dexter had healed to the point where he could walk with little hint of an injury, but he still tired easily. The bullet that Hicks had fired into Dexter's side had shattered a couple of ribs and nicked the lower portion of one lung. When he had started coughing up blood, Ann became terrified that he might die before the ambulance could get there. Much more terrified, she realized later, than she thought she would be.

A ceremonial flag was presented to Ann and Hallie, and then the stillness was filled with the stuttering glide of bagpipes coming to life. The sweet, uplifting strains of *Amazing Grace* welled up around them and rolled out over the valley. Ann felt her eyes moisten and without realizing it, placed her hand inside of Dexter's.

When they began the slow walk back to the church, Ann took care not to walk faster than she thought Dexter could comfortably manage.

"My boss called me this morning," she said. "It's official. Now that the suicide ruling was tossed out, they're opening a full investigation into Hicks's involvement in my father's death."

"Think you have enough to get him for murder?"

"Detective Perry's lab managed to lift some prints off the Luger that my father had. They got a positive match for Hicks, so the forensic evidence doesn't look good for him, and since my father was investigating him, there's certainly a motive."

"Even without that, they've still got him for the murders of Manning and Deal." Dexter put his hand over the wound in his side. "Not to mention attempting to murder both of us."

He paused for a few seconds while Ann waited for him to rest.

"I had lunch at Janet's yesterday," she said, "I saw Cara Lynn Grovsner."

"How's she doing?"

"Seems okay. She looks pretty good; no bruises or black eyes."

Dexter smiled, and then the smile disappeared.

"Is she in trouble?"

"What do you mean?"

"You know, with the law. She was willing to let Manning get away with murder in order to blackmail him, and her attempt at blackmail did lead to another murder."

"I don't see how justice would be served by prosecuting her."

"Justice? What about the law?"

"Isn't justice the point of the law? Besides, the only thing we have is her statement to me, and I judge her mental state at the time to be questionable at best."

"So there's no point in pursuing it?"

"Let's give her a chance to get her life back together."

They walked in silence for several minutes and then Dexter asked a question.

"Annie, when this started, you told me that when we found Muriel's killer, his motive would make sense." They paused on the path. "Did this make sense to Tom Manning?"

Ann thought about this for a minute. "Only in his panicked state of mind, but ultimately, no."

"I wonder what made Muriel believe she could actually get away with something like this?"

"People can believe anything. For a while, I was almost willing to believe that my father actually did kill himself."

Dexter put his hand on her arm. "You're human, doubt comes with the territory."

When they arrived back at the church, Dexter said, "C'mon with me for a minute, I have something for you."

He steered her out into the parking lot to his Cherokee. When they got there he said, "Close your eyes."

"Dexter, what—"

"C'mon, I said close your eyes."

Ann had no idea what to expect, but she did as he asked. She heard him open the Jeep door and a second later, he said, "Okay, you can look."

Just as she opened her eyes, Dexter dumped a tiny, furry bundle into her arms. It was a warm and squirming little puppy, and it was the most adorable thing Ann had ever seen. It immediately jumped up at Ann's face, its busy tongue licking her chin. Seldom had Ann been caught more off guard than at this moment.

"Dexter, what is this?"

"Annie, meet Asta, your new dog. Asta, Annie Summer, sleuth extraordinaire."

"Asta? Isn't that the name of—"

"Right, Nick and Nora Charles's dog in *The Thin Man*. And she's a Wire-Hair Terrier, just like the real Asta."

"But Dexter, why?"

"When you first came to town, you told me that the worst part of your job was not being able to have a dog. Well, I've solved that little problem for you."

Ann looked at Dexter and then at Asta. She scratched her behind the ears, generating a new wave of squirming. "God, she's so cute. But I explained how I couldn't keep a dog in Madison, because I travel too much. It's not practical, Dexter."

Dexter stroked Asta's head and smiled at Ann. "Sure it is. You can keep her if you stay here in Higgins Point, Annie.